# First Lady of the World

a novel

by

## Robert Muller

To Benita Esposito

with warmest wishes

Rob Muller

16 April 1993

# First Lady of the World

by
Robert Muller

Published by
World Happiness and Cooperation
P.O. Box 1153
Anacortes, Washington 98221
U.S.A.

First Edition

Library of Congress Catalog Card Number: 91-67790

ISBN  1-880455-01-3

*Front cover design:* The emblem of the **University for Peace**
**UNIPAZ  P.O. Box 138, Ciudad Colón, Costa Rica, C.A.**
This book is a work of fiction.  Any similarity between the fictional characters in this book and actual persons alive or dead is coincidental.

I dedicate this book
to my beloved
Margarita

# First Lady of the World

by

## Robert Muller

# Chapter 1

Lakshmi Narayan is kneeling in front of the iron ore altar of the UN Meditation Room in New York City, deeply absorbed in prayers and thoughts. It is her first day as the new Secretary-General of the United Nations. She has just arrived from New Delhi where a few days ago she received the astonishing news of her election to the highest office in the world.

A UN guard stands respectfully a few feet behind her in the dimly lit, silent cosmic prayer-room. He is contemplating her with curiosity. She is the first woman Secretary-General in the almost fifty years of existence of the world organization. Here, in this richest country and city of the Earth, a woman has arrived from one of the poorest nations on the other side of the globe to shoulder one of the most difficult jobs in the world. What changes have taken place on the planet since he joined the UN in 1948! Thoughts and images were reeling through his mind: what would Christopher Columbus and George Washington say if they came back to Earth? He himself whose black ancestors had been brought as slaves from Africa had seen accomplished in the UN the miracle of racial equality, of black delegates speaking as well as the other delegates, of Ralph Bunche receiving the Nobel Prize for Peace, of all African and other colonies becoming independent in less than fifty years, of the UN becoming universal. He still remembers that when he joined the UN as a young man, he heard a high official predict that decolonization would take

1

from 100 to 150 years! What a privilege it was to work for this organization. What an extraordinary, enriching life he had. And it was not the end.

Lakshmi Narayan was absorbed in her own thoughts. She remembered the poor Indian village she came from, the famines and epidemics, the wood shortage, the unhealthy water, the blindness due to smallpox, the miserable lot of the people when she was a child. But there had also been great lights of hope: Gandhi, Nehru, independence and her vast country taking finally its seat in the assembly of nations. How fervently she had prayed the Gods to enable her to do something good for the peace of this world and the happiness of the people. And the Gods heard her. She had won an essay contest of the United Nations Association of India, obtained a scholarship, studied law and international relations, was asked by the Indian Women's Congress to run for politics, became a member of Parliament and, at the early age of 34, was appointed Minister of Foreign Affairs of her country. And now, to crown it all, she was the new Secretary-General of the UN! She had dreamt to do good for this beautiful world and for its people? Well, the Gods had placed her right in front of that challenge in its toughest, world-wide dimension.

Tears of gratitude and of awe upwelled in her eyes. Gratitude for the miraculous course of her extraordinary life. Awe for the immense challenges and responsibilities expecting her. Her heart was full of prayers to all the Gods of the Indian Pantheon, especially to Lakshmi, the goddess of material and spiritual success, whose name she was bearing. Then she suddenly remembered something she wanted to do: out of her purse she took a statuette of Ganesha, the God-elephant who was bringing good luck when invoked at the beginning of a new task or undertaking. She placed him on the iron-ore altar brought over from Sweden by Dag Hammarskjøld and prayed the little God fervently to bring her good luck in her job. She needed it badly.

It was New Year's Day of 1992. The UN building was silent and empty when she finally arose from her knees and meditation. Andy Smith, the guard, asked her if she had any other wishes for the day.

She answered: "My first wish was fulfilled. I wanted to follow the example of my predecessor, Javier Perez de Cuellar, who when he became Secretary-General came first to this holy place to pray and meditate. I would like to visit my office next."

2

As they left the Meditation Room, Lakshmi had this comment: "As a Hindu I am trained and accustomed to sense the sacred radiations of certain places on Earth. They can come from the Earth as telluric energy as you call it, or from the cosmos, in particular from the sun, as cosmic energy. I feel rather strong vibrations at the UN, particularly in the Meditation Room. Is there anything special about the grounds on which the UN is built?"

Andy Smith answered: "As a matter of fact, there is. The UN stands on a piece of land called by the Manhattan Indians, Turtle Bay. Their legend was that floods of blood would drench that place but that there would come a time when many tribes will meet here to make peace. It happens that for many years the slaughter houses of Manhattan stood here and floods of blood were lost by hundreds of thousands of animals. When Mr. John Rockefeller bought the land, he got the slaughter houses destroyed and offered the grounds to the UN, the meeting place of many tribes. One could also add that the UN was born from the blood of the 30 million humans who died in World War II. These are the Earth vibrations noticeable at the UN. Regarding the cosmic radiations, it is also typical that the East River was called by the Indians the River of the Rising Sun. Our sun which shines for all peoples on Earth arises every day above the UN. A preferred time for photographers is the moment when the sun rises from behind the UN building in a glory of light which lends it a halo of sanctity, hope and resurrection. And indeed the UN is the world's House of Hope."

Andy then took her along the empty corridors of the UN, adorned with art treasures offered by governments and people in homage of the lofty ideals of the world organization: the Peace Dove mosaic given by Pope John Paul II, the reproduction of Hammurabi's Code, the statue of Sun-God Surya offered by Mrs. Indhira Gandhi, the Racial Equality mosaic by Norman Rockwell, tapestries, paintings, peace bells and many other symbols of humanity's aspirations. Lakshmi Narayan told Andy that she wanted to know the story and meaning of each of these gifts, to be inspired by them when she walked through the UN.

When they took the elevator, Andy told her: "The third elevator on the left is always kept at your disposal. When your limousine arrives at the entrance of the Secretariat Building, this elevator takes you directly to the thirty eighth floor." He added hesitatingly: "Only one Secretary-General decided to take the elevator with the staff in

3

order to be closer to his colleagues, Dag Hammarskjøld. He also introduced the practice that each new Secretary-General will go from floor to floor and office to office to meet and greet each Secretariat member." She commented: "Thank you for this precious advice. I will not fail to follow Dag Hammarskjøld's example and I count on you for any other good suggestions."

They arrived on the thirty eighth floor, the famous thirty eighth floor, a place which has probably seen more world history, heads of states, high dignitaries, peace advocates, scientists, artists, composers, writers, religious leaders and dreamers than any other place on Earth. They walked along the portraits of preceding Secretaries-General in the corridor at the end of which Andy unlocked for her the door of the Secretary-General's office.

She saw a large, but simple office made primarily to accommodate visitors and meetings with colleagues. There was nothing ostentatious or arrogant in it, no symbols of power, wealth or glory. Behind the simple desk of the Secretary-General there was a UN flag and a large bookcase with all the UN Yearbooks and numerous reports of the world organization.

Lakshmi was scanning the room with sharp, feminine eyes: this was primarily a man's room. She absolutely had to give it a womanly touch, something for the heart, for the soul and for the arts. She looked for closets. She found two big ones. A third door was locked. Andy Smith explained to her: "If that door is opened, you will see a hole that goes straight down to the ground floor of the UN building. The architects wanted to build here a personal elevator for the Secretary-General, but it was never done. Let me show you something else." And he took her to a little apartment next to the Secretary-General's office: a bedroom, a study, a kitchen, a bath and a shower-room. "This was foreseen by the architects so that the Secretary-General could stay here day and night in case of a crisis. The only Secretary-General who ever used it was Dag Hammarskjøld. John Kennedy also took a shower here before speaking to the General Assembly."

The unused bedroom was filled with lots of boxes containing UN documents. "These boxes must be removed," Lakshmi said. "I will arrange here a little Indian place of retreat where I can meditate, sleep, pray and rest." Her heart was jumping with joy. Here in this western skyscraper, she would organize a little Indian ashram to her heart's delight. Her mind was popping with ideas. "Here I want

4

statues of Lakshmi, Ganesha and Shiva; here I want a bust of Gandhi, here a picture of Nehru, etc."

Back in her office, she had a glance through one of the large windows and saw overpopulated, congested Long Island which reminded her of Bombay. She asked the guard about two islands - a sizeable one and a very tiny one - in the East River.

Andy continued his role as a guide: "The biggest, of which you see the southern tip, is Roosevelt Island. At the end of it, towards the UN, the city of New York tried to imitate Geneva by installing a water jet but it operates very seldom because the water it sprays from the East River is polluted and people from the neighborhood complained. On that southern tip Buckminster Fuller wanted to build a world globe electronically linked with the UN which would show the world population, the Earth's resources, pollution and other global data. Some people still suggest that the big globe from the former grounds of the World's Fair on Long island be moved to that spot."

"That is an excellent idea. And what about the little island just below my window?"

"Well, that could be an inspiration to you. One of your predecessors, Secretary-General U Thant from Burma, loved rivers which reminded him of his country. He used to contemplate the East River from his window. When he died, the UN Meditation Group, headed by a compatriot of yours, the Indian sage and guru Sri Chinmoy, asked the Governor of New York State to rename little Belmont Island, U Thant Island. The UN Meditation Group is entrusted with its maintenance. At the inauguration of U Thant Island, a box of memorabilia was buried into the ground. There was a plan to build on the island a Buddhist pagoda as a memorial to this deeply spiritual Secretary-General. He would amply deserve it, but so far governments have not done anything for him."

This remark threw her into thoughts. She had just read about the completion of a Memorial library for one of the former US Presidents at a cost of several million dollars, and she was pained to learn that nothing had been done for one of the finest and humblest Secretaries-General of the UN. She had to do something about it.

She asked if there was anything else Andy Smith wanted her to see on the thirty eighth floor.

"Yes, the office of the President of the General Assembly and the military map room."

These were located at the other end of the thirty eighth floor.

5

The office of the President of the General Assembly - a different person each year - was similar to that of the Secretary-General. Photographs of past Presidents of the Assembly were hanging on the walls. Various memorabilia and gifts to Presidents were also displayed. Again, it was definitely a male's room: 44 male Presidents and only two women had occupied it during the last forty-six years!

The military map room fascinated her: in a long windowless conference room, three walls were covered with maps of the world's conflicts and trouble spots with which the UN was concerned. Information on national contingents of UN peace-keeping forces was given on other displays. The last wall showed the photographs of UN generals and mediators since the beginning of the UN. There was not a single woman, not even among the mediators!

Lakshmi asked Andy: "How many military advisors does the UN have at Headquarters?"

"Four."

"Four only? You can't be serious," she exclaimed.

"Yes, I am serious. You will have many other such surprises regarding the stinginess of nations towards their world organization."

Her mind was working at high speed and she asked:

"Is there a thirty ninth floor on the UN building?"

"Yes, it is a mixture of empty spaces and rooms for yoga, gymnastics and art classes."

She remained silent, but was thinking:

"I want to get a world peace room up there, the counterpart of the war room they have in NATO. If necessary I will get Indian generals released to staff such a room. We must have an instantaneous high-technology surveillance, warning and communications center for all trouble spots on this planet."

Andy Smith for his part had simpler thoughts. He said to her: "You know, Madam, I have an old idea. I read and saw pictures that when a new Pope is elected by the College of Cardinals in Rome, they burn the ballots and when a column of white smoke arises from the roof of the Vatican building, the people gathered on St. Peter's Place rejoice and sing: Habemus Papam, we have a Pope. I often thought that we should do the same thing on our roof when a new Secretary-General is elected. It would be nice. The people would love it."

"You are right. I promise, we will do it next time. But I am very tired due to my long trip from New Delhi. Could you be so kind and drive me to my new home?"

When they reached the elevator, she had a last look at the East River through a large window, behind the desk of the security guard of the thirty eighth floor. A big white vessel was passing, blowing a whistle. Is this a salute to the UN?" she asked?

"Yes."

"Do we return the salute?"

"Alas, no, said Andy. I have often felt, sitting at this desk, that we should. The guard here could press a button which would activate a whistle or a horn. Such a system would not cost much."

"OK. It will be done too, I promise you. You are a gold-mine of ideas. You made my day. I appoint you my private idea-man. But how come that such suggestions have not been implemented? Don't you have suggestion boxes at the UN?"

"No, that idea too was turned down by petty bureaucrats who fear that they might be used for criticisms of the administration. It is a pity because there are so many good-hearted idealistic people in this house, who deeply love the UN and have wonderful ideas. Our administrative officers are always scared that it might cost money. They should have a look at what the military spend!"

"Andy, we will do all that. There will be suggestion boxes on each floor, including and especially the thirty eighth floor. I will open it myself every week. I thank you for having helped me so much on my first day."

They left the UN silently and when they arrived at the Secretary-General's mansion at Sutton Place, she folded her hands in the Hindu fashion, bowed her head towards Andy and thanked him again profusely for his help.

Andy answered: "And may I thank you, Madam, for having listened so patiently to one of your humble UN servants. And thank you above all for being so beautiful."

A little smile of vanity appeared on her lips. She knew how attractive she was and what effect she had on men. Alas, she had never fallen in love and was still a much coveted single woman. When asked about this aspect of her life, she usually answered: "It is because I am in love with humanity and married with the world. But some day it will happen too."

* * *

# Chapter 2

The following morning when Lakshmi arrived at the UN, a flock of journalists and cameramen was waiting for her, pushing each other to get close to her and bombard her with questions:

"What will be your main policy?"

"To love humanity and this beautiful planet."

"What about the Middle-East?"

"To love the Jews and the Arabs alike and to make them love each other.

"And Cyprus?"

"To love the Cypriot Greeks and the Cypriot Turks and to make them love each other."

An aide interjected that she would give a press conference in the next few days. The questions slowly died out while the cameras continued clicking. She lent herself graciously to picture-taking, while repeating to herself internally with conviction: "I love this Earth, I love you all," so that this love would show on her face in the pictures.

As the media dispersed, the New York Times journalist was complaining to a colleague: "What are we going to do with that female? Love! I have not heard this word in the UN for twenty years. U Thant was the last to use it. Love in world affairs! Can you imagine?"

His companion answered: "You must confess that we men have not been doing so well in world affairs. Perhaps a womanly touch will improve things."

"Damn it. How am I going to get copy on love, especially between Jews and Arabs, published by my paper?"

"Suggest to the top brass of the Times to read the famous 1936 exchange of letters between Einstein and Freud on the subject. They might learn from it that love for the world and humanity is indeed the answer."

\* \*

On the thirty eighth floor, the entire staff working there was waiting for Lakshmi at the exit of the elevator and applauded her warmly. The chef de cabinet, a former Indian diplomat, wanted to rush her away to her office, but she refused and said to the assembled group: "Come with me to my conference room."

There was not room enough for everyone to sit and some had to stand. She apologized and said:

"I want all of you to be my family. Consider me as your sister. You will all have direct access to me. If you have an idea, a dream, a wild proposal, put them down on paper for me. No one will be authorized to intercept them. I will meet each of your personally in the next few days. I want to know about your life, your family, your origin, your inclinations, loves, dreams and purposes, so that I can help you fulfill them for the benefit of humankind. We have only eight years left to the year 2000. Let us work day and night to change the course of history and to prepare a third millennium of planetary peace, cooperation and human fulfillment."

Then she greeted each one in the Hindu way with folded hands and the beautiful word Namaster (I recognize the divinity in you). Whereupon she accompanied the chef de cabinet who had a big file marked URGENT under his arm. A Secretary rushed into her office: "Madam, the Ambassador of the United States is on the phone. He wants to speak to you."

"Tell him that I have someone in my office. I will call him back a little later."

"He is not going to like that. You must know that he will be a presidential candidate and is likely to be the next President of the United States."

9

"Well, tell him that I love him and that I will call him back in a little while."

Then she turned to the chef de cabinet. The man who held this key position in the Secretariat was an elderly, gentle diplomat of the old school, impregnated with courtesy and affability, careful with every word and gesture.

He congratulated and welcomed her, especially as a compatriot from India, but added:

"Your position is a very frustrating and demanding one. Trygve Lie, the first Secretary-General, called it the most impossible job on Earth. You will need all the Gods on your side."

She answered: "Do not worry unduly about me. As a matter of fact, I love impossible jobs. One of my dreams is to be known as a specialist in impossibilities."

She asked him what kind of program he had foreseen for the day.

He answered: "It is customary that the new Secretary-General meets with his top-colleagues, the Under-Secretaries-General and Assistant-Secretaries-General, to make their acquaintance. I have advised them that you may wish to meet with them at eleven o'clock. That seemed to me to be the first priority. I hope you will agree with me."

She answered: "I have a slightly different priority. For me first come God, spirituality and my right place in the universe and in time. I hear that there is a Hindu guru at the UN. I will need him for my spiritual guidance. Please ask him to come and see me. After that, we will have our meeting with the top-aides. I must also make the acquaintance of my secretaries. Could both of us have luncheon together thereafter at a nearby Indian Restaurant?"

"I will be honored, Madam. But it is customary for the Secretary-General to dine up here on the thirty eighth floor or at the Delegates Dining Room, not in New York restaurants."

"Well, we will change that custom. Please ask a secretary to make a reservation at a Hindu restaurant in the neighborhood."

\* \*

Sri Chinmoy, the Hindu guru, arrived a little later, dressed in his Indian dhoti and Nehru-type jacket, gliding silently on his sandals. He folded his hands and bowed deeply in front of the new Secretary-General.

She responded: "Om shanti, Master. I know why you are here in this house. I know what brought you here from far away India and I am delighted that you came. Our western brothers may not understand your mission. They might even take you for a strange, mysterious fellow. But I thank you for the inspiration and spirituality you give to many young staff members, all considered to be among the best, as I have heard. I am asking you to be my guru, my teacher, my cosmic inspirer in the pure Auroville tradition in which you were trained. I will be subjected to such enormous pressures from western materialism and intellectualism that I need your help to keep me in union with the universe. What would be your advice on this first day, Master?"

"Revered daughter Lakshmi, may your thoughts be always impregnated with the spirit of our beloved Gandhi. Please have a bust of him in your office. Think, pray and work for the whole world and humanity as he did for India. A public servant of the young Indian government once asked him: "Gandhiji, I have to take many decisions, but often I do not know what is the right decision. What would you advise me to do?" Gandhi answered: "Remember the poorest, most abandoned, most miserable person you ever saw in your life. If you have a picture of that person, place it on your desk and when you take a decision, ask yourself the question: is it going to help that poor person or not? And you will get the right answer."

And the Secretary-General's new guru glided backwards on his sandals out of the office, folding his hands and bowing reverently before her.

* *

Eleven o'clock. Meeting with the Under-Secretaries and Assistant-Secretaries. There were more than two dozen of them, heading either logistical departments such as Personnel, Administration, Finance, Building Management etc. or substantive departments dealing with the world's major political, economic and social problems. As each of them was introduced to her with the name of his department, Lakshmi felt that she had all the dreams and miseries of Mother Earth and of humanity in front of her.

After the introductions, she spoke briefly:

"Dear colleagues, this is only a first get-together. We will have ample opportunities to know each other better. May I simply say this: I feel very privileged to be among you and to be allowed to give all

11

my strength, all my thoughts, all my love and all my soul to the service of the world and of humanity. Every day I will give thanks to God and ask this question: what more can I do? As a human being I will work for the peace and welfare of **all** humanity and of **all** the Earth, without prejudice towards any nation, culture, race, group or faith. But coming from India, I will also have two paramount preoccupations: the improvement of the fate of the very poor, and the spiritual dimension of life. The first aspect is well represented at the UN, being one of its highest priorities. But the second aspect is not, despite the prophetic teachings of my predecessors Dag Hammarskjøld and U Thant. We must always remember that we are not outside heaven, but in heaven. A cosmic experiment of the first importance is taking place on this planet. We must help fulfill its designs. Only a spiritual approach, only the soul can unite us with the universe and help us grasp our meaning. One of the western atheistic authors, Andre Malraux wrote at the end of his life: "The third millennium will be spiritual, or there will be no third millennium." Dag Hammarskjøld for his part said:

"I see no hope for permanent world peace. We have tried and failed miserably. Unless the world has a spiritual rebirth, civilization is doomed."

As for U Thant, from what I have read, all his life, from morning to evening, was spirituality, a constant, watchful, reverent communion with people and the universe. This is my philosophy and way of life too."

And she concluded: "The General Assembly had the vision to adopt as early as 1946 the following rule of procedure":

*Immediately after the opening of the first plenary meeting and immediately preceding the closing of the final plenary meeting of each session of the General Assembly, the President shall invite the representatives to observe one minute of silence dedicated to prayer or mediation.*

May I express the wish that every meeting and conference of the UN, including our own meetings, will start and end with a minute of silence for prayers or meditation. May I therefore ask you to bow your heads, to close your eyes and ask for God's guidance and help in the fulfillment of our awesome tasks. I am grateful to you for having come on such short notice for a first brief meeting. We will meet again soon. I wish you a good day and God's speed."

When the group of high officials left the conference room, Lakshmi had this internal remark:

"My God, there was only one woman in the whole crowd! No wonder that the UN is not very sentimental and spiritual. I will have to change that."

* *

Lakshmi then met her three secretaries: Francoise, a multilingual secretary born in Mauritius from a French father and an English mother. She was dealing with the immediate calls of the Secretary-General, her incoming and outgoing official correspondence, internal channelling of messages and memoranda, and filing. She was her principal secretary, a beautiful, highly intelligent and nice brunette in her early thirties.

Christina, her appointments secretary, was a blond girl from New Zealand. Her task was to establish the daily schedule of the Secretary-General - appointments, opening meetings, luncheons, receptions, etc. - as well as her long-term schedule and travels, of which there would be many.

The last secretary, Manuela, from Peru, was the private secretary of the former Secretary-General. She was in charge of his correspondence and relations with his home country, as well as his dictation of notes after meetings with heads of states, Ambassadors and other prominent personalities, his philosophical writings, even poetry which he would take with him as his personal papers for later possible publication. Manuela was being transferred to another position in the Secretariat so that Lakshmi could bring in her own personal Hindu secretary to take care of her correspondence and work in the Hindi language.

After learning about the backgrounds, lives and likings of the three girls, Lakshmi asked Francoise to give her the US Ambassador on the phone. She pressed the loudspeaker button so that the girls could hear the conversation.

The US Ambassador warmly greeted the Secretary-General and asked her for an appointment today to come and present his respects and congratulations.

She answered:

"Mr. Ambassador, this is awfully nice of you and I am deeply touched by your call. But I do not want you to use your precious time for a courtesy visit. Your telephone call will be in lieu of it and we can meet one of these next days at your convenience for a private working session with an agenda of items we both would like to discuss. Also, may I express a personal wish: if there is any problem at any time, my telephone line is always open to you. We can do a lot right over the telephone, that marvelous American invention which saves us so much time. I look forward to working with you with all my heart and mind. I have always liked and admired your great country."

Putting down the phone, she said to the secretaries:

"Spread the word that I am a great lover of the telephone instead of visits. Once they know that, the 166 Ambassadors and my top colleagues will cut down drastically their visits. Tell them that there is nothing I hate more than a visit which could have been avoided with a telephone call, and that people who make me lose my time are placed on a black list. You will see, it will work like a charm."

She kissed the three girls and returned to her office, saying:

"Here at least it is not a male world."

* *

Luncheon with the chef de cabinet. When they arrived at the New Delhi Delight, the whole staff of the restaurant was assembled to greet her and to place a necklace of yellow marigolds around her neck. The owner of the restaurant asked her to autograph a photograph which was quickly framed and hung on the wall above the table at which they were sitting. She was very touched and commented to her companion:

"Do you think I would have received such a nice reception at the UN Delegates Dining Room?"

"The staff there would have assembled too and applauded you."

"Yes, but they have no Indian food. They serve purely American and European food, which is not fair for a United Nations restaurant. Please ask the corporation that runs it that I want one day each week to be reserved for the best cooks in the city, of various cultural origins, to come to the UN and prepare for us dishes from their countries. We will have a Chinese day, a Hindu day, an African day,

14

an Indonesian day, etc. I am for unity in diversity. The culinary arts are one of the best illustrations. Also, chefs who will be selected and allowed to cook for us will feel very proud. It will be a sort of star for them. Incidentally, seeing these lovely, yellow flowers reminds me that one day I happened to be in New York on St. Patricks's day. I saw green carnations being sold everywhere for the Irish to wear. I want someone to get in touch with flower producers and ask them to develop, promote and sell light-blue carnations - the UN blue - for people to wear on 24 October, United Nations Day, the anniversary of the UN. And also remind me to address on that day my birthday wishes to all people on Earth who were born on a 24 October."

She seized a pencil and a piece of paper and made a rapid calculation:

"Suppose that the 5.3 billion people on this planet were born equally on each day of the year. It would mean that there are close to 15 million people who were born on a 24 October. Let us celebrate together with them and call them children of the United Nations. Incidentally, there was an early resolution of the General Assembly which asked all member-states to celebrate UN Day and to make it a holiday. I would like to get a report on the outcome of that resolution. Also, we should obtain that all people born on an International Day proclaimed by the UN, such as International Peace Day, Women's Day, Earth Day, Human Rights Day, etc. should celebrate these days. UNICEF should publish special birthday cards for these days."

And then she asked:

"What are the rules or traditions regarding the fate of my top-aides, the Under-Secretaries-General and Assistant-Secretaries-General?"

"In principle they should all offer you their resignation, so that you may choose your own collaborators. Some of them will actually do so. Legally, however, each of them has a fixed-term contract, and since they were recruited at different times, their contracts may extend as far as the next 2 or 3 years. There is nothing you can do if they want to stay. Many of them love their jobs and wish to stay. All of them are competent people and some have extremely valuable experience. It is not as if you were the Prime Minister of India and could select all your Ministers."

She answered:

"In India I would have to choose most Ministers on the basis of political considerations. I hear that at the UN national representation is the name for party representation."

"Yes, but it is not an iron-rule. Traditionally, nationals of the five permanent members of the Security Council are selected as Under-Secretaries-General in charge of the main UN organs: an American for the General Assembly, a Russian for the Security Council, a Frenchman for the Economic and Social Council, a Chinese for the Trusteeship Council. That leaves the British who are given Special Political Affairs and peace-keeping operations on the thirty eighth floor. And since the Trusteeship Council has practically completed its work, the Chinese wanted and received the Technical Cooperation Department. Each continent, each group, each nation wishes of course to be represented among your top aides. It is a question of national pride and honor more than of "representation". Your top-aides give the same oath as you and all UN staff members." And he took a slip of paper out of his wallet and read:

She seized a pencil and a piece of paper and made a rapid calculation:

*"I solemnly swear to exercise in all loyalty, discretion and con-science the functions entrusted to me as an international civil servant of the United Nations, to discharge these functions and regulate my conduct with the interest of the United Nations only in view, and not seek or accept instructions in regard to the performance of my duties from any Government or other authority external to the Organization."*

He continued:

"Of course, some of your top-aides are closer to their countries and delegations than others. In many cases it will be very useful for you to get informally the views and intentions of their delegations through them."

"Thank you. I have so much to learn. Could I ask you to get from the Chief of Personnel a table showing the end of their contracts so that I may think of people to replace them. I intend in particular to increase substantially the number of women so as to reach equality. The UN must practice what it preaches. I noticed this morning that among the two dozen of highest officials there was only one woman. What is the exact situation?"

The chef de cabinet took another slip of paper out of his wallet and said:

"I expected your question. The situation is as follows: this morning you saw only those top-ranking officials who are at headquarters. There are others in the European Office of the UN in Geneva, in Vienna and in other locations in the world. In total there are 26 Under-Secretaries-General, some heading world programs such as UNICEF, the United Nations Development Program, the UN Fund for Population Activities, the UN Fund against Drug Abuse, etc. In the 26 positions of Under-Secretaries-General there are only three women: the UN High Commissioner for Refugees, the head of the Vienna office and the head of the Fund for Population Activities. Of 18 Assistant-Secretaries-General there are only men, not one woman. In the Director category there are 71 men and 8 women. In the grade below there are 219 men and 16 women. In the next category there are 389 men and 73 women. The number of women increases substantially in the lower grades, making an average of 30% of women in the total staff. But in the leadership posts 92.9% are occupied by men and only 7.1% by women. If you take the whole United Nations system, including the specialized agencies, 95.4% of the leadership posts are occupied by men. To my knowledge, during the forty-six years since the UN was born, no woman has headed any of the specialized agencies".

When he saw consternation written all over her face, he added:

"A great fault lies with governments, because for top positions we receive usually government nominations and proposals. And these are consistently for men. But with your arrival, I am sure things will change."

She answered: "You bet they will. My mission is written right in my name, since Narayan means man and woman as partners."

The chef de cabinet after a silence said:

"This brings me to a personal subject. I must confess to you that I increasingly begin to feel like a tired, old man. World affairs wear you out. I am 68 years old and the UN retirement age is 60. I stayed at the request of your predecessor whom I have known for many years. But I would now like to go and start in India my Vanaprashta, my age of wisdom and preparation for the beyond. May I ask you the favor of accepting my resignation. The post of chef de cabinet is a very crucial one. You should therefore appoint to it someone who has your absolute confidence, someone of your personal choice."

She answered:

17

"I understand you and I accept respectfully your decision. You leave behind a good reputation of honesty, integrity and justice. You did credit to your country and to world service. I thank you from the bottom of my heart. Tell me, please, how does it feel leaving the UN?"

Tears came to his eyes. "It feels awful, as you will experience yourself when the time comes. Despite all the frustrations, immense obstacles, lack of power and the cynicism of the media, this is the most inspiring, exciting, fascinating, challenging, path-breaking institution ever created by humans. Here, for the first time in history, you are allowed to work for the entire Earth and human family. You will learn so much. It is the greatest University on Earth. You can do so much: for peace, for the poor, for the defenseless and down-trodden. It is the beginning of the fulfillment of the dreams of all great religious leaders, visionaries and philosophers. As your guru, Sri Chinmoy, whom you saw today, prophesied:

*"At the end of its voyage, there is every possibility that the United Nations will be the last word in human perfection. And then the United Nations can easily bloom in excellence and stand as the pinnacle of divine enlightenment."*

"My only consolation is that as an old sage in Auroville where I intend to retire, I will be able to teach young people from all over the world about this blessed organization and to make them love, respect and support it. If God allows me, I will try to leave behind my testament to the UN."

Lakshmi was deeply moved. She suddenly saw herself in his place, after her Secretary-Generalship. What will she think? What will she do? Where will she go? How will she transmit her wisdom and experience to the next generation?

They left pensively the restaurant, the older man holding the hand of the young, dynamic woman, full of dreams, ideals and vitality. He prayed all the Gods and saints in heaven to love her, to protect her and help her in her impossible task. He wished her to succeed in leading humanity peacefully into the third millennium and help this poor, bewildered, divided, mismanaged planet become the Planet of Peace, the Planet of God, the Planet of Civilization and Culture, a true showcase in the universe.

18

Lakshmi at one point broke the silence and had this comment: "Our oath of allegiance you read speaks of UN officials as servants. I think the title of Secretary-General should be changed to Servant-General."

* *

During the afternoon Lakshmi received her first visitors: the head of the UN Staff Association, the President of the UN Press Corps, the Director of the UN Women's Guild, and the Under-Secretary-General for Special Political Affairs to report on a flare-up in the Middle-East. Her secretaries were astonished by the time she devoted to each visitor. Francoise commented to her:

"Your predecessors often wanted to get rid of visitors. To do that, we entered with a slip of paper reminding the Secretary-General that he had another visitor waiting."

She answered:

"There is no need to do that. People are not fools. They know what those slips of paper mean, and I am supposed to know my schedule of appointments. For me every visitor is a precious human being, someone who might have something fundamental to say to me. As U Thant used to say:

*"I must empty myself of myself in order to receive fully my visitor. In return, they expect advice, a sign of hope, an idea, an inspiration, a message which they will never forget and on which they may work for the rest of their life."*

For me it is as important to speak to one person as it is to speak to thousands, because that one person might influence many others during a life-time. Let me be the judge. People wait in a doctor's and in a dentist's office. They can also wait a little in the Secretary-General's office. They will not regret it."

She had also a speech to deliver in the afternoon to the opening meeting of the UN World Food Program which channels surplus foods from the rich countries to the needy in the poor countries. Francoise gave her a draft speech prepared by the secretariat of that Program. Lakshmi had a little chat with her:

"How did my predecessors deal with speeches?"

"It varied. There are so many speeches to deliver that to read what the substantive departments have prepared is usually the only

19

way. You honor with your presence the opening of a UN meeting, you read the speech and you leave because you are supposed to be very busy and to have no time to participate in the debate. Important speeches you review ahead of time. Some Secretaries-General liked to add their personal remarks. The only Secretary-General who prepared most of his speeches himself was Dag Hammarskjøld. U Thant did it towards the end of his mandate."

"Well, to speak is so important that I want to follow their practice. Make sure that I get draft speeches or suggestions a few days ahead of time, together with the agenda of the meeting. I will read them in bed, just before going to sleep. My subconscious will work on them during the night and I wake up the following morning with a ready speech which I will dictate on a cassette, or at least the main ideas which I will develop. I will deliver most of my speeches impromptu without written texts, only a few notes on the main ideas. Make sure that they are taped and transcribed and I will then work on a written text for publication. In Hindu tradition, to speak is a cosmic communication of energy, a divine means to convey one's cosmic perceptions to other cosmic beings. One must speak as much with the heart and the soul as with the mind. Westerners are speaking too much with their head and hence communicate imperfectly. Sanskrit means "divine communication", and Devanagara, the written language, means words encapsulated in stone (nagar, the city). To speak freely and inspiringly is the true democracy."

She practiced immediately what she preached. She went down to the meeting and instead of reading the speech prepared for her, she spoke emotionally and from personal experience about what hunger really means. Her childhood experiences vibrated through her speech. When she finished, the delegates arose from their seats and applauded her in a long, standing ovation.

When she returned to her office, Francoise asked:

"How did it go?"

"I think it went alright. I saw a few people cry, which is the test of a good speech. You must touch the hearts of the people. They might forget what you said exactly, but they will never forget how they were moved and inspired to do good. And in turn they will move others to do good. That is what we call in India the law of Karma. Also, I learned a lot listening to myself. When we speak, ideas and enlightenments are born. Mysterious forces sometimes speak through us."

As is customary, television is very eager to get the views of new Secretaries-General, especially their origin, their youth, events in their lives which made them what they are and led them to this high world position. She accepted to be interviewed by CNN on her first working day. What impressed the public most was this statement of hers:

"When I was a child I always heard my parents speak of wars, enemies, foreign countries, border conflicts, occupation, colonialism and other similar evils. But when I looked up to the sky, I saw stars, a sun, a moon, clouds and birds who ignored all these divisions, borders and wards. And I dreamt that some day I would be on top of the world helping to create one human family in one planetary home. And my dream became true. Today, as Secretary-General, I have many more dreams. Dreams are stronger than armies. I dream that all human beings of this Earth will become instruments of peace, thus fulfilling the cosmic function for which they were born and allowed to live for a few years on this beautiful planet. I dream that humanity will hold a world-wide celebration of the year 2000 and of our entry into the third millennium, preceded by unparalleled thinking, perception, inspiration, elevation, planning and love for the achievement of a peaceful and happy human society on Earth. I want to be the Secretary-General of possible and impossible dreams. The only limits to the realization of our dreams will be our doubts and hesitations of today. We must move ahead with strong ideals and an active faith."

During the program, when asked if she would primarily represent the third world countries at the UN, she said that her guidelines would be this statement by former Secretary-General U Thant, speaking about his successor:

*As far as the nature of the Secretary-General's personality is concerned, I feel that he or she should be the kind of man or woman who looks to the future, a futurist, and has a global conception of problems. I do not believe in the importance of regional considerations in the choice of a Secretary-General. I do not believe that only an Asian or an African or a Latin American or a European should be the next Secretary-General. What I believe in are the qualities of the head as well as of the heart, like moral integrity, competence, and the ability to project in the future, to act within the framework of a global unit, and a genuine desire to see this organization develop into a really effective instrument of peace, justice and progress.*

\* \*

When she left the UN in the evening, both stimulated and exhausted by this first working day, accompanied by Andy Smith, she had only two thoughts on her mind which she confided to him:

"Andy, I will now arrive in this big house which was inhabited by the former Secretary-General. What will I do there with all those rooms and servants? My predecessors were married and had families. I am single and will be lost in there. In addition, I am a Gandhian, i.e. I favor simple, frugal living. What would you advise?"

He answered:

"Trygve Lie had an apartment in Manhattan. Dag Hammarskjøld too, but he rented a retreat house in Brewster, Connecticut, to be in nature during the week-ends. The house is now a museum in his memory. U Thant lived with his family in a rented house in Riverdale overlooking the Hudson river. He loved to dream and to meditate in front of the majestic river. The house burnt down after his death, but the estate has been preserved as U Thant Park. Mr. Waldheim and your predecessor Javier Perez de Cuellar and their families lived in the house you are to occupy now. It was a private mansion given to the United Nations Association of America which places it at the disposal of the Secretary-General."

"Well, I am much more tempted to live in the little apartment on the thirty eighth floor of the UN. It would be quite sufficient for me. We must give the example of simple and frugal life in order not to tax unduly the precious resources of this planet. As Gandhi said: "We must live simply so that others may simply live". For week-ends, I would like to follow the example of Dag Hammarskjøld and rent a room at the wonderful Lake Mohonk Mountain House, near New Paltz. It is located in the midst of magnificent nature, is owned by Quakers and has a remarkable history of peace initiatives and mediations. It would be a great relaxation and inspiration to me after my hard weeks at the UN."

"My second question is this: As I said on the television program, I wish to lay the foundations for a new millennium of peace and cooperation. I want to launch new initiatives, new bold ideas, create new world programs and institutions, develop a new thinking

22

and philosophy, strengthen world unity and consciousness, in other words help create as fast as possible a peaceful and better world. If not, this planet is likely to go to pieces or to become unlivable and the human species might vanish from it. I know that people like you have a good judgment of their higher-ups. You know who is really good, honest and reputed. Who do you think is a person or the persons to whom I should turn to help me with my grand design?"

Andy thought for a moment and then said:

"My advice would be to turn to a man named Louis Parizot, a Frenchman from Alsace-Lorraine, who served the UN for more than forty years, starting at the entrance grade and finishing as an Assistant Secretary-General. He has been given many nicknames: Mr. UN, the philosopher and prophet of the UN, the optimist-in-residence at the UN, and more. He has worked in several crucial fields, knows the UN and its specialized agencies inside out, was the collaborator of three Secretaries-General and before retirement organized the fortieth anniversary of the UN under the motto: The UN for a Better World. He has been a vocal advocate for the holding of a world-wide celebration of the year 2000. I think he would be your man."

"And where is he? I have never heard of him."

"He went down to Costa Rica to be the one-dollar-a-year Chancellor of the University for Peace created by the UN General Assembly, a new institution which has difficulties to get off the ground like all new visionary ventures started by the United Nations. Like you, he is fond of difficult, challenging tasks and eager to help the birth of new world institutions which he considers vital for a better world. He is down there in Costa Rica with his wife, a famous Chilean delegate who has done great work for the equality and rights of women and who was President of the UN's Women's Guild. Alas, in the last few years she has become afflicted with Alzheimer's disease."

"Well, I will send him a cable tomorrow, asking him to come and see me. Thank you again for your wonderful advice, dear Andy. You are an angel."

\* \* \*

# Chapter 3

A luxury boat is floating on the Potomac River near Washington, carrying a select group of prominent corporate leaders, wealthy people, top level US Administration officials and politicians. The group is staying together for two days, cruising on the river, concluding business deals and considering as the main subject of discussion the theme; how to keep the Republican Party in power for the next hundred years.

The group was the brainchild of Alexander Rumacher, a top Wall Street financier of immense wealth and power, one of the 157 billionaires of this planet, but also a great thinker, philosopher and supporter of the arts. He is a handsome, sportive man in his late forties, single, an avid reader, traveller and observer of humans and of the world. He has a boundless admiration for his father who started the fortune and imparted to him the conviction that economics and wealth rule the world. He studied economics, followed into his deceased father's footsteps, multiplied the fortune and never wavered from his fundamental beliefs. His two favored heroes are Alexander the Great and Baron de Rothchild, two men who had succeeded in ruling a great part of the world by different means: the first through power, armies and philosophy, the other through the behind-the-scenes political use of his wealth. Rumacher had the most unique collection of books on both heroes and he devoted all his vacations to retrace their steps and re-live their lives. His favorite voyage was to take his yacht on the sea-routes of Alexander the Great. In reality, in moments of confidence, he would avow that no one would ever reach again such power. Deep inside, he was a kind, loving and lonely man, but he would never budge an inch from the course mapped out for him by his father. He manipulated politics in far-away lands, bought companies and banks, launched and promoted new business ventures, values and philosophies through schools of economics, the media, politics and financial and other institutions around the world. He was the synthesis, reincarnation of both Alexander the Great and Baron de Rothchild, the personalized genius of modern business and money making. As part of his world strategy, using the key position and influence of the United States in the world, he had organized these occasional Potomac cruises, feeling wonderfully at home on boats.

One and a half days of the river voyage had been devoted to the main subject for which it had convened. The last afternoon was left to four more subjects: the demise of communism; the European Community; privatization; and the United Nations. Rumacher was sitting at the head table in the main salon of the vessel, presiding over the meeting. Next to him sat a young man, Felix White, the son of a banker and a fervent New Age advocate who challenged his father on every issue with radically opposed views. Alexander Rumacher appreciated his keen intelligence and had appointed him as the Devil's Advocate of these meetings. The young man sat there, his head sunk towards the table, looking crushed, powerless and disgusted by all the wealth and power represented in front of him.

Rumacher took the floor:

"Item No. 1: the demise of communism. There is not much more to say beyond our meetings over the last few years. We have finally won. President Reagan, our friend, followed our advice and pushed armaments to a point where the Russians could not follow or would be economically ruined. They finally capitulated. So this is done. We must hear at our next meeting the progress report and proposals of our task-force on The World After Communism which we were wise enough to establish as early as 1984. Now that communism is dead and will no longer be Enemy No. 1 and the scapegoat of all the world's evils, the people will be inclined to have a closer look at capitalism and at us, and we might fare worse than in the past. This must be avoided at all costs. We must establish a fast, clever, coherent, first class strategy to programme the public against other enemies. We have the means. The big media are in our hands. I am inclined to propose that we launch an all-out attack against ecologism as the new scourge of humanity, the new communism. I propose that we call it eco-communism, eco-leftism."

He turned to his young neighbour and asked:

"What does our devil's advocate have to say? Do you for once agree with us? Wasn't it a fantastic victory?"

Felix White:

"Yes, but with one big correction: the USSR is a vast, great country which has experimented with the perennial, deep-seated human dream of equality, while you used to the point of misuse and abuse the human dream of freedom, transforming it for your own benefit into unprecedented monopolies, compared with which all earlier forms of power look like peanuts. But do not underestimate them. You isolated them, you even supported Hitler against them, and they finally came to the good, old American conclusion: if you can't beat them, join them. You are going to get more trouble from the Russians than you ever had before. This time your monopolies and power over the people are going to be scrutinized and challenged from within. As for the reason for their demise, I have also a couple of corrections:

First, the Russians will make you believe that you got them on their knees, and it is true that their inefficient system, except for armaments and outer-space, would have never allowed them to catch up with you. But they knew that for a long time. The main reason why they changed course is that as good world analysts they came to the conclusion that the world was changing profoundly behind their backs, while they were engulfed in stupid, antiquated wars or footholds like Afghanistan, Cuba, Nicaragua, etc. They realized that the world environment is going to pieces, the climate is deteriorating. Their scientists gave them projections showing that the planet will become unlivable within a few decades if we continue on the present course. They got interested in the New Age thinking and perceptions of the youth of America and of the western world. They invited their most prominent spokespeople - mostly women - and saw that these were their new, natural allies, no longer the workers. The proof of what I say? Read Gorbachev's Perestroika: it could have been written by any leading New Ager. This is the new alliance, an alliance with deep-seated evolutionary, fundamental changes in values which are going to get **you** on your knees, because you don't care a bit

26

about the fate of the planet and humanity, you care only about your wealth, your profits, your bank accounts, your stocks and power. You can win against the poor devils in the street, but you cannot win against evolution. No one ever will. Just look at history, you Alexander Rumacher, who are so fond of it.

Secondly, on the occasion of the fortieth anniversary of the United Nations, Secretary-General Perez de Cuellar sent in 1984 to all governments a remarkable note in which he recommended that they ask their best thinkers to review the last forty years since World War II, to assess the achievements and failures of humanity, and to look to the year 2000 and third millennium. The Russians did it very seriously, while the US did not. And the Russians concluded that all their past foreign policy was wrong and that they had to change course. This is what you see since Gorbachev. He is not an accident, he is a product of the new policy. They are not on their knees. They are going to be active participants in the shaping of a new world, of a new age, of a new millennium, the features of which you are unable to grasp."

"Thank you, Felix, said Rumacher. This was useful. We too have to take evolution seriously. Dear friends, please think about it, all of you. This is no time for complacency. Let us establish a group on the subject: "What are the Russians likely to really do?" I now turn to Item No 2: the entry into force of the European Community. What are the implications for the US? I give the floor to our friend from the State Department."

Man from the State Department:

"The implications ar momentous. This Community is the most important single change in the world political structure since 1945. It has succeeded beyond belief and it will continue to succeed and expand. There is little doubt that after East Germany, every single former communist country of Europe will join it. And the apparent dismemberment of the USSR into more independent states might be quite welcome to their leaders because it will mean more members in that community. It will become the biggest economic and political block in the world. A whole series of non-European countries want to join it, especially African countries. Even some Latin-American countries are dreaming of joining it, and I am sure Spain and Portugal would welcome them. Also, do not forget that the USSR reaches far into Asia. It is not excluded that even China will eventually join it. My prediction is that by the year 2000, they will drop the adjective European and we will be faced with the most powerful conglomeration that ever existed on this planet, an irresistible political movement that will encompass ever growing areas of the globe. The US will be confronted with a new world order in the construction of which it has not participated. Let me read to you the final words of Jean Monnet's *Memoirs*, the man whose vision started it all after World War II, dreaming of the reconciliation of France and Germany, of a United Europe and finally of a World Community:

*Have I said clearly enough that the Community we have created is not an end in itself? It is a process of change, continuing in the same process which in an earlier period produced our national forms of life. The sovereign nations of the past can no longer solve the problems of the present: they cannot ensure their own progress or control their own future. And the Community itself is only a stage on the way to the organized world of tomorrow.*

What will be the consequences for the United States? First: we will be far outdistanced by this new political and economic power. Our political leadership in the world will be gone, as will be that of the USSR but they will be part of that new world order while we will not. We will hang alone in this world which we have helped so much for so long, without anyone being really grateful. As they say in the United Nations: there are no permanent friends, there are only permanent interests. Second: the European Community is creating one institution after the other, one legal order after the other in every political and economic field, from outer-space to the atom, from the entire social order to individual human rights, in which we do not participate and have no voice. As a result, we will be confronted some day with joining a new world order which we did not contribute to create. Then we will be really down on our knees. When you come in at the tail-end you are bound to lose. Ask the British: they fought the creation of the European Common Market, spent huge sums of money to campaign against it and then, after it succeeded, General de Gaulle made them pay the highest price for entering it: the abandonment of the Commonwealth preferences in favor of the agricultural products of the continent! If they had joined right at the beginning they would have never had to pay such a high price. You will ask me: "What can we do?"

Thank God, the first thing has already been done by President Bush when he announced the plan for a vast community of the Americas from Alaska to the Tierra del Fuego. Thus he has staved off the danger of seeing Latin American countries wanting to join the European Community, which was very close.

But more than that: while our preceding Presidents had their minds primarily in Moscow, Beijing, Tokyo and Europe, we are now discovering what the Americas really are: the richest continent on Earth, endowed with every conceivable resources, be it petroleum or other minerals; the richest agricultural lands, from Canada, the Mid-West, to Brazil and Argentina; the most diverse climates and vegetations, from the North and South Poles through all shades of temperate, sub-tropical, tropical and equatorial zones; a bicontinent with two of the most advanced scientific and technological countries on Earth - the US and Canada -, with a highly educated population, and well identified from the rest of the world by the vast expanses of the Atlantic and Pacific. What a jewel, what a model we can make out of this blessed continent!

As a result we will be able to match the European Community with an equally powerful American Community and will be at least an equal partner. I therefore recommend that top priority be given to an all-American Community. No time should be lost, because Europe is far ahead of us. All of you here, I beg you to invest in the Americas.

You will be shocked by my second remark, namely that we have a major trump-card in our hands: the presence of the United Nations on US soil. Instead of bickering against it, we should on the contrary, take the UN as the stepping stone to the world community we want to see established. President Bush should propose the creation of a true World Community to be worked out in the universal forum of the United Nations. If we do that, we will be thinking and acting right. We will be able to solve the problem of world poverty by having the Europeans take care of Africa, we of Latin America, and Japan and other rich Asian countries of Asian poverty. Instead of trailing behind the Europeans, we will be the leaders in shaping a true world community, with its capital in the United States. This would then be an orderly, well administered planet in lieu of the chaos we have at present. We would thus remain faithful to the mission of the US in the world, as shown so well by our founding fathers. We cannot forever live on their heritage. We must enrich it, we must go beyond it."

Alexander Rumacher: "Wow! That was mind-boggling. You hit me right into the stomach and I do not know what to say, except that I am glad that you are in the State Department and our friend. The subject is too big to be handled at the tail-end of our meeting. I put you in charge of a thinking group to prepare our next Potomac meeting on it. Thank you, thank you again. Our next subject is privatization. I give the floor to Joe Riches, President of the American Universal Bank.

Joe Riches:

"I am happy to report that all goes well on this front. As with communism, we are having a first class victory against socialism, trade unions, state enterprises and nationalized sectors. The incredible, unceasing, well-nurtured, insatiable craving for goods and services all around the world has prepared the world population to accept the fact that only private enterprise can provide these goods and not state enterprise. The era of nationalizations is gone and we have entered the golden age of privatization, entrepreneurship, marketing, advertising and big business.

Retroactively, I would also say that the strategy followed by US banks during the energy crisis was a stroke of genius. The added revenue received by the OPEC countries was tantamount to a taxation of the rich. If these revenues had been channelled through international agencies like the IMF, the World Bank, the Inter-American Bank and the UN regional banks and directed to the actual needs of the poor countries, we would have lost control over the money. The stroke of genius of the American banks was to get the money from the OPEC countries and to lend it to the backward countries for projects wanted primarily by US firms, even if they were useless, such as steel mills, atomic power plants, petrochemical plants, etc. And today, our banks hold their debts and we can impose privatization in return for debt reduction or forgiveness. We are thus regaining control over a large part of the natural resources of these countries, we can buy their profit-making enterprises and penetrate nationalized sectors such as insurance, medical services and even education. It is a fantastic success story."

Felix White interrupts him:

"You call a fantastic success story the creation of more misery, the taking over of entire countries, the creation of untold unnecessary waste, a rebirth of colonialism under the elegant name of privatization? From the world's point of view, I would call the strategy and actions of the US banks the greatest failure and self indictment of privatization in modern history. And of course, the US taxpayer has to pay for the debt reduction. You are not even funny anymore. You should be brought before a World Court for Economic Crimes. Furthermore, the issue is not of communism, nationalization and privatization. It is purely a question of good management. The French nationalized banks, railroads and automobile industry are among the best in the world, simply because they are managed to perfection. That is the main point the Soviets were missing, but you cannot fool all countries on that issue.

The current unholy alliance between nations and multinationals is going to break up. Nations will discover that they are no longer governing, but that government is in the hands of these new powers, many of which already outdo the majority of small nations. The world should on the contrary nationalize, decentralize, and privatize the large, monstrous, human values-deforming monopolies and oligarchies, the new enslavers of the people. Privatization should go at least hand in hand with demonopolization."

Alexander Rumacher:

"Enough of that. Time is running out. Let us take up the last subject; the UN, our greatest danger and enemy. I give the floor to John Fitzpatrick, head of the Golden Age Foundation."

John Fitzpatrick:

"Well on that score, as you all well know, we had only relative success. We have been able to stop the UN from growing and from meddling more in world affairs, but we have not been able to kill it, as was our objective. Why? Primarily because the US is not alone in this matter. We can programme the US public to disrespect the UN, to consider it ineffective, bureaucratic, duplicating, costly to the US taxpayer. That is working like a charm. We can plant adverse articles and news in the media of which we are by and large the masters. We can also, as we did, work on all US Congressmen and Senators, influenced already by the media and the opinion of their voters. But we are not in a position to do this abroad, except with a few like-minded conservative leaders. They cannot be fooled so easily. They know the UN through their own people, they find the UN and its agencies useful, often indispensable and irreplaceable. The only tactic that has worked therefore was to cut funds and delay payment of our dues. As a result, the UN and its agencies are for the moment close to paralysis, demoralized, unable to grow. But they are not disappearing. Our exit from UNESCO did not open the graveyard of that organization as we had hoped. Despite the enormous power of the US, only two conservative governments followed us and they consider re-joining, because UNESCO remains solid and they have no voice and role in it anymore, a fact which they consider detrimental to their interests.

Our original strategy to kill the UN was based on two consider- ations: the most important one was to destroy an official world platform where the communist countries were "recognized" and could propagandize their evil theories; secondly, the UN stands very often in the way of private business because its motives are not profit or capital accumulation but of a public service nature. A new world ethics is being born at the UN in which each nation has a voice. Business has no voice, except through the pro-business United States and a few conservative countries. As a result, the UN system is a serious and growing threat to our philosophy and world views.

We furthermore encounter the following obstacles: First, our ally Israel and the Jewish people do not want us to kill or quit the UN, although they have little love for it. But the UN recognized Israel and gave it its birth certificate and world identity. If the UN goes, Israel's recognition by the world community goes too. Only a handful of countries would continue to recognize Israel bilaterally.

Second, at one point we staged a heated campaign against communist infiltration in the UN, the size of the USSR delegation, and we raised the specter of a take-over of the US by the communists under the UN flag. The USSR in reaction notified the Secretary- General of the UN that if it continued they would request the move of the entire UN from the US to Vienna, where Mr. Waldheim would receive it with enthusiasm, in view of Austria's dream to play again a central role in North-South and East-West relations, and thus become the capital of the world. This threat brought about a change in the State Department policy. A move of the UN would be a big blow to US prestige as well as a loss of control over it. As a result we had to change our strategy. Our target is now: keep the UN as a useless debating society on the shores of the East River, cut funds, oppose any new programs, and proclaim our departure from UNESCO as irreversible and non-negotiable. UNESCO is indeed the greatest danger to the values we spread through the media, the multinational corporations and advertisement.

Third, an added recent element is that our new President knows the UN very well for having been our permanent representative to it for several years. We cannot fool him. He knows the value and the benefits he can derive from the UN, as was illustrated by his fast, successful move against Iraq in the Security Council.

A fourth element is the change of policy of the USSR which will make the UN work as proved in the Iraq-Kuwait crisis. With the end of the cold war, the UN can become an effective organization."

Alexander Rumacher:

"And what about this Indian woman who has been appointed Secretary-General? Was it wise for the US to support her? Women can be very sentimental, emotional and irrational. Their values are not usually profit and power. Moreover, coming from one of the poorest countries in the world which has opposed successfully the invasion of our products and culture, she might mean a lot of trouble to us."

John Fitzpatrick:

"Well, we had no choice. It was the turn of a woman and of an African. And an African woman would have been much worse. They are vocal, exalted, revolutionary, irrational and often anti-West. That was the real danger. Now we have to see and watch her closely. We have our insiders in the UN who will report on her very thoroughly. Most important will be her appointments of new Under-Secretaries-General and Assistant-Secretaries-General. We will, of course, plant our own candidates. She cannot do everything by herself. You will get a detailed report at a next meeting."

Alexander Rumacher:

"Thank you, dear friends, it has been a fruitful two days and we must soon meet again. Since we were speaking of India, it reminds me that Hindu political science considers that the caste system still exists today and that the same perennial groups seize or share the power: the kings or politicians, the merchants, the military, the priests and the poor. Politics is an eternal variation in this struggle. We are the merchants, allied with the politicians and the military, and our theatre of operations is the entire world. I think it is great to be living today and to have wealth and power."

At that point he wanted to close the meeting but Felix White handed him a sheet of paper.

Alexander Rumacher:

"Wait a minute, our young devil's advocate wants to have the last word."

Felix White:

"Yes, while I listened to you, I scribbled this drawing: it shows our globe and, jutting out of it, several clusters of sky-scrapers: Manhattan, Los Angeles, Dallas, Hong Kong, Sao Paolo, Singapore, etc. In between are the seas and oceans and the continents on which I have marked the word: desert. You are like giant suction machines, big vampires, huge vacuum cleaners who will clean out the whole world of its nature, elements and species, leave it a vast desert and for what? To accumulate useless paper money, bank accounts and stock certificates in your sky-insulting buildings. If you don't revise your course, these buildings will be your tombstones on an empty planet floating life-less in the universe without a single one of your names ever to be remembered, except as a curse."

Alexander Rumacher:

"Dear Felix, you play an important role in humiliating us. We need it once in a while. I will have a poster made of your drawing and we will distribute it at our next meeting. We need such warnings and a little modesty. Goodbye, dear friends. It was a great meeting. We hammered out a strategy for the next 100 years. We are the power of this century and we intend to remain it for the next millennium. The Golden Calf will not be overturned this time. It will be the permanent world God of the future. It is wonderful to be alive in these times. I wish you great joys, much power and huge profits."

\* \* \*

# Chapter 4

Louis Parizot is sitting in an airplane flying from Costa Rica to New York. He is man in his late sixties, very sturdy and broad shouldered, of strong Alsatian stock, with still abundant blond-grayish hair, blue eyes and pink, healthy cheeks in a wide-open, optimistic, trustworthy face. In his strong, energetic hands he holds a file entitled *2000 ideas for the year 2000*. He closed the file for a moment and began to ponder:

"Why am I called to New York by the new Secretary-General? How does she even know of my existence? What can be the motive of her cable: Would be grateful if you could come to New York for consultations, I need your advice."

He reviewed several possibilities but quickly gave up, saying to himself: "Never mind. In a few hours I will know. In any case, God has always such mysterious ways to use me and to move me around the world. I better leave things in His good hands."

Nevertheless, in order to be prepared for any eventuality, he had taken along a few files containing his numerous ideas, plans and proposals for a peaceful and better world. He had just finished reading his Plan 2010 submitted in 1984 to a Christian Science Monitor contest. He was half-pleased and half-sad: some of his major recommendations and hopes had been fulfilled, in particular the end of the cold war between the US and the USSR. This was of momentous importance for the future of the world and of the UN.

35

But there remained so much to do and progress was so slow. Moreover there had been the setbacks of the US unilateral military intervention in Panama and of Iraq in Kuwait. What a mess! What were humans doing to each other and to this beautiful planet so recklessly, so unnecessarily, so primitively!

At times he was beginning to feel the burden of growing age. He had lived 68 years filled with events, sufferings, war, evacuations, nazi occupation, prison, studies and finally four decades of world service with the UN. What an incredible and demanding life it had been. His wildest imagination could not have dreamt such a life when as a boy he looked out of his window at the stars, the moon and the clouds and wished to be some day on top of the world. Love for life, peace and happiness had been his constant obsession and God used him fully as His instrument. It seemed never to end. After retiring from the UN, he was now the Chancellor of the University for Peace created by the UN in Costa Rica. He loved difficult and impossible tasks, those which no one else wanted to tackle. He was always on the front lines of new world ventures, dreams and institutions and when they worked he left for others. His last dreams were to give wings to this first supra-national University, to see it become a school for heads of states, to see scores of students from all the world trained in it, and to be buried someday in demilitarized Costa Rica, the country on Earth which came closest to his ideals.

His retirement from the UN was saddened by the decline of his wonderful life-companion, Margarita, his Latin-American wife, afflicted for the last several years with Alzheimer's disease. As a young girl in the North of Chile, she too was possessed with a magnificent obsession: to study at a university, to go out into the world and to fight for equal rights for women. Despite her father's opposition, she became one of the first women Doctors of Law and women diplomats of her country. As a delegate to the UN, she worked with Eleanor Roosevelt, Gabriela Mistral and many other remarkable women to obtain the equality of women with men in the world. What a beautiful, intelligent, fiery, energetic, passionate and God-loving person she was! He remembered that when they got married, she refused to accept the French nationality law which she considered discriminatory to women. She took up the matter in the UN's Commission on Women's Rights, got a convention on the nationality of women adopted, and the French had to change their law! That was the kind of woman he had married. And what beautiful four children she gave him and raised single-handed, resigning from her diplomatic post, placing her love and care for her children above her career. And when the children had grown up, she resumed her fight for women's rights as a volunteer delegate of Chile and President of the UN Women's Guild. Then, after the age of sixty her memory and mind began to decline. He took care of her for five years up to the point when specialized care became indispensable. After a long, careful search, he found a remarkable, small nursing home in Costa Rica, conceived by a top Costa Rican gerontologist who considered love, kindness, affectionate care and good nutrition to be the main help that could be given to Alzheimer patients. So they moved to Costa Rica. He spent his mornings at his beloved University for Peace on an inspired hill in the midst of tropical forests, and his afternoons and week-ends with his beloved wife in a beautiful Spanish hacienda converted into a nursing home.

He was still dreaming and reminiscing when the pilot announced the plane's landing at Kennedy airport. It was only midday and he decided to go straight to the UN to try to meet a tentative appointment with the Secretary-General in the afternoon.

He was so happy to see again the tall UN building where he had dreamt, thought, loved and worked so much for the world and humanity. For him this was a truly holy place, the dream of Christ and of all great sages become true, the meeting place where all humanity was seeking its unity and ways on this blessed planet in the vast universe.

The UN guards at the entrance greeted him warmly. He was one of their heroes, having helped them out in difficult situations. A newly recruited guard wanted to be introduced to him: "Mr. Parizot, I want to have the pleasure of shaking your hand. As part of my briefing I was given to read a book by the UN Meditation Group on the UN Security Service. I read in it your speech. It is so inspiring and encouraging to us. Thanks to you, I am proud to be a UN guard."

He was deeply moved by this welcome and the memory came back how he once managed to convince Viet-Nam war protesters who had chained themselves to the seats of the Security Council to leave peacefully and to stage their protest in front of the US Mission. Ever since, the UN guards, who did not have to use force, saluted him with respect.

* *

When he arrived on the thirty eighth floor, Francoise told him that the Secretary-General had a better idea than an appointment in her office. She was now living in the little apartment on that floor and she invited him for a tete-a-tete Hindu dinner which she would prepare herself. She had read his novel *"Sima Mon Amour"* unfolding in India and knew of his love for Indian food and traditions. In the meantime he could pay visits to friends and do a pilgrimage in the UN.

This is exactly what he did. He paid a visit to the nearby room where he had acted as the Director of the Secretary-General's Executive Office. There he had served 3 Secretaries-General, was involved in many crises, devised long-term plans for the success of humankind and of the UN, written many speeches and seen innumerable people. But he left that office quickly to prevent tears from coming to his eyes. The memories were too overpowering.

He got a message that a customer wanted him to autograph one of his books at the UN Bookshop where his memories were still alive in his numerous works on happiness, war and peace, spirituality, hope and even good humor. His books were best-selling items in the Bookstore. He even designed their covers in order to convey to readers and perusers an immediate message to do something for peace and a better world. Sometimes, when he used to autograph large numbers of books in the evening while watching television, his wife asked him why he was doing that, and he answered: "Because an autographed book is not likely to be thrown away. One of my books might show up in a garage sale many years after my death. Perhaps a young person will have the curiosity to read it, might be touched by it and will implement one of my proposals. The ways of the universe are mysterious. Perhaps God will guide these books into the right hands, under the right eyes, into the right hearts and souls."

His friends at the Bookshop greeted him warmly. They were his best salespersons. And as usual they had some nice comments in reserve for him: "This morning a lady came in to buy five more copies of *Most of All, They Taught Me Happiness* for her grandchildren". "A priest bought ten copies of *New Genesis* for gifts to his parishioners". And they asked him if more books were coming out, which he happily confirmed, especially now that he had more time to think and to reminisce at his beloved University for Peace.

He then went to visit his old office on the twenty ninth floor of the UN, facing the skyscrapers of Manhattan, a sight which often made him dream and think, especially in the winter when the night fell early. He loved to close the lights in his room and watch the tall buildings with their innumerable occupants and lights, busy like ants changing the world for better or for worse. What would the Buddha, Confucius, Socrates, Jesus, Julius Caesar, Napoleon say at the view of such an incredible sight? He had just read a letter sent by a New York priest who had gone to work in a poor village in Malaysia: in view of the inefficiency, lack of interest and concern of the villagers the priest was ready to give up. But then he woke up one day with this thought: "This village will still be here in 2000 years, but Manhattan will not."...Louis Parizot had occupied that office already as a young man when the UN moved from Lake Success to Manhattan. It was in that office that visitors could see a framed poster showing Christ knocking at the tall UN Secretariat building. His secretary had bought it and offered it to him with this comment: "I counted the floors and the windows, and it is at your window that Jesus is knocking." He had kept the poster ever since as a reminder of that message. Later, when he was in charge of the visit of Pope John Paul II to the United Nations in 1979, his counterpart in the Vatican bought a copy of the poster and gave it to the Pope with these words: "This is what you are supposed to do at the UN." But Parizot disagreed with him: "The painting is wrong. Christ is already *inside* the UN. He has always been!"

Then he went to the conference rooms where he had spent so many years of his life: to the Economic and Social Council of which he had been the Secretary, to Conference rooms 1, 2 and 3 where he had been Secretary of one of the main committees of the General Assembly, and finally to the large General Assembly Hall where he had sat at the podium a few times. What flocks of memories came back to his mind! He could visualize himself sitting up there, listening intently to speakers and debates, and always writing. People sometimes asked him: "After so many years don't you get tired of listening to all these speeches?" And he would answer: "How could I? This is the first time in human history that all nations are talking to each other, trying to find their way on this planet. Think of what a Socrates would say if he were sitting in my place, listening to dialogues between 166 delegates representing every nation on Earth?"

39

"And what are you writing all the time? Reports on these meetings?"
"Yes, but also my personal thoughts, dreams, conclusions and even sometimes poetry."

In the General Assembly Hall, he remembered two dreams, one fulfilled, the other not: the first was to stand up once on the podium and to play the Ode to Joy of Beethoven on his small harmonica which his grandfather and father had taught him to play. It happened shortly before he left the UN. A children's gathering took place in the great hall of nations to announce the yearly awards of Golden Balloons to peacemakers who had worked particularly for children. He was one of the recipients, in recognition of a new world educational system he had proposed. He had brought with him one of his grandsons to be amongst the children and to see his grandfather honored. And as usual, when he was with his grandchildren, he had his harmonica in his pocket. He noticed that the singing of the Ode to Joy was on the children's program. When that moment came, sitting at the high podium, he seized his harmonica, played the Ode to Joy and all the children joined in! It was the high-point of the ceremony! And when he left the podium he said to his grandson: "You see, all dreams sooner or later come true."

His second dream remained unfulfilled. Several years ago he had been invited by the Hopi Indians in Arizona to listen to their prophecies and to share with their elders his own vision of the future. The Hopis loved him because he had opened for them the doors of the UN to deliver their famous prophccy that either the white men will join with their red brethren in a spiritual rebirth of the world, or gourds of ashes would fall from the heavens and destroy all humans. They had given him an eagle's feather - one from the top of the head which is nearest to God - and the name Koogun Deyo, Spider Boy, with the task of catching all evil on Earth in his web and to throw it far away into the universe. As he sat for many hours with the Hopi elders in their kivas, he observed that there was an opening in the cupolas of those half-buried circular meeting places, as well as a hole in the ground, exactly below the opening in the ceiling. When the meetings started, a stone slab covering the hole in the floor was removed. Thus, the Hopis were sitting around a line that came from the far universe through the opening in the cupola, straight down to the center of the Earth. As a result, they had to think and deliberate in cosmic terms. When the meeting ended, the stone slab was placed again on the hole in the floor, and the Hopis or Peaceful Ones, left for their earthly occupations.

Well, the great General Assembly Hall of the UN has exactly the form of a gigantic kiva in which all the tribes of Earth get together. It has even an opening in the ceiling through which one can see the sky. But it does not have a hole in the floor. Parizot's dream was to see a hole bored into it and covered with a slab which would be removed before each meeting, so that the delegates would be conscious of their place in the universe and of their cosmic responsibilities. But no one listened to him and to his crazy proposal. Perhaps the new Secretary-General coming from India, would have a better feeling for it and might give instructions to implement it. He made a mental note to mention it to her at an opportune time.

His last visit was to the UN Meditation Room. O' God, what memories upwelled in him there! He didn't really like Dag Hammarskjøld's modernistic concept of the room, a reflection of a vanishing, analytical, dissecting age. He preferred Trygve Lie's original nature-evoking meditation room in Lake Success, now preserved at Wainwright House in Rye, New York: a big section of a mahogany tree from Africa on which was always displayed a large bowl with flowers or greenery. But nevertheless he liked Hammarskjøld's cosmic concept of the room, its lines, lights and forms originating from a distant point in the universe. The huge, heavy slab of pure iron ore brought from Sweden was truly a cosmic altar. Stanley Kubrik used it as a symbol in his film 2001, showing the slab floating in the universe at the end of the film. On his last day at the UN, Parizot placed on this altar his Testament to the UN, praying God and the universe to bless the peace organization to which he had given so many years of his life and love.

\* \*

At seven o'clock he was on the thirty eighth floor, every cell of his being still vibrating from the emotions of his pilgrimage. He had to shake himself and switch from the past to the future since the lady who invited him expected him to be worthy of his reputation, and to offer her his visions, plans, strategies, ideas and concrete proposals for the future.

She welcomed and received him with keen expectation. They looked at each other with searching, evaluating eyes. He was struck by her extraordinary beauty, her wide, open face drenched with intelligence, avid to know, to receive, to understand the entire Creation. Her deep, large, brown eyes were living cameras bridging her deeper inner self with the outside world. The vivacity and grace of her gestures reflected her passion and joy for life. How she reminded him of Sima, the ideal Hindu woman with whom he had fallen in love in his novel about India! Tears were coming to his eyes. He felt like taking her in his arms and embracing her.

She, on her side, knew instinctively whom she had in front of her: a Westerner who had reached the states of trilokinath and trikaldarshi, a being who was living fully his inner life, his outer life and his life in the universe; his past life, his present life and his future life, even beyond death. He was truly Purushottama, the name given to him by guru Chinmoy, i.e. the seeker of the origin, reason and cause of all things. He was not young anymore, but his spirit took off several years and a part of his present sufferings from his shoulders.

All this took only a few fleeting minutes in view of their high capacity to communicate as living units extremely sensitive to the cosmic currents of the universe.

She invited him to sit down on a divan in her Indian living-dining room, offered him natural fruit juices - she was totally against alcohol- and got busy preparing for him in the little adjacent kitchen a series of delightful vegetarian dishes which often surpass the flavors and pleasures derived by Westerners from meats. He was happy and at ease in this oriental atmosphere which reminded him so much of his stay in India. This woman was more than the Secretary-General of the UN, she was a blossoming human being enjoying fully the miracle of life.

After the delicious dinner, she served him tea and then they began to talk seriously:

She opened the discussion:

"Here I am, a feeble woman, in this new, immense, incredibly difficult job about which I know so little, for which I have been imperfectly prepared, ready to give five to ten years of my life. Except for my eagerness to do good and my love for humanity and this planet, I am at a loss. I can see myself drowning in a multitude of daily problems and demands in fields in which I have no expertise. The danger that my years at the UN will be lost is great. You have been called the prophet of hope of the UN, its optimist-in-residence.

This is why I have called you to my help. Please give me guidance and tell me how to carry out my job efficiently."

She looked at him with keen expectation. What would he respond to her question?

He answered:

"It is very simple. Consider your task as a unique historical opportunity and privilege  Consider the complexity and challenges of the problems facing you and the UN as a wonderful manifestation of human progress. Each of them is a sign of humanity's increasing consciousness of the marvels and complexity of Creation. Consider right from the beginning that humanity is expanding its knowledge and concerns into three directions:

- from the infinitely small to the infinitely large;
- from the total human person to the individual human family;
- from the infinite past to the infinite future.

Put each problem at its right place in that trimurti (trinity) of our magnificent, ever expanding and ever more diverse and refined knowledge of the universe. Each day you will be enriched by it to an incredible degree. On the same day you might be seized with a problem of outer-space and of the atom, of overpopulation and the violation of human rights, of the preservation of the past and a projection into the future. Think how richer, how wiser, how more knowledgeable you will be every evening! More than any head of state on this planet, you will be at the center of an incredible world brain which is being born to the human race at this phase of our evolution.

In your Departments and in the UN's main organs converge practically all the information and world knowledge of humanity:

- the General Assembly gives you a yearly diagnosis of the human journey and of the state of the planet;
- the Economic and social Council digests the world information received from 32 specialized agencies and world programs, from a host of functional commissions covering practically everything under the sun, and from regional commissions for each continent;
- then you have the world conferences and international years;

- the reports from eminent persons on vital world issues;
- your meetings with heads of states;
- the visits and reports to you from the most prominent people, scientists and thinkers on Earth;
-   the work of hundreds of international non-governmental organizations accredited to the UN.

The perceptions, reactions, messages and warnings of this global brain use the channels or nervous system of governments, the media, associations and education to inform and obtain the participation of the people on problems as varied as peace and war, sickness or health, well-being and hunger, a good or a bad environment, drugs, the elderly, the handicapped, etc.

What is still missing is a global heart, the love for our beautiful planet and for the human family, and a global soul, i.e. the love for God and the heavens and our role as living cosmic units in the universe. It could be your great contribution as a woman and as an Indian to bring the world a step further into the sentimental and spiritual spheres, beyond the mental and material successes achieved so far.

Lakshmi:

"This is beautifully said, but the people are looking for action and this is an organization which has no power to act."

Louis Parizot:

"Yes, perhaps luckily so at this stage. I once delivered a speech on the subject: "The UN, the least powerful and most influential organization on Earth." Being powerless, we are more truthful, for as someone once said: power corrupts and absolute power corrupts absolutely. Member states want to remain absolutely sovereign. So let them implement or not the recommendations of the UN and take the responsibility of the fate of this Earth and of its people. This planet has the most outdated, chaotic and Earth-damaging political system in the universe. But this is all you get at this stage of history. You must make the best of it. You will of course have to deal with this problem too and propose a totally new political system for the planet. It will be an essential part of your mandate. We will take this up some other time".

Lakshmi:

"What you mean to say is that the human species is finding its characteristics as a one-species and is developing global organs or meta-organs such as a global sight, global hearing, a global brain, a global nervous system? This is very close to our ancient Hindu philosophy which extended this view into the universe by making us manifestations or incarnations of the vital forces of the cosmos, including the consciousness of our earthly home."

Louis Parizot:

"Yes, and it will be your role to convey this to the people. What we are living is something extraordinary. We are becoming a new species which will be the consciousness and the life of the planet and of the universe. Compared with the primitive species we were a few thousand years ago, we have extended the scope of our eyes millions of times into the infinitely large and the infinitely small through giant telescopes, satellites, space probes, microscopes, picoscopes and atomic bubble chambers. We have extended the scope of our hearing through telephones, radio, satellite communications. We have extended the power of our hands through incredible machines and factories, multiplied the scope and speed of our legs with boats, cars, airplanes and satellites. And most recently we have extended the capacity and power of our memory and brain through incredible computers. We are developing our global organs, brain, nervous system, heart and soul. It is the most fantastic story, ever, on Earth, the birth of a meta-species, of a cosmos-concious species and you are at the birthplace of it. You must therefore never complain, never be sad, never be frustrated, never be pessimistic or despair. You must be happy to serve the UN, the new meta-organism of the human species, of the earth and of the cosmic evolution and conciousness. You must rejoice, be grateful and be ready to serve that evolution and its main institutional manifestations. Every morning when you wake up, look at the sun, fill your lungs with love and express to God your happiness to be alive and readiness to serve."

Lakshmi:

"It shows that you have been in India! What I learn from you is a better understanding of the western way and success in science and technology expressed in evolutionary, cosmological terms. I am indeed beginning to be excited. You have given me a lot of food for thought. But accepting this hopeful, ascending, cosmic framework, how can I best plan my five or ten years of Secretary-Generalship? What can I hope to achieve in those years? How would you proceed?"

Louis Parizot:

"Every Secretary-General comes to this job with his or her innate virtues, capacities, inclinations, loves and skills, and with a cultural background. Do not betray any of them, because they are your strength and your vocation, they are the cosmic forces, evolution and current realities incarnated in you. Secondly, you come as you are at a particular epoch of human history, into a dominant, powerful historical situation with underlying no less powerful, new evolutionary trends. The successful molding of these three elements should be your preoccupation. Regarding the first, you know yourself infinitely better than I. Regarding the powers of our epoch, you know them well too, since you were a Minister of Foreign Affairs of your country. It is on the third element that I can help you best and this is what I would suggest:

We are in January 1992. There are eight years left to the year 2000. You are the luckiest of all Secretaries-General, because you will be able to use these years to shape the fate of the world at the turn of a millennium. Beyond the turmoil, agitations and headlines of the day, you must discern those facts, trends and tendencies which are fundamental to our time and set aside whatever is accidental, secondary, ephemeral and anachronistic. Your life might be rendered totally ineffective by over-attention to the accidental, while it will be incredibly aggrandized by a correct understanding of the new, emerging evolutionary trends. And you are here in a house where both this danger and this opportunity are great. As in private business, you must think about the demand and success of tomorrow and not of yesterday. I would advise you, therefore, to do four things:

1. propose a new item on the agenda of the next General Assembly, entitled: "Preparation and celebration of the Year 2000", with an explanatory note to all member governments in which you outline your perceived needs and proposals;

2. begin to prepare yourself a Peace Plan 2000 and beyond , outlining your vision, steps and proposals to bring about universal and definitive peace and a better world. You have a good example in this regard: Trygve Lie submitted in 1946 a ten year plan to the big powers. Today two-thirds of his proposals have been implemented although the three most important ones: peace, security and disarmament were not and remain high on your list."

She interrupted him:

"Please wait a minute. What you say might be of utmost importance to me, but you have lived all this so intimately that it is quite natural to you, but not to me. Tomorrow in the turmoil of affairs, I might forget what you tell me today. Would you allow me to tape-record what you say so that I may return to it at leisure?"

"Of course."

And she placed a little tape-recorder in front of him.

He continued:

"3. begin to think of a testament you will leave behind at the end of your mandate. No Secretary-General has done this so far, and it is a pity. Think of your unique position in the world. It is your sacred duty to leave behind your thinking, conclusions and proposals to the next generation. You must begin now. I strongly advise you, I beg you to keep a notebook with you, and whenever a fundamental thought or idea occurs to you, write it down. It is important for your journey and for the world. Read Dag Hammarskjøld's Markings and you will see how precious his brief thoughts are to humanity, especially to youth. Remember the Latin advice: Nullus dies sine linea; not a day without a line. Your testament will be a most precious document for humanity. You owe it especially to women, since you are the first woman Secretary-General. Open a file tonight: "My Testament" and jot in it any idea, thought, text or anecdote which you feel is important and a gift to the world. You may even use your tape-recorder and have a secretary transcribe your dictation. It will be faster. When you retire you will be happy to have this record, to work on it, to edit it, to re-live your fascinating life and to give the world a unique legacy. Remember the laws of karma and the duty of great, privileged people to do good even after death."

Lakshmi:

"You have given me a lot. I would even say you have "bombarded me" with a lot. I will require a little time to digest all this. May I suggest to you the following: wherever you are, be it at the University for Peace in Costa Rica or here at the UN where I will give you an office on my floor, please help me, especially on number 2, the Peace Plan 2000 and beyond. Give me your ideas as soon as possible and do not hesitate to send me separate notes at any time. My Journal, Markings and Testament will be my own personal responsibility, but on my future action and strategy I need your help. On that particular score, is there anything else you would like to say or propose?"

Louis Parizot:

"Yes. During your ten years of mandate - I assume that you will be re-elected for a second term - you will have a few fundamental dates from which you can greatly profit:

**1992** is a very important year for four reasons:

First, it is the year of Europe, when the only major postwar change in the political structure of this planet will take place: the entry into force of a United Europe, after centuries of wars on that continent. This will be a great stepping stone towards the birth of a true world community. The President of the United States has already responded to the challenge by proposing an American Community from Alaska to the Tierra del Fuego. In your Plan 2000 you can recommend the formation of further regional communities for Africa, Asia and the Middle-East as building blocks to the transformation of the United Nations into a true world community, a United World.

Second, it is the year of commemoration of the discovery of the New World 500 years ago. This has aroused a lot of thinking about these last 500 years and about the future. It would be appropriate for you to raise the question: "What is the New World that remains to be discovered? What are the new frontiers of humanity?"

Third, it is the year of the second UN world conference on the environment and development, in Brazil, twenty years after the first one held in Stockholm in 1972. It will force humanity to take stock of our progress and regress in the environmental field in the last twenty years. It is a path-breaking conference in human evolution, because it will redefine our basic relations with our planet and make us realize that this planet was not created for us but that we were created for it, for reasons which we have not even tried to determine.

Fourth, it will be also the International Year of Outer-Space which gives us an opportunity to take stock of our immense success in penetrating the far reaches of the universe, to see and study our planet from the outside, with all its psychological consequences towards a one-world-view. Combined with the Brazil conference on the environment that year should be considered as the first cosmic year of the United Nations, since it deals with our current knowledge of the universe, our place in it and our relationships with the particular celestial body on which we live and evolve. It could lead to mind-boggling conclusions and changes of behavior.

**1993**: this year will have significance to you, since you are a deeply spiritual person and come from the Orient. One hundred years ago, a great Indian sage, Vivekananda, came from your country and at the first world congress of religions in Chicago in 1893, proclaimed the unity of all great religions. In 1993, to commemorate that momentous event, a second world congress of religions will be held in Chicago. You should be the main speaker at that conference to proclaim the need for a spiritual Renaissance and propose the creation of a world spiritual agency as part of the UN.

**1994** has been proclaimed International Year of the Family, the basic natural, biological social unit of the human species. Pope John Paul II pleaded so much for UN action on the family. You must invite him to address the General Assembly. He should seize that occasion to give the world his vision of a third Christian, spiritual millennium. He could lift the spirits, sights and wills of governments to a new spiritual, united, peaceful millennium, just and equitable to all humans admitted to the miracle of life on this extraordinary planet.

**1995** will be the fiftieth anniversary of the United Nations, a landmark in recent world history. It should be the year of the Family of Nations, a great year of stock-taking of a half-century packed with the most intensive changes in the evolution of this planet since the appearance of the human species; it should trigger off long-term prospective thinking and be a major stepping stone to the all-important year 2000. The cities of San Francisco and Berlin are already preparing special events for that anniversary.

The years **1996** to **1997** are still free of major events. It gives you an occasion to propose some other building blocks to the year 2000.

The year **1998** will be the fiftieth anniversary of the Universal Declaration of Human Rights, a landmark in human history. It could be celebrated by the addition of a Universal Declaration of Human Responsibilities, as several hundreds of young people have done at the Council of Europe in Strasbourg in 1989, on the bicentennial of the French Declaration of Human Rights:

The year **1999** will mark the hundredth anniversary of the First World Peace Conference in the Hague in 1899. What a wonderful overture this will be on the eve of the Bimillennium! Also the new Panama Canal Treaty will come into effect on 31 December 1999.

The year **2000** will be the culmination and coronation of your mandate. You must constantly keep that date in mind and make the eight coming years its nourishing blood and flesh. Fortunately, a lot of preparatory work has already been done: practically all the UN specialized agencies and world programs have prepared plans for the year 2000: Food 2000, Health 2000, Literacy 2000, Employment 2000, Industrialization 2000, Telecommunications 2000, Environment 2000, etc. The UN has proclaimed economic development decades and general prospects for the year 2000, as well as long-term projections for the children, women, the elderly, the handicapped, etc. What are missing are targets and projections in the crucial political fields and in disarmament. This is where you can play a fundamental role. The decade of 1990 has also been declared Decade of International Law. This gives you an opportunity to assert the absolute need for world law, the enforcement of the judgments of the International Court of Justice and the creation at long last, of a system of world law above and beyond national legal orders. Last year also ended the International Decade of Cultural Development, a basis from which you can recommend a much needed world cultural Renaissance, a millennium of Pericles."

Lakshmi remained pensive and looked at the graying, elderly gentleman. How knowledgeable, enthusiastic, relaxed and sure of himself he was! It was as if the world and humanity were married to him, a beloved wife whom he knew intimately. He seemed to be saying to her: "Don't worry, all will go well; all we have to do is to believe in you and to work hard for you." It was quite a sight! There was no hesitation in him, no scare of not knowing, no pessimism, no frustration, no hopelessness, no acceptance of the impossible. She thought for herself: "I must read all his books and get acquainted with his extraordinary life and journey as a world servant. Here is the "idea-person" I have been looking for. The same way as Franklin Roosevelt used "idea-men" to take his country out of depression, I will use him and others to take the Earth out of her depression."

It was getting late and she felt tired. She took his two hands, looked deep into his eyes and said with an enchanting smile: "Thank you, thank you, thank you. You have opened the windows of my mind, heart and soul to the great vistas of humanity's future. You have elevated me to the heights of the world and of humanity and of our incredible meaning in the universe. I have marked your words in golden letters in my mind. I will work with you and help you fulfill your vision. You are a great man. I am only a small diplomat eager to be of use."

He patted her hands gently and said:

"Dear Lakshmi, you are great, every human being is great, a unique miracle in the universe, never to be repeated again in the entire eternity in exactly the same form and circumstances. One of your roles will be to validate humans, to make them feel great about themselves, happy to be alive at this time of maximum knowledge and consciousness, part of the great human adventure, responsible universal entities in the vast evolutionary changes taking place on this planet after billions of years. You can and will be the greatest woman ever. You will be the First Lady of the World, I assure you. Sleep well, Rest well. Put a last great thought or love into your mind and heart before you sleep, and your sub-conscious will work for you faithfully and happily all night.

And near your bed, on your night-table, have a notebook to write down the thoughts and ideas whispered to you by the forces of the universe.

And tomorrow morning, as on every day of your resurrection, ask God this question: "What more can I do for your beautiful Creation and your beloved, divine children!" And you will receive the answer."

* * *

51

# Chapter 5

At the headquarters of the Golden Age Foundation in Washington, about twenty people are sitting around a table, listening to John Fitzpatrick, the President. The subject of the meeting is: the United Nations.

"Dear friends and co-workers, this is our first meeting in 1992 of the anti-UN task force of our Foundation. We can be relatively proud of our successes during the last few years: we stopped the UN from growing at a time when a host of new global problems could have meant a greater recourse to the UN, we prevented a strengthening of the Organization and the creation of new agencies. Furthermore, we stopped the entry into force of the UN Law of the Sea and of the Law of Outer-Space which would have meant the birth of two unprecedented world commons. We stopped any world action in favor of the handicapped and the elderly, despite the noise made by the UN for these two new global problems in the International Year for the Disabled and in the first World Conference on Aging. We left a good part of the UN paralyzed and demoralized by the nonpayment of US contributions to the budget. We terminated the US contributions to the UN Fund for Population Activities. We put the FAO on the defensive and above all we got the US out of UNESCO and made a return to it practically non-negotiable.

But before I continue, let me introduce to you our new friend and activist, Napoleon Ames, our first black staff member whose ambition is to play a prominent role for America and the defense and promotion of our most cherished values. For his benefit, I would like to re-state briefly the origins and aims of our Foundation:

Dear Napoleon, this Foundation was created by a number of very prominent businessmen from some of the oldest American families who have built this country and shaped our noble ideals, values and virtues. Thanks to them, the American way of life has become a household word in the world. But in this century, especially since World War II, our leadership has run into threats of erosion by all kinds of foreign ideas and philosophies, such as socialism, liberalism, nationalization, public enterprise, social security, and the worst of all, communism. Government is getting into everything, killing or impeding seriously private enterprise and liberty. On the world level, we were able to make a quantum jump of private enterprise through the extraordinary growth of multinational corporations which conquered immense markets before governments became aware of it. But the problem was finally raised in the UN, that devilish invention by Democrat Franklin Roosevelt. Today the UN system stands in our way in innumerable sectors and places of the world. We wanted to kill it because it gave legitimacy to the communist countries, another mischief by Franklin Roosevelt and the Democrats. Thank God, communism is now out of the way. It has capitulated to the American ideology. But the UN is still around with its horde of underdeveloped countries and attempts at world social justice. It constitutes one of the main threats to the dominance of our philosophy and values in the world. It might no longer have to be killed, because if we do so, something even worse might be created to replace it. Planetary consciousness and the one-world concepts have grown during the last few years to an unprecedented degree and it is likely that the old devilish idea of world government might return to the fore. So it might be in our interest to let the UN survive, but it must be stopped from growing, it must be put on the defensive and besmeared with American public opinion. Our meeting today has been called to assess more particularly the effects of the election of a new Secretary-General, of all people a woman and on top of it from India! But before opening the discussion, I would like to give the floor to our new friend Napoleon Ames."

Napoleon Ames:

"Mr. President, dear friends. I am glad that you accepted me in your midst and I want to assure you that you will not regret it. My story and motives are very simple: since I was a child, I could not understand that I was black. I hated to be a black. I developed a hatred for all the blacks around me. I just could not accept that while there were so many white people, anyone had to be black. It was an intolerable, unbelievable injustice by God. So I began to hate God too. I tried everything at the beginning: black churches, black colleges, black activism, black demonstrations, and the more I tried, the more I hated the blacks. They are an underdeveloped, cursed race. So I decided to leave them for good and to devote my life to fight for the whites' causes. I looked for the most extreme rightist group in the country and I found you. I was accepted in your ranks and put on the anti-UN task force, especially in view of the growing influence of the black countries in the UN. I hate the UN because it has made the black race acceptable. Without the UN they would have never received the recognition they have now. It is the same phenomenon you underlined with regard to communism. I hate the UN because it favors all the values I hate. I am therefore all yours in your fight. I expect to find in your Foundation a relief, an outlet for the incredible frustrations I have harbored for so long. Thank you for admitting me."

John Fitzpatrick:

"Thank you, dear Napoleon. You can fully count on us. Now I would like to hear the report of our friend from the UN Secretariat on the newly elected Secretary-General. I give him the floor."

Secretariat member:

"Here are the main points: she wants to be popular with the UN staff and rekindle their morale and ideals; she wants to hire more women; she wants to surround herself with idea-people as Franklin and Eleanor Roosevelt did - they are her heroes; she wants to lift the UN far above the heights and sights of nations. She is quite a lovable dynamo of a woman, and most staff members and delegates consider her a winner."

John Fitzpatrick:

"Well, this is of bad omen. In these circumstances, our strategy should be this:

1. Plant as many women as possible among the candidates for the posts she wants to fill with women. As with national governments, we should follow the example of our friend Alexander Rumacher and get "iron-women", really "non-women", into command. Contact a number

of conservative women who are our friends and get them appointed. They will boycott her and pursue exactly the opposite policies she wants;

2. Plant our own idea-people on the thirty eighth floor to undermine her scheme. Get really the very best of our friends and if need be, send them to me so that I can explain to them the importance of their acceptance;

3. Spread the rumor all over the UN Secretariat that the morale has never been so low, that the US is less likely than ever to return to UNESCO and to pay its full share of contributions to the UN which it considers more than ever to be anti-American.

4. Continue and intensify the campaign that we pay too much for the UN, that it is extravagant, inefficient, bureaucratic, duplicating, top-heavy, that there are too many agencies and that as distinct from communist countries, which are abandoning communism, the communist staff members in the UN have not changed and remain enemies of the US;

5. Step-up the campaign that the UN is anti-semitic and pro-Arab;

6. In view of the growing role and success of the peace movements, infiltrate with our people every single non-governmental organization accredited with the UN and the specialized agencies; they are becoming an increasingly important danger;

7. Ridicule her Hindu customs and criticize heavily her alliance with the developing world and her sympathy for their cultures. Underline the danger of her Hinduism for Catholicism and all Christianity. Accuse her for wanting to promote Hinduism as the most valid world spirituality and philosophy;

8. Last but not least, continue our campaign of hand-delivered criticisms of the UN and of its agencies to all US Senators and Congressmen.

And he turned again to the Secretariat member:

"In order to evaluate correctly what we are facing, could you give us an evaluation of how the Iraq-Kuwait crisis has affected the UN?"

Secretariat member:

"To be honest, contrary to our expectations, it has done the organization a lot of good. We are witnessing a fundamental new trend: the world is tired of unilateral interventions by states in violation of their Charter obligations. This has happened all too often since World War II, causing more than 100 conflicts and 20 million dead. The cold war had paralyzed the UN because the US and the USSR supported and took position for opposing parties in such conflicts and vetoed any action by the Security Council. All this has changed. The UN declared and imposed within hours a world boycott on Iraq by a unanimous decision of the Security Council. This is a major change in recent history. From now on no nation will dare again to intervene unilaterally and invade another country. Even a new temporary incursion such as that of the US in Panama for specific purposes is unthinkable in the future. In other words, with the end of the cold war, the UN works.

Also, the Iraq-Kuwait crisis gave a substantial boost to an old idea: that the UN should have its own military peace-keeping forces on a round-the-clock basis, especially to begin with a UN navy. Several countries came out in favor of this idea. Also a key instrument of the UN has been revived: the Military Staff Committee of the Security Council. Few people remember that immediately after World War II, the chiefs of staff of the allied armies met at Hunter College in New York, together with some of the finest political brains of the time, to do two things according to the Charter:

1. To devise a world security system which would protect every member-state against foreign unilateral actions;

2. After that, to disarm the planet.

The cold war killed all that. The US and the USSR stopped cooperating with each other on the implementation of that plan. Since then, you can see each fortnight at the UN, a few uniformed military officers meet in that Committee, just to keep it alive but without having anything to do. Well, the Military Staff Committee has been revitalized: as a result of the Iraq-Kuwait crisis, it was given the supervision of the boycott and eventually of military action and surveillance in that area. This is a new important page in UN history."

John Fitzpatrick:

"Well, there might be some hope with the UN after all. But I doubt it. I have infinitely greater confidence in America, in its strength and in its values. An effective UN would be even more dangerous to the US than an ineffective one. That is my opinion. We must therefore intensify our anti-UN action, boycott and belittle the UN by every means at our disposal, get it out of the world's business. In the light of our discussion I would like each of you to submit a list of specific action proposals against the UN and its agencies, which we will discuss at a next meeting. I want to have an overall strategy which takes into account what the Russians may be up to. Never forget the danger of the UN becoming a world government. Please work hard for God and for our country. We will meet again once I have received and studied your proposals."

* * *

# Chapter 6

It was the dawn of a marvelous, sunny, exceptionally clear day. Ice cold winds from the North Pole and Canada had cleaned Manhattan of all its dust and pollution. Lakshmi was snuggled voluptuously among the soft silk cushions of her warm Indian bed and was reading with keen attention the world peace plan 2010 given to her by Louis Parizot. He had written it late in 1984, on the eve of the fortieth anniversary of the UN, in response to a Christian Science Monitor contest which called on "future historians to write from the year 2010 and describe how peace came to Earth during the preceding 25 years".

She was overwhelmed by the number of coherent proposals and prophetic predictions outlined in the document, for example the end of the cold war, the revival of the UN and in particular of the Military Staff Committee, which had all taken place. She read and re-read these concluding remarks:

"The Charter of the UN drafted after World War II at the initiative of the United States proved to be one of the most remarkable documents of all times. From the moment the cold war between the US and the USSR ended and all governments decided to implement the Charter faithfully, the world entered a definitive era of peace and of orderly management of planet Earth for the greatest happiness of all those admitted to the miracle of life."

She jumped out of her bed, all excited, talking to herself, pacing up and down the little apartment, exclaiming: "This is it. This is the plan for my tenure. I am not going to wait for his additional ideas in the light of recent events. This document should be known to every top official in the UN, to every head of state. I am sure they took him for a fool, a dreamer and an idealist. On the contrary, he is a man with his head in heaven and his feet on Earth, a Machiavellian Utopian."

She remembered that during their dinner he said to her:

"Nowadays when I visit the UN, former colleagues and diplomats stop me and say: Mr. Parizot, we can tell you now that when we heard you deliver years ago your optimistic, hopeful and prophetic speeches about the future of the UN and the world, we thought that you were a little crazy. But today we realize that you were right and that many of the things you predicted have come true." And his answer was: "Well, we must now predict further new good things, so that they too will become a reality."

She did her ablutions in the strict Hindu way, remembering that good care of the human body is a religious obligation, not merely a question of hygiene and self-interest. To maintain the body clean, to nourish it well with strictly vegetarian food, to abstain from all deleterious substances such as alcohol, carbonated drinks, tobacco and drugs is a sacred duty. "Our body is a temple", she murmured. "We can serve God only if it is clean, pure, healthy and beautiful. A good bodily life is the first rung of the ladder leading to happiness and spirituality."

She believed also that we must eat primarily the products of our own region to which our body is accustomed. Her breakfast therefore consisted of mangoes, pineapple (for the prevention of memory loss), japathies and Indian tea.

To celebrate Parizot's writing she selected one of her brightest gold-embroidered, light-blue sarees from her vast collection. Like all Indian women, the more sarees she possessed, the happier she was. On that point, she could not agree with Gandhi. She brightened her dark carbuncle eyes with the skillful application of kol, and affixed a diamond at her forefront, remembering Parizot's love for Sima and her jewelry. She went all out to adorn herself with bracelets, rings and even a "glove" of jewelry on her left hand as one can see them only in India.

She continued talking to herself:

"Cultural diversity is essential. Humanity needs unity in diversity, following the wonderful example of nature. There is nothing sadder in the world than to see the youth of so many countries abandon the beautiful traditions and vestments of their culture and wear instead those horrible "blue-jeans" meant originally for factory workers, smoke American cigarettes, drink whiskey or Coca-Cola, listen to ear and mind-damaging, deafening music, and read the horrible magazines and so called bestsellers mass-produced in this country. Even if I cannot change the world, I can at least give the example of someone who does not capitulate to the neo-enslavement by advertisement and big business."

At 9:30, when the three secretaries arrived, they gasped at her beauty! She smiled and said to them: "Girls, we are the eternal feminine. We are not inferior to men. We are superior. We lead them, we dominate them and make them run after us. Our beauty is our main asset. When God created Adam, he saw that he had made a mistake with many shortcomings. So he started all over again and made the women, adding the miracles of motherhood, love and beauty, as he did for his earlier creation, the Earth, which in all languages is a woman. Please do not neglect your beauty and remain proud of your origins and culture. We are here at the top of the world. We must give the good example."

She then changed the subject and said:

"Here is an important document which I have just read. Have it photocopied, divide the phones between the three of you and ask all Under-Secretaries-General and Assistant-Secretaries-General to come to a meeting in my conference room this afternoon at three o'clock. Have the document hand-delivered to all of them with my plea to read it before the meeting."

The three secretaries got busy. Lakshmi locked herself up in her office, asking not to be disturbed. She wanted to devote the whole morning to a thorough study and revision of Louis Parizot's Plan, to determine what was obsolete or already achieved, what remained to be implemented, make corrections and add her own ideas and proposals. Then in the afternoon she would get the comments of her top colleagues who were dealing with practically every conceivable world problem.

As she corrected and redrafted the plan, she wrote down her own observations on separate sheets of paper. At the end, she took a pair of scissors, cut out the plan's proposals and opened a set of files

# A note from **Robert Muller**

and

# **World Happiness and Cooperation**

As a result of the major changes that have occurred in the political structure of Eastern Europe, please make the following minor changes in the World Peace Plan 1992 - 2010:

page 61    Section 1, first sentence, change end of sentence to read: ... *between the Presidents of the US and of Russia.*

page 62    Section 4, change the third line to read: ...*jointly by the Presidents of the US and Russia to draft proposals for* ...

page 63    Section 8, paragraph ii, change end of sentence to read: ... *as was proposed by the USSR in 1988.*

which she would keep on her desk for further elaboration, additions, corrections and discussion with heads of states, diplomats and prominent visitors. She was happy like a child and worked in her Secretary-General's office in the same spirit as she did as a school-girl in her tiny room on the other side of the globe in her parents' home. The only difference was that this time the whole world was her school.

When she finished, late beyond lunch hour, this is the text she had produced:

# WORLD PEACE PLAN 1992-2010

## 1992

1. Several personal summit meetings are held between Presidents Bush and Gorbachev:

   i. They decide to chart a new course for humanity and the Earth, a Global Renaissance, a new Planetary Deal.

   ii. New world priorities are set to be met with the huge resources released by disarmament and demilitarization.

   iii. The two countries plan jointly total nuclear disarmament by the year 2000 and total disarmament and demilitarization by 2010.

   iv. The two countries agree to stop all arms sales and to call for a United Nations conference on the world-wide prohibition of arms sales and production.

   v. High-technology video and sound communications systems are established between the offices and the homes of the two Presidents in order to be in direct, instantaneous communication at any time on any crisis, problem, idea, proposal or action for peace and a better world.

   vi. The two leaders solemnly rededicate themselves and their people to the United Nations Charter.

2.    The US scraps all plans for a Star War.

3.    The US ratifies the UN Law of the Sea which creates an unprecedented legal order for the largest world commons, the seas and oceans which cover two-thirds of the planet.

4.    The US returns to UNESCO and pays all its arrears to the UN and its specialized agencies. A group of experts is appointed jointly by Presidents Bush and Gorbachev to draft proposals for a renaissance, forward-look and quantum jump in the role and resources of the UN system, to enable it to deal effectively with the host of global problems confronting humanity and the planet at an accelerating pace.

5.    In view of the top urgency of world population control, the US renews its support to the UN Fund for Population Activities and increases tenfold its former contribution to it. A UN specialized agency on Population is created.

6.    The Second World Conference on Climate which met in Geneva gave the world the necessary warnings and action proposals. The UN World Meteorological Organization is renamed and transformed into the World Climate Organization.

7.    Following the path-breaking reports of Eminent Persons on North-South relations (the Brandt report), on Disarmament (the Palme report) and Our Common Future, on environment and development (the Brundtland report), three further groups of Eminent Persons are established:

   i.    On the elimination of all forms of violence in the human society.

   ii.   On a New World Deal and course for humanity, including world priorities.

   iii.  On world governance and the creation of a true world community, to include the existing, successful European community, and planned new regional communities for Africa, America, Asia and the Middle East.

8.   The UN General Assembly takes four major decisions:

i.   It adopts a turning point declaration requesting the Secretary-General, in consultation with governments, world agencies and the best minds of the planet, to prepare a plan for world peace by the year 2010. All member states are requested to submit their proposals. National committees are established with peoples' participation for the formulation of ideas and concrete action proposals towards "Total World Peace 2000" and "Total World Disarmament and Demilitarization 2010". The General Assembly requests that all existing UN plans 2000 (Food 2000, Health 2000, Literacy 2000, Industry 2000, Employment 2000, Environment 2000, and the Economic Development Decades) be put together into a **World Action Plan 2000**. The Assembly takes note of the recent settlement of most conflicts, and calls for the rapid solution of all remaining ones to enable humanity to enter the next millennium with a clean slate. A world-wide cease-fire is proclaimed in the meantime under UN control.

ii.  It decides to abolish the Trusteeship Council which has completed its work and to replace it by an Environmental Security Council as proposed by the USSR.

iii. The Assembly decides to celebrate in 1995 the fiftieth anniversary of the United Nations, both as a retrospective of the successes and failures of the world community during the past fifty years, and as a forward look to the year 2000 and third millennium.

iv.  In 2000 a world-wide Bimillennium Celebration will be held, preceded by unparalleled thinking, perception, inspiration, elevation, planning and love for the achievement of a peaceful and happy human society on a well-preserved planet. For the first time in history humanity is entering a new millennium with most of the necessary planetary and human information at its disposal. For the first time it can intelligently plan and prepare its future evolution. All nations, professions, arts, media, firms, religions and people are invited by the UN to participate in this celebration and to contribute their ideals, visions, wishes, proposals and ideas to it.

The following progress is also achieved in 1992:

1.    The second world conference on the environment and development held in Brazil twenty years after the first one in Stockholm, constitutes a major turning point in human history and in the planet's evolution. The conference adopts a bold World Environment Action Plan, both immediate and reaching far into the third millennium. The United Nations Environment Program becomes a specialized agency with vastly increased resources, including taxes on environmentally detrimental activities. The UN Trusteeship Council has become the World Environmental Security Council. Further accelerated world conferences on environmental issues are decided for the coming years.

2.    In 1992, International Year of Outer-Space, a long overdue decision is taken to create a UN Outer-Space Agency as proposed by Austria.

3.    1992, being the 500th anniversary of the discovery of the New World, eminent thinkers meet during the year to draft a World Constitution as a step towards discovering the next new world. Provisions are made for world democracy, world elections, world public opinion polls and referenda to give people a direct voice in the world's affairs, a step rendered possible by modern communication technologies.

## 1993

On the basis of governmental proposals and the Year 2000 Peace Plan presented by the Secretary-General, the following Ten Major World Steps are set into motion:

1.    The UN Security Council meets several times a year at the heads of states level to review the world political and security situation, to take decisions, settle disputes, finalize agreements and initiate further action, especially by the Secretary-General and

the Military Staff Committee. The Council meets in various cities of the world, to be closer to the people, especially in troubled areas.

2. The summit meetings of Eastern, Western and non-Aligned countries are abolished and replaced by a yearly world summit meeting of all heads of states during the UN General Assembly, preceded by continental or regional summit meetings (African, American, Asian, European, Middle-Eastern).

3. Incessant meetings, visits and communications are taking place between heads of states. Reports on their outcomes are submitted to the Security Council and to the General Assembly. The UN establishes a special office to receive and publish such information. United Nations offices in New York, Geneva, Vienna, Africa, Latin America, Asia and the Middle-East are organized and used as supra-national grounds for meetings between heads of states.

4. A World conference on Security is decided, to remain in session like the Law of the Sea Conference did, until it has hammered out a proper world security system (target: 1995).

5. The Military Staff Committee of the Security Council meets again at the chiefs of staff level and undertakes these immediate tasks: 1. planning of the World Disarmament Agency foreseen in the McCloy-Zorin agreement; 2. adoption of immediate measures to prevent a nuclear war by accident; 3. planning and implementation of world-wide military cooperation in multiple fields, starting with the creation of a UN fleet to control the seas and oceans, and of a UN satellite system to control disarmament as proposed by France.

6. Preparation of a Marshall Plan for massive help to the poor countries, with savings from disarmament and demilitarization both in rich and in poor countries. Premium aid and debt reduction and forgiveness are granted to those poor countries who decide to disarm and demilitarize under UN protection and guarantees. A whole series of major world engineering and power projects are implemented to improve dramatically the

overall productivity, efficiency and environmental conditions of the world economy.

7. Immediate fostering of nuclear free zones, peace zones and demilitarized areas guaranteed by the UN, all to be given premium economic aid.

8. Setting up of high-technology direct communication, video and teleconferencing systems between **all** heads of states, especially the members of the Security Council, and the Secretary-General.

9. Bold strengthening of the Secretary-General's office for conflict information and prevention. Establishment of a high-technology World Peace Room at the UN, jointly run by the Secretary-General and the Military Staff Committee of the Security Council, in order to prevent, track, contain and solve conflicts swiftly in any place on Earth. UN political offices are established in each capital.

10. All UN agencies and world programs are requested to revive major plans and projects for world cooperation which had been shelved as a consequence of the cold war. The concept of risk capital is applied to world cooperation. New bold ideas and financial and management approaches, commensurate with the magnitude and acceleration of global problems, are introduced.

During the year 1993, the UN Secretary-General addresses the second World Congress of Religions in Chicago, one hundred years after the first one in 1893. The world's religions pledge to put an end to all religious conflicts, to support peace, disarmament and demilitarization, to cooperate on a global world spirituality and to draft in common a world code of ethics and a new cosmology as guides to governments and world agencies within the larger framework of the universe and eternity. The United Nations creates a world spiritual agency which brings the resources, inspirations, visions and wisdom of the spiritual traditions to bear on the solution of world problems.

The International Year of the World's Indigenous People reminds humanity of some fundamental human values and traditions which need to be restored:

*Strong family ties and values;*
*Love for Mother Earth;*
*Respect for Nature;*
*Love for the Creator;*

## 1994

1.    The Military Staff Committee completes its work on the prevention of nuclear accidents, on a UN satellite system for disarmament control and on a UN fleet. The implementation of these proposals is set into motion by the General Assembly. The blueprints for a World Disarmament Agency are well advanced and will be ready for 1995.

2.    Three further world environmental conferences are held during 1994:

   i.    A world conference of scientists from crucial environmental fields (oceanography, atmospheric science, hydrology, climatology, biology, land use, deforestation, radiation, immunology, toxicity, etc.). The scientists are asked in how many years they expect planet Earth to become unlivable if present trends continue unchecked, and what measures they propose.

   ii.    A world conference of education ministers adopts measures for urgent environmental education in all countries of the planet.

   iii.    A world conference on garbage is held.

3.    Celebration of the International Year of the Family, restored to its natural, central, universal role in the human society.

4.    Visit of the Pope to the United Nations on the occasion of that year. In a major historical address, in the name of all religions, he outlines the vision of a united family of nations and of a spiritual peaceful, just third millennium.

5.   A world conference on Voluntary Simplicity and Frugality is held in order to save the planet's resources from over consumption, human greed and monumental, accelerating, unnecessary waste and garbaging.

6.   A third, world conference on population and development is held.

## 1995

1.   Celebration of the fiftieth anniversary of the United Nations. The General Assembly meets at the heads of states level and receives from the Secretary-General a state of the world report reviewing the successes and failures of the world community during the last fifty years and outlining the visions and proposals for a peaceful, better world and family of nations in the decades ahead. A solemn rededication of all member states to the Charter takes place during the anniversary ceremony on 24 October 1995, transmitted by television and the media world-wide. World prayers are held for the UN by all religions.

2.   A fourth, world conference on women is held.

3.   The Marshall Plan for the dramatic improvement of the standards of living of the poor countries drafted by the UN Economic and Social Council is endorsed by the General Assembly and put into operation.

4.   The Conference on World Security has completed its work and submits a treaty for ratification by member states within a year. The Military Staff Committee submits to the Assembly a blueprint for a World Disarmament Agency as part of that treaty.

5.   All other Ten World Steps are implemented, or well underway, creating a good deal of enthusiasm, emulation and stimulation among governments who are now convinced that world peace is possible and that an entirely new period of human history can begin, marked by an unprecedented synergetic cooperation in a

world society no longer stifled by absolute and abusive national sovereignty.

## 1995-2000

During the entire period 1995-2000, an unprecedented flourishing and outbidding of ideas, initiatives, activities, projects and achievements takes place in an astonishing euphoria of explosive world consciousness which breaks up old barriers and takes the Earth and humanity on an incredible bandwagon into a new age. For example:

1.  Several countries have their delegates to the United Nations elected by popular vote.

2.  The majority of countries change the name of their ministries of "foreign" affairs to Ministries of Peace or Ministries of World Affairs and Cooperation. In some countries, the Vice-President is put in charge of world affairs and cooperation.

3.  The United Nations flag and emblem gain world-wide affection as the planetary symbols of one world and one human family. The UN emblem is displayed on all vessels, aircrafts and satellites to discourage piracy, highjacking and terrorism. Some countries adopt a new flag showing their national flag on one side and the UN flag on the other. The UN's world hymn composed by Pablo Casals is better known.

4.  More and more nations decide to celebrate the world days proclaimed by the United Nations, such as Earth Day, the International Day of Peace, United Nations Day, Human Rights Day, World Health Day, World Food Day, International Children's Day, International Women's Day, the Day of the Elderly, etc. All National war memorial days are shifted to United Nations Day, a symbol of hope and rebirth from all past wars. Monuments to known and unknown peacemakers, peace parks and peace museums are created in many cities. National hymns are rewritten in peaceful, global terms.

5.  A world-wide minute of silence for prayer or meditation is held by all peoples of the world, together with their delegates to the General Assembly when it opens each year on the third Tuesday of September (International Day of Peace). The event is televised world-wide. All religions join in prayers. Church and temple bells, muezzins, gongs and chofars contribute their cosmic vibrations to this world pentecost.

6.  A World Peace Service is created allowing young people to do world service, especially in poor countries and in world agencies, in lieu of the abolished military service.

7.  A World Core Curriculum and a Planetary Management Curriculum are adopted by UNESCO as common guides for proper Global Education in all schools and universities of Earth. 1996 is proclaimed International Year of Global Education.

8.  All countries follow the example of the US and Canada and create National Peace Academies or Institutes. The University for Peace in Costa Rica develops a comprehensive peace science (irenology) and strategy and training programs concerned with every layer of our planetary reality, (outer-space, the atmosphere, the seas and oceans, the continents, down to the atom) and of the human family (world peace, peace between nations, races, sexes, generations, religions, cultures, political systems, minorities, corporations, the family, etc.). National peace academies and institutes meet every three years at the University for Peace to coordinate their action.

9.  Following the creation of the International Institute for Training in Nuclear Physics in Trieste, the United Nations University in Tokyo, the University for Peace in Costa Rica, and the International Maritime University in Malmo, many more world universities are created under the auspices of the United Nations and its specialized agencies: on aviation, on outer-space, on the oceans, on the deserts, on population, on reforestation, on the biosphere, on planetary management, on world spirituality, etc.

10. The University for Peace in Costa Rica becomes a school of heads of states, ministers of peace and world affairs, world

servants, corporate heads and diplomats. A Center is created at it for the study, collection and exchange of experience in the function of head of state. Regional UN peace universities are created on each continent.

11. More and more countries disarm, demilitarize and have their borders protected by UN observers under regional and international guarantees. The savings are devoted to development, the environment, education and social services.

12. The world's regional organizations and the regional provisions in the Charter of the United Nations are considerably strengthened.

13. The US the USSR and other countries relinquish their claims of total righteousness and agree to have their performance judged by the international community in the United Nations and in its specialized agencies.

14. More world ministerial councils are established along the pattern of the UN's World Food Council and the World Environmental Security Council.

15. A host of new world conferences are convened at an accelerated pace: on soil erosion, on mountain areas, reforestation, the world's cold zones, consumer protection, standardization, world commons, a world tax system, etc.

16. Several new world agencies are created: a World Transport Agency, a World Organization of National Parks, a World Organization for the Handicapped, a United Nations Fund for the Elderly (UNIFELD) on the pattern of UNICEF; the UN Institute for Training and Research (UNITAR) is transformed into a World Academy; UN statistical and data services are integrated into a World Data and Optimal Designs Agency. The International Bureau of Informatics in Rome is made part of it. A UN Institute for the study of national and world management (gaia or geo-management) is established.

17. The world community decides to tackle the fundamental, ominous question of truthful, objective information, the exercise of democracy being possible only if people are objectively informed. The UN and its specialized agencies and world programs are major contributors to such information.

18. A world cadastre of property registration is established in order to determine what the exact legal status of ownership is in the world: world commons, national and state properties, municipal properties, corporate properties, religious properties, private associations ownership, family and individual ownership.

19. Following the example of the world navigation satellite of the UN International Maritime Organization, several other global satellite systems have been created and joint space ventures are organized by the world community.

20. The International Court of Justice's judgments are now enforceable and no nation can take exception. The Court is reorganized as the World Supreme Court. The UN Secretary-General is entitled to submit cases to it.

21. Regional Courts of Human Rights have been established on the pattern of the European Court of Human Rights, empowered to render verdicts in favor of individuals against governments. A World Court of Human Rights is created as an appeal's court on human rights.

22. A World Ethics Chamber determines what is ethical from the world's and humanity's point of view rather than that of nations, sub-groups and special interest groups. A Sub-Chamber on Media Ethics receives complaints against unethical treatments by the media.

23. A Commission on Subversion has been created in the United Nations to which governments can submit complaints against foreign subversion.

24. A World Foundation has been created to allow private citizens, organizations, firms and corporations to contribute to world peace

and cooperation through the United Nations and its specialized agencies and world programs.

25. World standardization makes considerable progress: e.g. the UN convention on road signals and traffic rules is applied world-wide as well as the World Health Organization's standard nomenclature of pharmaceutical products. The International Standardization Organization has become a specialized agency of the UN.

26. World consumer protection is promoted through world-wide cooperation of national consumer agencies and the creation of a World Consumer Protection Agency with tri-partite representation of governments, producers and consumers.

27. The UN publishes each year a world budget showing the total national and world expenditures on every aspect of humanity's and of the Earth's condition.

28. The taboo subject of world taxation appears at long last on the world agenda. Strong measures are taken to combat world fiscal evasion. The US formalized its proposal for the establishment of a World Bureau on Income Information. A percentage of the proceeds from effective international control of fiscal evasion is allotted to international humanitarian programs. A world tax system is planned.

# Year 2000

An unprecedented, hopeful, optimistic world-wide celebration of the Bimillennium takes place all over the Earth, preceded by much public and governmental preparation and excitement. Gratitude is expressed and prayers are held for having overcome one of the most dangerous and promethean periods of change on any planet in the universe. Innumerable, rich materials have been published on the human journey and ascent over the last 5000 years and on hopes and remaining challenges for the future. The UN state of the world report 2000 highlights the following accomplishments and failures:

1.  World population down to 5.8 billion people (against forecasts of 7.3 billion in 1970, during the twenty-fifth anniversary of the UN, and 6.1 billion during the fortieth anniversary); early child mortality reduced in 9/10th of the world; longevity progresses world-wide; racial and sexual equality nearly achieved; decolonization achieved; UN universality achieved; UN world plan for the handicapped implemented; environmental deterioration slowed down, the pendulum swinging back to improvement in many places; soil erosion, loss of tree cover and desertification considerably reduced; agriculture and economic conditions improve worldwide. The world's global warning systems work more satisfactorily. There is better coordination between global, national, regional, local and individual policies and behavior. More accurate, truthful information is available as well as a vastly improved global education in the world's schools.

2.  There are no conflicts anywhere; all wars and disputes of the 1980s are resolved; a world security system is now in place; UN land, air and naval peace-keeping forces are ready to intervene anywhere to guarantee the territories of all nations; a World Disarmament Agency has begun to operate; reconversion of defense and arms industries is in full swing; the military are being used for constructive activities, help to natural disasters, environmental conservation and are demobilized or transformed into police forces; nuclear weapons have been destroyed on an increasing scale; transfer of military expenditures to greater world productivity and help to the poor is under way; conventional armaments are being destroyed by ten percent each year, in order to achieve total disarmament of the planet by 2010.

3.  Yearly states of the world reports are issued by all UN agencies on every global facet of our planetary home and of the human family. Plans and targets for each next decade throughout the century are prepared and a general outlook 3000 will be issued in 2025.

4.  The UN has produced a new planetary ideology and spirituality consisting of five basic harmonies.

a.   Harmony between humanity and the planet (population, conservation, environment,no armaments.)

b.   Harmony of the human family and of its natural and human-made groups (races, sexes, generations, nations, cultures, languages, religions, corporations, no wars, no violence, all conflicts and differences being resolved with civilized, peaceful means).

c.   Harmony with the past and with the future (preservation of genetic material, of nature's elements, of the Earth's living species' and flora, of cultures, preservation and preparation of a better, safer and more beautiful planet for future generations).

d.   Harmony with the heavens: the religions have produced a code of cosmic laws to be followed by all peoples and groups on our celestial body.

e.   The fulfillment, happiness, harmony and contribution of each human being to the human family, to the planet, to the universe and to the stream of eternal time. The art of peaceful, happy, responsible and contributing living is taught to all.

5.   A Parliamentary Chamber has been added to the UN. Steps have been taken to introduce a new system of planetary governance: Harold Stassen's redraft of the UN Charter calling for an executive ministerial council composed of ministers appointed by the different regions, to administer the two first world commons - outer-space and the seas and oceans - is being implemented. Strong world-wide revival of parliamentarism.

6.   On the negative side: there are still 300 million malnourished people on the planet and 600 million illiterates; misery and unemployment are still far from being eradicated world-wide; urban growth remains unchecked in many places; mortality due to accidents, especially automobile accidents, and to environmental diseases are rampant. All nuclear armaments are not yet destroyed. The environment is still unhealed. Species' continue

to disappear. World accidents and degenerative diseases are on the increase. There are signs of a breakdown of the immunological system of the human body under the rapidity and intensity of environmental changes. Some big cities have become environmentally unlivable and are being abandoned. Epidemics have reappeared in poor countries. World governance is still primitive and imperfect in the face of growing world problems. There is still no world budget and no proper world tax system for the benefit of the Earth and humanity as a whole.

# 2010

1. The first decade of the New Planetary Age is now over. There are no more wars and conflicts in the world. The rate of arms destruction has continued unabated. All governments recognize that their people and the world are much better off after each phase of arms destruction. A totally disarmed planet is now in sight.

2. The state of the world reports show progress on all fronts. The world is in an optimistic phase and there is progress in achieving right relationships between the human species and the Earth.

3. World trusteeship and management is improving everywhere. The UN World Climate Organization has devised methods and techniques to detect and prevent climatic changes. We are becoming intelligent, knowledgeable caretakers of our planetary home, living children of the Earth taking good care of their mother, as was meant to be.

4. Humanity is happier physically, mentally, morally and spiritually. More and more people are enjoying life in its rich, astonishing diversity and understand that life is a privilege, a true miracle. No other planet with life has as yet been detected in the universe. It is becoming increasingly evident that the cosmos has produced unique, rare phenomena on this planet, especially human life with its constantly transcending consciousness and knowledge of the entire universe, from the infinitely large to the infinitely small. We have succeeded in becoming a new species by extending

incredibly the power of our senses, physical strength, memory and mental capacity through science and technology. We are a unique cosmic phenomenon as part of the evolution of the universe. Our duty is to help the cosmos succeed in its evolutionary experiment on this planet. Heads of state recognize that they have a duty not only towards their people, towards the planet and towards humanity, but also towards the success of cosmic evolution on Planet Earth.

5.    The next phase of our evolution will therefore be a cosmic, spiritual age in which the Earth becomes a true showcase in the universe with human beings in perfect physical, mental, moral, affective and spiritual union with the universe and time. Humans at long last recognize that they are living cosmic instruments, part of the universes's evolution on a particular, miraculous, lucky, life-teeming planet circling in the fathomless and mysterious universe.

* *

When Lakshmi finished this redraft of Parizot's plan, she felt totally exhausted. It was just too much for her to absorb, to digest and to improve. Any one of these proposals could occupy many energies and talents for quite some time. Also, what were the priorities? What are the most urgent and overpowering planetary problems to tackle first? She just could not face meeting her high officials in the afternoon and go on grinding on this colossal task. She was simply worn out.

She went over to the secretaries' office, held out her redraft and said:

"Please type this text and postpone this afternoon's meeting to tomorrow at 3 pm. Extend my apologies to the invitees and tell them that they will receive by the end of today, my redraft of Parizot's plan. This should facilitate our discussion. Also ask them to think about priorities."

And she added:

"I am worn out. Ask Andy Smith to bring the car in front of the Secretariat building and to drive me to Lake Mohonk. I want to walk in nature and to be alone, to let things settle. It is just too much and too fast for me. I will be back tomorrow by mid-morning. Tell the people who want to see me or to talk to me that I feel sick. If there is anything really urgent, you know where to reach me. Thank you for your kind help and patience. See you tomorrow morning."

And she fluttered away, her beautiful, blue silken saree floating prettily behind her admirable, voluptuous, oriental body.

\* \* \*

# Chapter 7

**5 am.**

Lakshmi Narayan is walking briskly on the path leading to the top of Lake Mohonk Mountain. Her thoughts are with Suryia, the Sun God whom tens of millions of her Indian compatriots revere and pray every morning when the sun resurrects above the horizon to give again light and life to the world. She wanted to keep this tradition both in her UN skyscraper in New York and especially here in the midst of God's beautiful, unspoiled nature. She loved Lake Mohonk Mountain, an extraordinary remnant of a volcanic eruption millions of years ago in the Hudson Valley. The crater of the ancient, extinct volcano is filled with a magnificent lake, captured in perennial stillness, surrounded by a profusion of nature paths and gazebos with the most beautiful panoramas. The majestic, antique, high hotel on its shores reminded her of the great romantic hotels built in India at the turn of the century.

She reached the top of the mountain just in time for sunrise, knelt down and quickly lit an Agni Suryia incense bowl to greet the rebirth of our Father Sun. How precious this moment was! She felt the vibrations and love of Mother Earth penetrate through her knees, radiating through every cell of her body, while the warm, cosmic rays of Father Sun entered through her face and eyes; she felt re-created, resurrected, in total union with the universe and time. She was indeed an instrument of God, of the cosmos. Her life had meaning only through total surrender and unselfish service to this planet and to humanity.

After meditation, she arose and offered a bowl of rice to the God of the day who never ceases to shine generously for rich and poor alike during the hundreds of millions of years of the Year of Brahma. She could visualize the multitudes of her compatriots who were performing the same ritual at sunrise in the innumerable villages of her country.

She then walked down slowly and pensively the path to the hotel, meditating and dreaming. What was her role going to be at the UN? What did the Gods have in mind for her? How would she proceed this afternoon at the meeting with her top colleagues? A remark of Louis Parizot came back to her mind:

"You will be the head of the most powerless organization on Earth. It does not even possess the sovereignty of the smallest nation. It has no legislative power, no executive power, no judicial power, no taxing power. It cannot even borrow money. The tiny speck of land on which it is built is only "lent" to it for 99 years. But it has one great power: the power of ideas. And as Napoleon said: "Ideas are stronger than the sword." Make, therefore, your Secretary-Generalship a flourishing garden of ideas. Change the world through ideas. Any idea whose time has come will sooner or later be accepted and implemented. Do not be afraid to launch ideas. And remember what Schopenhauer said: "All truth passes through three stages: first, it is ridiculed; second, it is violently opposed; third, it is accepted as being self-evident."

He was right. She smiled to herself and stamped energetically her pretty feet on the ground when she arrived at the hotel to have breakfast. "I will build my Secretary-Generalship on this trimurti: the power of ideas, the power of love and the power of the soul."

Keith and Ruth Smiley, the wonderful Quaker couple who own Lake Mohonk Mountain House were also just returning from their early morning walk in nature. They invited her at their table in the huge dining room with its breathtaking views. They were honored to have her as a guest. She had rented a room year-round to escape as frequently as possible from Manhattan and its burdens. They knew that she was in a hurry and they promised to tell her on another occasion how one of their ancestors was taken by the beauty of this place, bought it, built a hotel, started the first conferences of Friends of the Indians and from 1895 to 1916 the Annual Conferences on

Arbitration. Still today Mohonk is a beloved meeting place for informal meetings between UN delegates. This is how she knew about it and had fallen in love with it. Last year she had been invited by the Stanley Foundation to a meeting on the strengthening of the UN. God has given her the best of two world: she was now working for the strengthening of the UN, and she was enjoying Lake Mohonk as her second home.

During most of the trip back to New York, she remained silent, deeply absorbed in her thoughts and plans. She jotted down ideas and markings, remembering Louis Parizot's advice: Nullus dies sine linea. Andy Smith respected her silence. He had his rich harvest when she told him at the beginning of the trip:

"Andy, I have it. I know exactly what I will do. My trinity will be: ideas, love and spirituality."

This was a big enough subject for him to reflect upon. He decided to begin to formulate his own ideas and to collect ideas and suggestions from colleagues. Once the UN staff would know that she was keen on ideas, there would be a flood of them. UN staff members have been waiting for such a signal for a long time.

* *

At the UN there was a full attendance at the afternoon meeting. No Under-Secretary-General or Assistant-Secretary-General had excused himself. Some had been elated, others shocked by the boldness of her plan. All of them were dying to see how it would go.

After greeting her colleagues, Lakshmi opened the meeting with these comments:

"This morning at sunrise in the beautiful Hudson valley, while praying God Suryia, the pillars of my Secretary-Generalship became clear to me: first, we must use our intelligence to the fullest and have ideas for the construction of a peaceful and better world; second, we must use our heart and love humanity and all Creation; third, we must use the spirit and understand our responsibility towards God and the universe to make the evolutionary cosmic experiment on this planet a success. And to wrap it all up, we must be of unreserved, unselfish service to this cause and work, work, work. Today's meeting will be devoted to the first subject, the power and development of ideas.

Let me tell you right away that one of my great heroes is Franklin Roosevelt, the master of great ideas. He extracted ideas from every visitor; he surrounded himself with idea-men; he solicited ideas ; he produced ideas; he communicated enthusiasm for new ideas. As a result, with his New Deal he took the US out of depression and with the UN Charter he ushered humanity into a New Deal. Being handicapped and in a wheel-chair, he knew well the power of ideas and ideals to overcome his handicap and to do more than a normal person, as did blind Homer, blind Milton and deaf Beethoven. Just to give you an example: there were many unemployed graduates of literature during the depression. Someone suggested to him to appropriate modest sums of money to jobs which consisted of going to remote areas of the US and collect the stories of old people. The young graduates did it and several of them became the great writers of the US!

Incidentally, meditation and prayer have the same effect: when you meditate you are in union with Creation and ideas will arise how you can help its further evolution; when you pray you submit a vision or wish to God and by doing that quite naturally the ways and ideas of accomplishing it come to your mind.

Hence, my first recommendation: in all your speeches and in the speeches you propose to me, I want to see ideas, concrete, inspiring ideas on which governments, delegates and people can start to work. It might take years until some of them are accepted, but we must begin somewhere. So let us start now.

Prior to examining my Peace Plan 2010 which is an update of the Plan of your former colleague Louis Parizot, I intended to discuss with you priorities of world problems. But I gave up the idea, after seeing whole collections of priorities established by a great number of organizations and people. For example, the Union of International Associations in Brussels has published a thick inventory of world problems in which they list a total of 13,167 world political, social and economic problems classified in 14 categories of which I mention as examples: armaments and wars, poverty and homelessness, illiteracy, disease, pollution, endangered species, unemployment. Louis Parizot has given me his list of ten major problems: actual wars, armaments, world population, hunger and poverty, health, environment, world accidents, violence, terrorism and crime, human rights and lack of meaning of life. The western countries generally consider overpopulation, climatic changes, pollution, deforestation and human rights to be the top priorities, whereas poor countries have on their list western armaments, poverty, hunger, illiteracy, disease, unemployment and homelessness. I learned that on the occasion of the fortieth anniversary of the UN, a preparatory committee tried to establish a list of priorities, but the divergences of views among governments were such that the only common motto they could agree upon for the anniversary was: United Nations for a Better World!

Under these circumstances, I think the best solution is to work hard on all fronts without worrying too much about priorities. The more irons we put in the fire, the more results we will get. Each of your Departments is a priority in itself and you know perfectly well what your priorities are. Political events will anyway dictate them to us. So let us turn immediately to the paper submitted to you, for your reactions, comments, corrections, additions and ideas."

There was a long silence and hesitation among the attendees to take the floor. Most of them were thinking about what she had just said.

To break the ice, the lady representing the Center for Social and Humanitarian Affairs took the floor.

"My comments are these: first, the subject of youth is omitted in the plan. A new world conference of youth should be included to seek the ideas and inputs of youth regarding the third millennium which will be their millennium. Youth has a very special and natural perceptory and anticipatory role to play in social evolution. This source of ideas should be tapped. Secondly, it is well-known that the Ministries between which there is the least international cooperation are the Ministries of War or Defense, the Ministries of Justice and the Ministries of Interior, all three being very closely linked with national sovereignty. Your plan provides for breakthroughs in military cooperation and in the field of justice, but nothing is envisaged for the Ministries of Interior. I would recommend adding the creation of a World Police Agency where all national police information would be coordinated, exchanged and computerized as a means to track criminals and offenders world-wide. Common action would be taken by all national polices intimately cooperating with each other. Nowadays, terrorists, criminals, maffias, arms and drug dealers are better organized internationally than nations. There is also need to bring the police forces closer to the people and to return to the old French concept of "agents de la paix" or peace-agents rather than the discredited word of police. Ideally, if the military are suppressed, the UN Peace-keeping services could be merged with police forces to constitute a World Peace Ensuring Agency dealing with all forms of violence on our planet, with national and local services down to the cities and neighborhoods. Since your plan is very ambitious, perhaps one could think afresh this whole area and conceive entirely new structures taking into account the unity, interdependence and diversity of our globe."

Encouraged by this first statement, the head of the Department of Economic and Social Affairs took the floor:

"I like your plan very much, Madam. It holds many keys to the problems of poverty and under-development. I like in particular your idea of a Marshall Plan and we will work on it right away. But I would like to suggest an amendment to it: it should be conceived from the start as a revolving fund. In other words, if an assisted country succeeds and becomes rich, it should reimburse all or part of the aid it has received, so as to help other new areas of distress. It was a great mistake of the US Marshall Plan not to be conceived in that way. If it had, today most European countries would be obligated to reimburse interest-free the huge sums they received from the US. The new Marshall Plan should therefore obtain its major resources from countries like Germany, France, Italy, Japan which were helped on a large scale by the US after World War II."

The head of the UN Statistical Office:

"Madam, may I say that I just love your proposals on world data and information. I could kiss you for them. At long last, there are fresh winds of change in this house. I predict that you will succeed beyond any expectation, because your proposals are all ideas whose time has come. You will have my full, enthusiastic cooperation and that of the UN Statistical Commission."

The Under-Secretary-General for Economic and Social Affairs took the floor again:

"Yes, it seems very important to me that during these coming years we re-evaluate our statistics and value measurements. I would add a recommendation for a World Values Measurements Conference to review the entire field. We speak of economic progress and development which often are regress and destruction from a planetary and future generations' point of view. The famous Gross National Product is filled with non-products. For example, military expenditures are included. Also waste is included. The enormous packaging industry is included. We include the costs of waste removal and transportation as a "product". And then we include recycling and waste disposal as a product. In reality all this should be removed from the Gross National Product. If we did so, we would see that the GNP is in reality not growing and in many cases even declining! We need entirely new statistics and standards. Often when I see the sign "construction", I replace it in my mind by the word "destruction". We introduced recently a new index, the Human Development Index (HDI), based on longevity, knowledge and decent living. But it is not enough. It is no fun anymore to be an economist. I think that the Economic and Social Council and my Department should be renamed and drastically revamped. When I see one of our glowing reports that international trade has increased by so many percents, I wonder who gave us the right to rejoice at something that might be damaging to the Earth and be only partly necessary or useful to humans. I have more and more sleepless nights. There are many areas in the world where there is still room for a lot of development but there are others where development should slow down or be stopped altogether. I am glad, Madam, that you brought us an eye-opening, revolutionary plan. It might save the world and our sanity."

The Secretary of the Economic and Social Council:

"I love your plan too. The world underestimates the enormous contribution of the UN system to human evolution. You are right, we need many more world agencies. The world needs at least as many agencies as nations have ministries. Instead of that, we hear only criticism from some countries threatened in their power that there are too many UN agencies, programs and world servants. This is utter non-sense. Governments should look into their own face. Incredible savings could be achieved world-wide if there were more global cooperation and coordination through central common agencies and instruments. Just think of the national savings achieved due to the fact that the UN and its agencies collect, coordinate and publish all needed world statistics and that national statistical offices no longer have to do this work, duplicating each other 166 times. In addition, think of the 2 billion dollars saved each year through the eradication of smallpox thanks to the work of the World Health Organization. This alone represents several times the budget of that Organization. Just to give you an example of national duplication: I learned recently from UNESCO that the money spent in national universities to teach international relations and the UN system is more than the total cost of that system! Coordination of such studies through the

University for Peace in Costa Rica and the UN University in Tokyo would save the world substantial resources and duplication. Some criticize the tiny UN for duplication, but no one ever looks at the colossal duplications and lack of coordination between 166 nations! It is incredible what could be achieved if the whole world were taken as a unit and organized as one human society. It is becoming imperative if we want to survive. We need, indeed urgently, to concentrate our attention on proper world governance, management and conservation as we move towards the third millennium. The situation is becoming critical and will soon be cataclysmic. We must think afresh many things, and change course fundamentally."

The official in charge of Perspectives 2000 then took the floor: "Dear Sister Lakshmi, as one entrusted with preparing the annual document for the General Assembly on perspectives for the year 2000, I have one criticism to address to your otherwise remarkable plan: it does not go far enough in time. The main problem on this planet is the blindness of governments and of international institutions to the distant future. And yet that distant future is of great consequence not only for future generations but also for today's life. Every day more than 300,000 children are born on this globe. In the rich countries they have a life-expectancy of more than seventy years and in the poor countries of more than sixty years. Are governments, are we not responsible for the entire life duration of these children? They will live to the year 2060. In what conditions? In what kind of world and society? Who on Earth is thinking of the year 2060? No one. And yet, the humans who will live then are already amongst us. I am thinking sometimes that we need to proclaim a new human right, the right of each human being to proper foresight and planning by governments and world agencies of the conditions of life for the duration of *his or her* life expectancy. The Iroquois took their decisions taking into account the effects on the seventh generation. We should at least take into account the effects of our decisions on the next generation."

The representative of the UN Environment Program:

"Sister Lakshmi, I like your idea of a conference of scientists who will be asked in their respective fields how long they think it will take until the planet will become unlivable for the human species. In my many years of world service for the first time I hear raised the possibility that the human race might become extinct if we continue

86

on the present course. I have estimates that go from 20 to 100 years, which are mere specks of time in the multibillion years history of this planet. Like the dinosaurs we might disappear because we did not grow a big enough brain to assess our planetary environment and the effects of our actions for a long time to come. Any species which does not preserve its habitat is doomed. One can already envisage that on this planet other species will continue to evolve without us. Perhaps the Earth and its biological riches will be better off without us. Perhaps humans, unable to chart correctly their planetary role and evolution, will turn out to be evolutionary misfits instead of the evolutionary spearhead and success we were supposed to be. If we want to survive, we must drastically reduce our population growth and life-styles, our monumental waste and built-in obsolescence, our greed, our so-called "growth" and economic development. I therefore also support wholeheartedly your proposal for a world conference on simple and frugal living. We need a more humble and natural life on this planet. We are getting wronger and wronger, more deeply into trouble every day that passes. Your proposals on the political level should even be stronger than they are. Governments must drastically change course and abandon urgently their antiquated quarrels and military build-ups. They appear to me as total madmen. Who do they think they are? The political system of this planet is a chaos on the verge of total collapse."

There was a silence. An angel of peace was passing.

Lakshmi Narayan asked:

"Does the Under-Secretary-General for Political Affairs have any comments?"

He took the floor hesitatingly:

"There are many far-reaching, courageous proposals in your plan, Madam. It will be interesting to see the reactions of governments. A remark of Gunnar Myrdal to his friend Dag Hammarskjøld comes to my mind. He said: *A Secretary-General of the UN must always be ahead of governments, but not too much.* Personally, when I read the proposal to draft a World Constitution, I am reminded of some very humble changes I would like to see introduced, for example that all governments would hold their elections in the same year and for the same duration of office. You will soon see why, when you deal with the Middle-East or Cyprus: many times you will be told that you cannot take any initiative because there will be elections in Israel, in

Egypt, in the United States, in Turkey, in Greece, all in different years. This fact alone renders negotiations impossible more than half of the time. Perhaps the eminent group dealing with a World Constitution could have a look at that. Of course, if there was a world parliament, elections would be world-wide or at least simultaneously held in all countries of a world federation. This would solve my problems."

There was a silence.

The head of the UN Translation Services:

"Why do you call world management "gaiamanagement" instead of "geomanagement" which would be understandable to the people, since we use the words geography (the description of the Earth), geology (the study of the Earth), geometry (the measurement of the Earth), geophysics, geopolitics, etc.?"

Lakshmi:

"Because the Greeks called the Earth Gaia, the Goddess of Light - probably a galaxy - who whirled in the universe until she took the form of the Earth. Men of course hastened to change the feminine Gaia into the masculine geo! Personally I have decided to always use the words gaiagraphy, gaialogy, gaiametry, etc. and I would love to see all UN services and agencies, and why not all women of the world, do the same. Incidentally, in most languages of the world, the word Earth (germanic: the Goddess Eartha) is a woman, a goddess or a mother. It just shows how the instinct of the so-called primitive people was right. Perhaps the UN Linguistics Club could study all etymologies and issue a paper on the subject. We have people here in the house from practically every language on Earth. Did Georges Schmidt, our world record holder of languages ever write or speak about it? You may wish to check."

The chef de cabinet was the last to take the floor:

"As an old man I do not agree that youth was left out of the Secretary-General's plan. On the contrary, the proposal for a World Peace Service instead of military service is one of the most beautiful ideas I have heard in a long time. May I also mention that a number of young people have recently established in Holland a United Nations of Youth (UNOY). They might be asked to provide the input for the third millennium mentioned by our colleague from the Center of Social and Humanitarian Affairs. And I would like to make another observation. The young people of the world organized a very strong, vocal movement in the 1960s telling the people in power what kind of a world they wanted: peace, an end to the cold war, disarmament, the protection of the environment, war on poverty. Well, most of these issues are today on the front-pages of the media and they had several victories. What I regret is that the youth of today seems to be asleep. We badly need a youth movement of the 1990s which will give the views and visions of youth of the future, of the third millennium. I do not know who can start that, but I pray God that youth organizations will."

The other attendees did not venture to speak. The meeting was already dense enough. There would be other opportunities to return to the subject. Lakshmi felt that this was all she could get for the moment. She therefore took the floor to close the meeting:

"I thank you all from the bottom of my heart. I know that you have a lot more to say and there will be other opportunities. This is only a beginning. Do not hesitate to send me notes with your thoughts and proposals. I will appreciate them immensely. We are part of the world brain. We are component neurons of it. This requires constant interchange and communications. The comments that came to my mind as I listened to you were these: world consciousness has progressed to such an extent in the last few years that we no longer have to speak in broad, philosophical, lofty terms. The people are fully aware of the need for peace, disarmament, demilitarization, a better environment, a new political system, etc. What they need now is concrete steps and action proposals. They want to participate in the making of a better world. This is the emerging new world democracy. More and more books on world affairs I read recently have long lists of things which people can do: 500 ways to improve the environment, 60 proposals to help disarmament, 100 occasions to plant trees, etc. Louis Parizot, when he received recently the UNESCO Peace Education Prize, was asked to deliver an acceptance speech of a maximum of twenty minutes. He managed to submit to UNESCO in those twenty minutes twenty-four concrete proposals. I am tempted to believe that in the UN we should prepare and publish a volume entitled:" 2000 ideas for the next millennium." Perhaps all of us should write down our proposals. If the people begin to act, the leaders will follow. There are innumerable ideas to improve the world situation. As regards the remark of Gunnar Myrdal to Dag Hammarskjøld, I will correct it by saying: 'A Secretary-General must always be far ahead of governments.' It is our fundamental duty to assert the precedence of the world and of humanity, those two orphans of all past history. Nations must be put at their secondary place where they belong. A total revolution in thinking and approach is needed if we want to get out of the present chaos. For example someone who opts for the planet and humanity rather than for a nation is called a traitor. Why don't we wake up and call those who are ready to kill other human beings for a nation traitors to humanity? And a final remark: even if this plan is not fully implemented by the year 2010, at least a large part of it will, and we can hope that all of it will become a reality by the year 2020. Let us not discount the phenomenon of take-offs and sudden accelerations after certain points. A sportsman will beat his record only if he reaches for the impossible and tries incessantly. We must do the same in the UN. The UN will win, because we are in the right currents of evolution, while nations are not. Whatever they try, they will be subordinated to the primordial needs of this planet and of the human species. In this connection , since we have still a little time, I cannot resist reading to you a preface to a remarkable book I read last night, entitled "Planethood" by Benjamin Ferencz, a former prosecutor at the Nuremberg trials, and Ken Keyes, a peace activist. The book advocates the creation of a United States of the World, the same way as the American Confederacy which did not work, was transformed at the request of George Washington into the United States of America."

With a glow in her eyes and the excitement of a child, she read the following text:

If a divine or extra-terrestrial committee of experts in planetary management visited our Earth, they would not believe their eyes.

"You are insane!" they would exclaim. "This is no way to administer a planet! We give you the lowest mark in planetary management in the entire universe."

We would look at them with surprise, astonished by the vehemence of their attack.

"Look at what you are doing!" they would add with gentleness and pity. "You were given one of the most beautiful planets in the cosmos - one of the rare celestial homes at the right distance from a sun, endowed with marvelous forms of life. It is a living planet with an atmosphere, fertile soils, waters, and oceans. It is vibrant and interdependent, with elements all interlinked in the most marvelous ways. A true jewel in the universe. And look what you have done with it:

1.  You have divided this planet into more than 160 separate territorial segments without rhyme or reason - without geographic, ecological, human, or any other logic. All these segments are sovereign; i.e., **each of them considers itself more important than the planet and the rest of humanity.**

2.  You have armed these fragments to their teeth in order to defend their so-called "integrity." They often steal a piece of land from their neighbors.

3.  You let two of the biggest parts of this international jigsaw puzzle stuff the surface and the inside of the earth, the waters, the seas, the airs, and tomorrow the heavens and the stars with nuclear devices capable of destroying most of the life on this planet.

4.  You permit ego driven tyrants to snuff out the lives of people with poison gas.

5.  You put some of your best minds to work designing more efficient ways to kill - instead of better ways to nurture one's body, mind, and spirit.

6.  You spend huge sums of money for each of these sovereign territories, and almost nothing to safeguard and provide for the needs of the planet as a whole. You do not even have a planetary budget! What an aberration!

7.  You let many of your scientists, industrialists, developers, builders, promoters, merchants, and military progressively destroy the fundamental resources of your planet so that within a few decades it will become unlivable - and you will die like flies.

8.  You educate your children as if each of these territories were an autonomous island floating on an ocean - instead of teaching them about their planet which is their home - and about humanity, which is their family.

91

They would have a long list of other grievances: the gaps between the rich and the poor, between the overfed and the hungry, violence in so many forms, self-destructive drugs, the radioactive and chemical poisoning of the planet, ruthless greed for money and power regardless of the harm to fellow humans and animals, the violation by states of individual human rights, refugees, tortures, abandoned children, the homeless, the absence of a philosophy of life, of ethics, of planetary morals, a youth without ideals, racism, misinformation by the media and governments, abusive monopolies, and an unlimited imagination to attribute to our own nation every possible virtue and greatness while at the same time denigrating and dividing other nations and groups, etc.

We could find many arguments to try to justify ourselves: our checkered history; the current nation-states being the result of conquests, murders, stealings, invasions, wars and marriages; the recent discovery, only 500 years ago, that we are a globe turning around its sun rather than the contrary; the dearth of global data until the United Nations and its specialized agencies were born; a total inexperience in planetary management; the absence of any precedents; the novelty of the crises, challenges, and global problems to which we react like little children burning our fingers; a first very weak world organization, misunderstood, used as a scapegoat by its masters who monopolize all fiscal resources of the planet; belief in obsolete values and ideologies; the multitude of tongues, cultures, beliefs, and religions which we have inherited from the past, etc.

The extra-terrestrials would answer, "Alright. You have extenuating circumstances due to your history and slow evolution. But this has lasted long enough. You have until the year 2000 - the date of entry into your third millennium. Sit down. Think. Bring together your best minds. Consult your populations. And make a blueprint for a better system of planetary management. Luckily you have many excellent resources available.

The latest is *"PlanetHood"*, a book by Benjamin Ferencz and Ken Keyes. *"PlanetHood"* seems to us a good point of departure. That book raises in effect the following fundamental question: What would be the fate of the United States if each of its fifty states were sovereign, possessed an army, a President, a Supreme Court, a State Department, a national hymn, a national flag, national days, and the exclusive power to levy taxes on its citizens? What if the United States government were no more than a United Nations without sovereignty, without legislative, executive, judicial, and fiscal powers, unable to make decisions and laws, but only recommendations and exhortations? You would exclaim: "What an indescribable mess it would be!" Well, this is exactly the state of your planet torn up into 166 pieces!

"We will return in ten years, during your celebration of the Bimillennium. We hope that by then you will have drawn up a proper political and administrative regime for this planet."

"Do not lose any time. Be courageous. Do not get stopped by the antiquated beliefs carefully nurtured by the existing powers and all those who benefit from the present disorder."

"You are on the eve of major potential nuclear, ecological, and climatic disasters. May God protect you, bless you, and guide you. After all, you are our brothers. May cosmic enlightenment finally illuminate your marvelous little planet circling faithfully around its sun in the vast universe."

"And please remember," they would advise as they left, "this planet has not been created for you. You were created to take good care of it."

When she finished reading, she arose and brandished the book in her hand saying: Dear friends, miracles are expected from us. We will make the UN the miracle organization on this Earth. I thank you from the bottom of my heart. I love you."

\* \*

As the attendants of the meeting were leaving, Lakshmi asked the Chief of Finance to stay behind, because she wanted to have a few words with him.

She said to him:

"One thing annoys me supremely: the US criticism that the UN costs too much, that it is a burden to the US taxpayer, that we are a bureaucracy, that there is waste and duplication, that there are too many agencies and programs, that the UN is inefficient. That seems so much rubbish to me, having worked for a national government, that I want your frank opinion and ideas for a well-conceived counter strategy and campaign."

Chief of Finance:

"First of all, this position is not a US monopoly. You will find a similar speech by the USSR one year after the UN was created! It is almost a built-in ingredient of big power politics. They are basically scared of the potential growth of the UN which is much more in line with the trends and necessities of evolution than their own nations. A US State Department official once told me: 'We have a rule of thumb in the Service saying that we should not let the UN become too popular with the US public and not too unpopular.' Therefore, when there are anti-UN campaigns you might even conclude that the UN is not doing so badly. As U Thant used to say: 'When I am equally criticized by the US and the USSR, I know that I am right.' Also, do not underestimate the fact that many politicians and government officials are jealous of the UN and of its agencies: they know that the whole world and humanity are the new great page of history, that we are lucky to be in the midst of it while they are stuck in their national structures which do not have much future. This applies even to Academia. I once heard the Rector of the University of Brasilia say: "We are jealous of the UN, because it is the only really universal University on this planet.' Another problem is the fact that contributions to the UN are part of the budgets of the Ministries of Foreign Affairs. They inflate these budgets and the officials of these ministries are not very happy. Such contributions should be in a separate budget. They are no longer "foreign affairs" of nations. Finally, one should not underestimate the effective campaigns of isolationist, extreme right movements, and the pride of the American people in their country and their sensitivity to criticisms often levied against the United States by the third world.

Regarding a counter strategy, there are three levels of action: your own as the Secretary-General; my own as the head of financial services; and that of the Department of Public Information."

Lakshmi:

"Excellent. So what can I do? I am impatient to get this ludicrous annoyance out of the way."

Chief of Finance:

"Here are some suggestions:

1.    Express your annoyance to the heads of states, Ministers and Ambassadors you meet. They will be surprised and impressed, and will convey your annoyance and ask questions to their subordinates. Do not forget that often some very little people are

involved in such campaigns. In one of the Ministries of foreign affairs of a big country, which I will not name, they call the UN budget "petty cash." But it gives them a chance to exercise their power.

2.    If you really want something badly, like your Peace Room or high-tech communications with heads of States, simply threaten to resign. That is a crisis which the big powers do not want to hear of. The designation of a new Secretary-General and the crisis of a resignation are nightmare to them. It would show the public how right you are and how petty they are. They will therefore readily grant you what you want. It will not mean much to them anyway and they know that you are right. Try it and you will be surprised. As a matter of fact we had in the UN system a man who used this tool very successfully: Wyndham White, the Executive Director of GATT. He threatened to resign, on average, two or three times a year and always got from governments what he wanted.

3.    Address yourself directly to the public in your speeches. Do not fail to mention the UN financial stringencies. Give some good, hardhitting comparisons; for example, that the US contribution to the UN budget is equivalent to one-third of the cost of an atomic Trident sub-marine, or equal to the budget of the Fire Department of New York City, or equal to the cost of military bands in the US armed services. U Thant used to say that the whole UN budget was equal to the cost of one day of war in Vietnam. Ralph Bunche had wonderful techniques to answer the classical criticisms: when someone spoke against the UN in an audience, he told the person that his or her contribution to the UN was 25 cents a year, and gave the person a quarter, saying: 'And now please shut up.' When you hear criticisms that the UN is a papermill, just tell the people that the whole paper consumption of the UN in one year, dealing with a host of world problems in several languages, is less than the paper used for one Sunday edition of the New York Times! You can also say that the US gets back three times the sums it pays to the UN, since delegations have to spend a lot of money in the US and the UN spends the largest part of its money in the US. New York City would be terribly hit if the UN moved to another, cheaper country. Each

time we want to transfer a few officials to other locations in the world, we have a diplomatic problem with the US. It is the same when we want to hold meetings away from headquarters."

Lakshmi:

"What about the criticism that the US contribution of 25% to the UN budget is too high?"

Chief of Finance:

"That is a classical criticism too. Until 1970, the US paid 33% of the UN budget. Then, upon the recommendation of a Congressional Committee, the contribution was reduced to 25%. When Mr. Waldheim was Secretary-General, he proposed informally that an effort be made to reduce the US contribution to 15%, in view of the wide-spread criticism that the contribution was too high. The US Mission to the UN declined to consider the proposal, because it would reduce the US influence in the UN. This reminds me that when Mr. Waldheim visited China, Zhou En Lai asked him why China's contribution was only 6% while the US and USSR contributions were 25% and 14%. The Chinese Premier said: "I want the Chinese contribution increased, because as the Americans say: who pays the fiddler, sets the tune.""

Lakshmi:

"This has been very useful. Please send me all the ammunition you have and also ask the Department of Public Information to send me theirs. I am ready to give a battle. The UN budget seems ridiculously low to me given the world problems we have to face."

Chief of Finance:

"It reminds me of Louis Parizot who was Director of the Budget for a while. He created such trouble by publishing information about the growth of military budgets and the stagnation of the UN budget that he did not last more than three months in his position and was kicked upstairs as Director of the Secretary-General's Executive Office. There he started a much more ambitious general campaign for the growth of the UN and became one of U Thant's most trusted and beloved co-workers."

Lakshmi:

"Good for him. I am not surprised. But I did not know that detail. I will ask for his advice and views too. Thank you for this most helpful briefing."

* * *

96

# Chapter 8

Napoleon Ames was pacing up and down the living room of his small apartment in Washington D.C. He had read last night Lakshmi Narayan's Peace Plan 2010 leaked out already to the Golden Age Foundation. He woke up with his heart full of hatred for that woman. Hate was his normal and preferred attitude. He just loved to hate. And the objectives of his hatred were not missing: he hated the world, he hated life, he hated humanity, he hated his race, he hated himself. It did not bother him a bit. On the contrary he felt well only when he hated. The more violently he hated, the better he felt. Hatred was his nature. He did not wonder why. He just accepted it as the natural characteristic of his being. It made him feel good. It gave him a lot of satisfaction and relaxation. It was like an inside force that possessed him and every cell, thought, movement, attitude of his being. He had to let it go out, to be released. This was particularly the case in the morning, when he woke up and was thinking of his day. The subconscious dominated him completely and charted for him the path of hatred he was to follow during the day. He was talking to himself as he was pacing up and down: "That Golden Age Foundation is all very well. They will be delighted to use my hatred for their ugly, narrow interests, like everyone else. Where will it lead me? To a job, perhaps to a position of influence inside the US administration? So what! My life will go with it in an unfolding flow of mediocrity, little games and victories without real world importance and impact. I will get old, lose my time in all their games and die without leaving a name. What am I going to do? God, help me."

As he pronounced the word God, a light went on in his mind: he hated God too! The image of Jesus came to him and with it that of Judas who hated Jesus and betrayed him. This was it! Judas was his ideal, the personification of hatred . All traitors and great killers of history out of sheer hatred should be his models and ideals. Since he was so possessed by hatred, why not give it full dominion? Why not become another great figure of hatred in the history of this planet? The face of Gandhi's killer in Attenborough's film came back to him: this was the face of perfect, total, unexplained, pure hatred, without need for a single word. It did not even seem to bear any relation with the person killed. The role of the latter was simply, through his prominence, to give occasion to the hatred to be shown world-wide, as a reality of life in certain cursed individuals of whom he was one.

He jumped with pleasure: "I am going to get any books I can get hold of and study all great traitors and killers of famous people throughout history: Judas, the killers of Caesar, Gandhi, Martin Luther King, John Kennedy, etc. And I am going to be the next in the Hall of Fame of great haters and killers. I will be the first ever to kill a Secretary-General of the UN, a female Gandhi, in a higher position than any US President or other head of State, surpassed in prestige only by the Pope. But I have no way of getting close to the Pope, while I have a way of getting close to her thanks to my relationship with the Golden Age Foundation, the perfect UN-hate organization. This is going to be thrilling and fun!"

He rubbed his hands with delight and exclaimed: "I am going to get myself a job in the UN and I will commit the crime of the century. I will be famous. I will be in all the newspapers and media of the world. I do not mind getting killed or condemned to electrocution in Sing Sing. Since I hate myself it will be the perfect exit from life, my last laugh in the face of God who gave me life without asking me. This is going to be great!"

He dressed up quickly, took a taxi and drove to the US National Library where he would spend the next weeks studying every book and report he could find on his new heroes. In the meantime, the Foundation will submit his candidacy for a UN job through the US delegation. He wanted to be hired for the Buildings Management

Service which would give him an opportunity to get fully familiar with the UN building and select the perfect spot for his crime.

* * *

# Chapter 9

Louis Parizot came to say goodbye to Lakshmi. He apologized that he had to return to Costa Rica so early. His wife needed his presence and was asking for him every day in the nursing home. They had no other family in Costa Rica, and he felt very badly when he was absent for too long. He assured Lakshmi that he would be at her disposal either by telephone or telefax at any moment. He congratulated her on her redraft and updating of his Year 2010 Plan and the many novel ideas and proposals she had included in it. He asked her also how the meeting with her top officials went.

She answered:

"It went very well. Most of my colleagues are deeply devoted to the UN and fascinated by their work. They need encouragement from the top and I will give it to them. I am much more confident today than on our first evening. You gave me the right advice, namely to be on the offensive for peace all the time. It seems that we have entered a period when peace is becoming the wish of the vast majority of governments and peoples. The next big battle to be won is demilitarization in order to get the resources necessary to heal our many other wounds. I wish you all the best in Costa Rica, and an improvement or at least a stabilization of your poor wife's condition. I will think of you often. I have placed one of your poems on my desk to remind me never to despair and to get the maximum out of every situation. I will turn to you much more often than you think and I hope to come and visit your University some day. I have one question on my mind before you leave: when I read and worked on your Peace 2010 Plan I wondered how you could have so many ideas, all of them appropriate and responding to the needs of our time. You must have a special head to produce so much. Please tell me. I am sure I will learn from it."

Parizot:

"It is true that God must have given me imagination as one of my gifts. I remember that on most of my essays, the teachers wrote the comment: a lot of ideas and imagination. But more important is the fact that since early childhood I deeply loved life, people and nature all around me. I considered life to be "divine" (in German gɵttlich, since we spoke that language at home). Therefore, any sickness or misery I saw became a challenge. As a little boy I was asking myself constantly: how can this misery be avoided? What can I do? What would I do, if I had the power? The occasions were plentiful: there was talk of war all along the border; we lived in the poorest neighborhood of our town where workers were getting drunk on payday and were beating their wives and children. My father could not buy me glasses because he was too poor and there was no social security, etc.

These images have stayed with me all my life. As I go around the world, my mind constantly works at imagining solutions to our problems. There are endless occasions to have ideas in the light of specific situations. There are also so many people who have ideas and projects for a better world. We must be open to them and help them. I continue to do that now at the University for Peace, after having done it for more than forty years at the UN. In the end, it counts and one reaps many, many positive results and satisfactions."

Lakshmi:

"Please give me some specific illustrations. For example how did you get the idea of high-tech direct communications between heads of states and the Secretary-General, one of your ideas which I am determined to implement."

Parizot:

"It came about as follows: In July 1972, I was invited to accompany Secretary-General Waldheim to Beijing as his political adviser. I had played an active role with his predecessor U Thant to get China to occupy its seat again in the United Nations. Without the presence of China in the UN, the world situation did not make much sense, in my view. When we arrived in Beijing, we were invited to spend a long evening with Premier Zhou En Lai. He apologized for receiving us so late - it was ten o'clock in the evening - and said 'I cannot afford to be asleep when they are awake in Washington. Therefore I have my watch set on Washington time.' His Minister of Foreign Affairs, an elderly gentleman, complained to us later: 'I have to spend most of the nights in meetings with the Premier, and then in the morning I have to go to the airport to receive dignitaries like you. I cannot go on for long.' And indeed, a few weeks later he resigned from his position. At the beginning of the talk, Mr. Waldheim expressed his misgiving that the Secretary-General of the UN had very little power and influence. Zhou En Lai said to him:

'I cannot agree with you. On the contrary, you have a very important role. What do you think I am doing here every evening late into the night? With my colleagues we are trying to figure out what they are scheming against us in Washington and in Moscow. But often the thought crosses my mind that since we are not scheming anything against them, it is quite possible that they are not scheming anything against us either. But we are not sure. We do not trust each other. Therefore, it is important that people like you visit us and reassure us about each other. You have therefore a very important role which is to calm our relations and create confidence among the big powers.' As I heard him say that, I wondered how primitive and retrograde heads of states can be. I looked at the huge blank wall behind the Premier and I visualized a big screen on which the images of the Presidents of the United States and of the USSR would appear in order to have a person-to-person conversation with Mr. Zhou En Lai. I imagined the following conversation":

Zhou En Lai: "Mr. President, what are you concocting against us in Korea? I have very specific reports that something will happen there."

President of the US: "My dear Zhou, I have no idea. Let me find out and I will call you back."

A little later, the screen lights up again and the President of the United States says to Zhou En Lai:

"I checked what you said and I am so grateful that you called me. Indeed, my people were scheming there something of which I had no idea. You know how it is. Our policies are misinterpreted by so many of our inferiors. They are eager beavers as we call them in the United States. I stopped the whole business right away and I am grateful and apologize. Please let me know whenever something like that is going on, and I will do the same."

Parizot continued:

"We had the same situation in Europe where the chiefs of states rarely spoke to each other. They sent their Ambassadors who very often create more trouble and complicate things because they want to look important. Today, if there is a problem, the heads of states of Europe talk to each other on the phone and see each other very frequently. The same has to happen between all heads of states of the world.

And since China is far away from Washington and they cannot see each other as frequently as in Europe, why not have direct video telecommunications systems which they would use practically every day, in order to avoid trouble, solve problems and cooperate ever more actively among themselves. Can you image what kind of a better world it would be if one of them woke up in the morning, switched on his screen and said to one or several of the others: 'I have an idea. What do you think of it?' The heads of big multinational businesses operate that way. There is no reason why the heads of states should not do the same and take full advantage of the most modern means of communication."

Lakshmi loved the story, and said:

"You are a good story teller. You must have dozens of others. Tell me one more. Fore example, how did you come about the idea of a World Peace Service for youth in lieu of military service?"

Parizot:

"Yes, I love story-telling. That is why I write so many books and give so many speeches. I want to tell the people that many good things are possible and that they should be story-makers and storytellers. I say to them: if you have a good idea, send it to your President or to the Secretary-General of the UN. They have all a colleague who is in charge of collecting ideas. They turn to him for ideas to include in their speeches. Your idea, if it is good and timely, has a good chance of being proposed and adopted.

The idea of a world peace service came to me in the following circumstances:

Once I visited with my wife the refugee camp of Colomoncagua in Honduras which was run by our daughter Solange, a child nutritionist. I was amazed that this extraordinary camp of 8000 Salvadorean refugees was entirely run by about fifty young people of various nationalities. none of them more than thirty years old. They were doctors, teachers, social workers, agronomists, nutritionists, handicrafts specialists, etc. They were living in the village of Colomoncagua without electricity, far removed from urban centers. No adult foreign expert would have accepted their poor living conditions. They were sponsored by charitable aid organizations such as Catholic Relief Services, the Quakers, Medecins sans Frontieres, etc. They received very low salaries. But they deeply loved their work and were happy to be of service. At six o'clock in the morning, next to our room, the doctors gave already free medical consultations to the local population of Colomoncagua before taking their tour of duty in the camp. I asked them if they had any complaints or wishes. Yes, they wished the UN High Commissioner for Refugees to give them a minimum of protection against arbitrary arrest, molesting or expulsion. They were only tolerated by the government and could be harassed by the military at any moment, as was our daughter later under very dramatic circumstances.

There was plenty of material aid and food in the camp. I saw big piles of bags of food labelled "European Economic Community" and had a grateful, pious thought for my saintly compatriot Robert Schuman who had created that community, proving that former enemies like France, Germany and England could perfectly live in peace and cooperate with each other. But there was not enough personnel available for the needs of the camp. Our daughter told us that she could use two or three times the number of volunteers she had. I then remembered that several European countries allowed their young men of military age to do their service in humanitarian agencies or in bilateral technical assistance programs in poor countries. The following idea was therefore born during an evening with these young people around a fire and a barbecue in the open air under a starry sky:

Why not create a World Peace Service under the auspices of the United Nations whose Volunteer Service could easily be converted into such a program? UN agencies such as UNICEF, the High Commissioner for Refugees, the Food and Agriculture Organization, the World Health Organization and UNESCO could indicate yearly how many young people with given qualifications they could use in their programs in the poor countries, for example in refugee camps where many are needed. Countries would offer their young people to work with these UN agencies in lieu of military service. They would receive a small stipend and their travel would be paid by the military budget. The UN for its part would provide them with a UN laissez-passer or document giving them the necessary protection. Each young peace worker would deliver the oath of allegiance to the UN, swearing that they would work for the UN ideals only and not for any government or private interest. The whole United States Peace Corps could be integrated into such a truly World Peace Service. And since the US and the USSR have become friendly to each other, it would be wonderful to see young Russians and Americans work together in such a service.

In January 1987, during the session of the Council of the University for Peace, the Director of the Spanish Red Cross visited Costa Rica to sign an agreement of cooperation with the University. I asked him how many young Spaniards served in the Spanish Red Cross. He answered: 8000. He was in the process of obtaining legislation which would allow him to send such young people abroad. I suggested to him therefore to send a first group of young Spaniards for peace service with the University for Peace or to be placed by the University in local programs in Costa Rica. He promised to do so. Also noteworthy is the fact that the French government allows already a dozen or so of young Frenchmen to do service with UN agencies located in the developing regions of the world instead of military service.

Parizot concluded:

"I am so glad that you have mentioned such a program in your Peace Plan 2010. I hope your colleagues will work out a detailed plan for consideration by governments in the General Assembly. It would go a long way in restoring the faith of youth in a better world. It would be a great tribute to the idealistic young people endowed with such devotion and human love I saw in Colomoncagua, and to so many others like them who are working as volunteers in numerous places around the world and would love to work for such a service. May the year 2000 not come without having seen the birth of a World Peace Service on this planet. As a matter of fact, I think it is essential, since otherwise we will see the birth of a US/USSR Peace Service and the national games will start all over again, although in improved form."

When he finished, Lakshmi looked at him and commented: "This is all so fascinating. It confirms me in my intention to launch constantly new ideas and to make this planet a planet of dreams, prayers, ideas and visions. We have neglected these powerful ways to achieve a peaceful and better world. In Hindu philosophy, ideas, visions, dreams and prayers are forms of individual conciousness to use the all-pervading, immenent cosmic energy in us and around us, and transform it into new realities and manifestations. The greatness of humans is to possess this conciousness and to be co-creators of cosmic evolution. But it has to be rightly channeled. I am glad that I will have my high-tech telecommunications screen and I will use it generously. Anyway, since I am a woman, the heads of states have to be polite and cannot refuse to see me and to listen to me on their screens."

Parizot:

"It is all the more important due to the fact that huge establishments of people are working to implement the policies decided at the top. It reminds me of another anecdote which has always stuck in my mind: when I was U Thant's assistant, we had often chats on why certain heads of states were following this or that policy. When Willy Brandt tried to get a reunification of the two Germanies, I asked U Thant if his decision was his own, or whether it had been suggested to him by one of the big powers, U Thant did not have any opinion on it. Then one day, Willy Brandt came to visit the Secretary-General and I was present at the meeting. U Thant remembered my question and he put it to Willy Brandt.

The Chancellor of Germany answered: "Having been Mayor of Berlin and knowing what the division of a people and a wall mean, the first thing I did when I became Chancellor was to get my colleagues together and I told them: you are going to work for the reunification of Germany and I want files, proposals and new policies to be worked out and submitted to me." They almost all shouted unanimously: 'That is impossible!' I answered: The more impossible something seems to be, the harder one must work on it. A few weeks later the same people who had thought that it was impossible and had worked on making it impossible submitted to me files showing that it was possible and how it could be done!"

Parizot added:

"Can you imagine how these files must have proved useful and timely when the reunification took place on such a short notice recently?"

Lakshmi looked at the old man with tenderness:

"You are really in love with the world as you were as a child. You have not ceased to be a child and as Jesus said: Let the children come to me. You must be very close to His heart. May He protect you and keep you well for many, many years. We need you so much. Take good care of yourself and of your beloved wife."

* * *

# Chapter 10

July 1992. Lakshmi Narayan is in Geneva to open at the Palais
des Nations the summer session of the UN Economic and Social
Council and to preside over a coordinating meeting of all the heads
of the UN agencies and world programs. At dawn she quietly slips
out of the Hotel Intercontinental to take a stroll in the magnificent
park surrounding the UN Palace, an entire hill donated by a peace-
loving Swiss land-owner for the seat of the first League of Nations.
From that hill one enjoys a prestigious view of Lake Geneva and of
the Mont Blanc, the highest peak of Europe, emerging from behind
pine-covered, dark forerunners of the Alps.

She engaged briskly into several paths to find a particular bench
described by Louis Parizot in a story entitled *"The Dwarf with the
Silver Hands"*. It was one of his anecdotes of extra-sensory perceptions he had experienced in his life. In it he tells how he liked to
arrive early at the UN when he was stationed in Geneva and to sit on
a particular bench offering a breathtaking view of the lake and the
mountains. He often sat there, meditating, dreaming, thinking, and
writing about a peaceful and better world. One morning, in spring,
as he was contemplating a group of little daisies turning their heads
towards the sun, he had the impression that a dwarf was trying to
emerge from under the ground near the bench. The dwarf had silver
hands stretched out towards the sky. From that day on, experiencing
this feeling every morning, he wrote his journal in the form of

dialogues with the Dwarf with the Silver Hands. A year later, when he was transferred back to New York, he forgot about the little dwarf, and his journal of that time remained stored in a cupboard. A few years later, when he accompanied the Secretary-General to Geneva for the summer session of the Economic and Social Council, he slipped out of the Hotel Intercontinental at dawn to pay a visit to his beloved bench and to reminisce in front of the magnificent scenery of lake and mountains. When he arrived at that spot he could not believe his eyes: the bench had disappeared and on its place stood an enormous monument of steel and iron: a shining, sloping triangle of polished steel, ending in a needle, was pointing to the universe, like a launching pad. Next to it, stood an iron space capsule out of which a helmeted astronaut was stretching his two metal hands towards the heavens, exactly as he had seen him underground! Here stood in front of him the Dwarf with the Silver Hands! It was a monument donated to the United Nations by the USSR in honor of all astronauts and of the human dream to reach the stars and the heavens. He took a picture of it and when he returned to New York he showed it to his wife, went to the cupboard and extracted from it old envelopes with notes entitled *Dialogues with the Dwarf with the Silver Hands*. His wife was not surprised and simply commented: "You do not have to prove to me your extra-sensory perceptions. I have seen them at work so many times."

A new bench had been built next to the monument. Lakshmi sat on it and did her early morning meditations and prayers. She was about to participate in two great meetings on these blessed grounds, in a Palace filled with the dreams, wisdom, efforts and ghosts of many great men and women from all nations. It was her turn to take place in the chain of these lives devoted to peace and a better world. She prayed God Suryia with every fiber of her heart to help her, to bless her, to inspire her, to make her a worthy and beloved instrument of the universe. She stretched her arms towards the heavens, like the *Dwarf with the Silver Hands*, in the same urge and dream to return to God, to home, to the paradise we came from. How beautiful and powerful it would be, she thought, if all UN delegates, world servants and peoples of the planet would stretch out their arms and lift them to the heavens. She did it symbolically for all of them at the very moment when the sun arose above the horizon.

\* \*

109

When Lakshmi returned to the hotel, the first thing she did was to send a cable to Louis Parizot in Costa Rica: "I would be eternally grateful if you could join me in Geneva for the session of the Economic and Social Council and the coordinating meetings of the specialized agencies. These meetings are essential for my enlightenment and preparation for the coming General Assembly. Your presence would be most important and precious to me. I pray God that you will accept."

At the Palais des Nations she was given a beautiful, luxurious office overlooking the park, the lake and the mountains. When the first League of Nations was created after World War I, diplomacy and international civil service were still considered an aristocratic activity, often reserved to an elite and unfolding in relative luxury. Today, world affairs have been democratized and brought down to the people. The UN in New York is much more functional, business-like and people-oriented. She preferred New York, except for the wonderful natural grounds of the Palais des Nations in Geneva.

During her fruit-and-juice breakfast she quickly refreshed her memory before going to the agencies meeting, by perusing a basic working document which she had read carefully in the plane from New York. My God, what a document that was! From it all the world's crying pains were appealing to her. It was the product of the year-round cooperation between officials of all the UN Departments and specialized agencies under the leadership of an Assistant-Secretary-General attached directly to her office. It was this crucial, mind-boggling position that Louis Parizot held for several years, giving him his extraordinary knowledge and intimacy with the world's needs and problems. The role of the meeting of the heads of agencies under her presidency was to review the planetary situation and to draw conclusions and future plans from that crucial document. She was to open the meeting with an overview of the world political situation.

When she entered the conference room, the chiefs of the specialized agencies arose and applauded her. Her sharp eyes went around and immediately noted that there was only woman among them! This was worse than anything she had seen before! How could governments ever let such a distorted situation develop when presenting their candidates for high international offices? But she was consoled that at least the world and humanity were represented here and not nations or political groups. She had no idea that such a meeting even existed on this planet. This was a true world cabinet meeting dealing not with India, as she was accustomed to, but with the entire globe and human species. Why was this not known to the world's public? Such a meeting should be televised world-wide for all people to see, to learn from and to act in consequence.

* *

Well, it was quite a day. She would never forget that meeting. In the evening, when she went to bed, totally exhausted, like beaten, her head ringing with facts and figures, she re-read to herself the notes she had taken during the meeting:

"In my opening speech I underlined the beneficial effects of the end of the cold war for the UN. The organization, at long last, is able to function as was foreseen by the drafters of the Charter who had assumed that the US and the USSR would cooperate in ensuring world peace and order. I mentioned also my trimurti approach to my task.

The head of the UN Fund for Population activities reported that we had reached 5.5 billion people in 1991, compared with 2.5 billion in 1951 when the UN published the first world population figure. We are likely to be 6.2 billion in the year 2000, and 8.5 billion in 2025. More than 90 million people are added each year to the world population. On the present trajectory, the world population would stabilize only at 14 billion. With an heroic effort we could achieve stabilization at 9 billion. A country like Nigeria could grow from 30 million in 1950 to 280 million in 2025. In that year, 7.1 billion people will live in the developing countries and 1.4 billion in the developed ones. Life expectancy has increased from 43 years in 1950 to 64 years (74 years in the developed countries, 61 years in the developing ones). As a result a substantial aging of the world population will take place: 400 million more elderly people over 60 will be added to the world population by the year 2025.

The Director General of International Economic Relations surveyed the world economic and social situation. He reported a narrowing of the income gap between the poor and the rich countries; a substantial reduction of infant mortality in poor countries; an increase in life expectancy and in world literacy. Despite these significant improvements, most serious problems remain:

111

* more than 1.75 billion people live without safe drinking water;

* 1.5 billion persons are without access to primary health care.

* 1 billion people live in absolute poverty often homeless;

* 900 million persons cannot read or write;

* 800 million persons suffer from hunger;

* 150 million children under the age of five (one in three) are malnourished;

* 14 million children die before the age of five;


He also reported on the damaging effects of the Iraq-Kuwait crisis on the world economy.

The Director General of UNESCO:

The absolute number of illiterate people is still increasing, due to the rapid increase of population in the poor countries. This is a battle we are losing every year. But in relative terms, the situation is improving: the average adult literacy rate for the world increased from 43 percent in 1970 to 60 percent in 1985. He also reported that 161 governments had approved the changes he introduced in UNESCO and that the two countries which had left UNESCO, at the same time as the US, will join again this year.

The head of the World Meteorological Organization:

The second World Conference on the Climate held in 1989, confirmed our critical findings and predictions at the first one in 1982. This planet's climate is in trouble, due to human over-activity and lack of foresight. Global warming is a sure fact. Further increases in the average temperature of the atmosphere around the globe are likely to range between 1.5 to 4.5 degrees centigrade by the year 2000. This will have a major impact on weather and climate. It would also lead to a sea level rise of 20 to 165 cm. By the year 2010 sea currents could change direction, a fact which would remain irreversible for thousands of years. Depletion of the ozonosphere is another confirmed fact to which most governments have fortunately reacted by adopting drastic measures. We wish that similar measures were adopted for the reduction of carbon dioxide emission into the atmosphere, the main cause of the greenhouse effect. The whole field of meteorology has been overtaken by climatology. We must indeed soon change our name to World Climate Organization.

The Director General of the World Health Organization:

Epidemics and infectious diseases are on the decrease; alcoholism, drugs and accidents are on the increase; progress in longevity will create one of the biggest world sociological problems on this planet, second only to the world population explosion; the number of handicapped (more than 300 million) will increase as a result of the handicaps of the elderly. This is another battle which we are losing every year. AIDS might be the first signal of the breakdown of the human immunological system; the human body seems to be giving up under the stress of too numerous, intensive changes in his environment over too short a period of time. Evolution and adaptation can no longer catch up. As already pointed out, 1.5 billion people are still without access to primary health care. One billion persons suffer from iodine deficiency. He was mad that the world was spending more for the military and armaments than for health and education together. For every 80 military there is only one doctor in the world.

The Director General of the Food and Agriculture Organization:

It is becoming increasingly difficult to feed the growing world population. Loss of topsoil and deforestation have become major problems. Each year the world's farmers lose 24 billion tons of topsoil from their croplands in excess of new soil formation. In the 1980's this meant a loss of more than 240 billion tons, an amount more than half that of US cropland. Worldwide the number of acres in cropland has now diminished. Regarding our forests, at the present rates of destruction, virtually all our rain forests will be gone by the year 2032, only 40 years from now.

The Director General of UNICEF:

The summit meeting of heads of states on the occasion of the adoption of the Declaration of the Rights of the Child, was a great success. Abandoned children and traffic of children for profit from the sale of organs, are new substantial problems to be added on top of those already affecting the world's children. On the good side: developing countries have reduced their infant mortality from nearly 200 deaths per 1000 live births to about 79 from 1950 to 1985, a feat that the industrialized countries took nearly a century to accomplish.

The head of the International Civil Aviation Organization:

World aviation will nearly double by the year 2000. A switch to hydrogen fuel is being seriously considered.

The head of the International Maritime Organization:

The world navigation satellite, the first of the UN system, is a great success and means substantial savings to governments. It could be a good example to follow by governments in other fields. The World Maritime University created in Malmo, Sweden, similarly demonstrates the usefulness of creating world universities in global fields.

The head of the International Monetary Fund:

The developing countries suffer particularly from the increases in oil prices, from the inflationary increase in the prices of their industrial imports and the decrease in the prices of their primary commodities. This curse in the world economic situation since World War II, aggravated by indebtedness of these countries, remains unchanged.

The head of the UN Environment Program read out this planetary ecological clock:

**Each minute....**

*   21 hectares of tropical forests are destroyed

*   we consume 34,725 barrels of oil

*   50 tons of fertile soil are washed or blown off cropland

*   we add 12,000 tons of carbon dioxide which warm up the atmosphere


**Each hour....**

*   685 hectares of potentially productive dryland become desert

*   1,800 children die of malnutrition and hunger

*   120 million dollars are wasted on military expenditures

* 55 people are poisoned by the pesticides they use and 5 are killed

* 60 new cases of cancer are diagnosed in the US alone, over 500,000 cases each year with 20,000 cases leading to death, because of the thinning of the ozone layer; that thinning also affects the immunological system of the human body and might destroy the diatoms or microscopic algae of the seas and oceans which provide two thirds of the oxygen of this planet

* about every five hours a species becomes extinct

**Each day....**

* 25,000 people die of water shortage and contamination

* 10 tons of nuclear waste are generated by 360 existing nuclear plants

* 250,000 tons of sulfuric acid fall as acid rain in the northern hemisphere, killing lakes and devastating millions of hectares of forests

On that gloomy note, Lakshmi stopped reading her notes. Still 22 more UN agencies and world programs reported on the world situation! As she turned off her bedside lamp, she thought about the next meeting which would consider actions to try to remedy this situation, including her World Plan 2010 which suddenly appeared to her much too timid to cope with such colossal problems.

Her last words were addressed to God:

"Dear God, why do you allow the incredible division of this planet into nations and the astronomic military and governmental waste it entails? The United Nations is doing its best, but it is totally under-equipped to deal efficiently and with urgency with such colossal problems. Please save our beautiful planet and provoke a revolution in the political system."

\* \*

Louis Parizot arrived two days later, on the day when Lakshmi was to open the summer session of the Economic and Social Council. She welcomed him with relief and asked him to accompany her to the opening ceremony of a UN organ of which he had been the Secretary for many years. She was already at a loss and was reconciled to simply read the speech written for her on the world economic situation and then to leave the meeting immediately after the speech by the President of the Council.

He said to her: "Do not give up so easily. Read the speech but at the end of it express your own, deep, womanly feelings. Tell them that the women of the world are tired of wars, of seeing their sons killed, their children hungry, uneducated and with a frightening, uncertain future. Tell them point blank that the military should vanish from this planet with all their paraphernalia and that our beautiful Earth must be totally demilitarized and disarmed, following the excellent example of Costa Rica which has lived in peace ever since it abolished its army in 1949. Give them your cri-du-coeur. It is your right and duty. And it is about time that a woman does it. It is bound to have an effect, because the time is ripe. And do not leave the meeting. Stay with them. Listen to them. Become one with them. Spend at least a couple of hours with them each day. You will learn enormously. You will get a first-class assessment of the world economic, social, environmental and human situation from governments, from thirty two specialized agencies and programs, from reports on several world conferences, from five continental commissions and from a good dozen of functional commissions of the Council. This is one of the most incredible world meetings and think-tanks that has ever existed on this planet."

She looked at him with fondness, smiled with gratitude and said: "I won't give up, I promise."

* *

Lakshmi had indeed an incredible month in Geneva and was able to get action in the Economic and Social Council and in the specialized agencies on a good number of her proposals. In particular, the Council approved the proposal for a Marshall Plan for the poor countries and established a preparatory committee to that effect.

She was happy. She was cheerful. During the week-ends she visited some of the beautiful natural and cultural highpoints not far from Geneva: the Mont Blanc, the Plateau d' Assy, Aosta and its Roman ruins, Annecy, the medieval villages of Yvoire and Gruyeres. Parizot even took her on a visit to his beloved Strasbourg and Alsatian villages. She was thinking how beautiful this planet was, how creative, imaginative and artistic humans are. Yes, it was the sacred duty of leaders in the Palais des Nations to preserve all that for future generations, to pursue the marvelous human journey, to foster all that is good and beautiful and to prevent and eradicate all that is destructive, cruel, ugly, wasteful, painful, wounding and a blemish on the surface of this celestial body. It was indeed a great month in her life and a good preparation for the General Assembly. Louis Parizot who knew this region inside out from the years he worked for the UN in Geneva, was her guide and told her many moving, unforgettable stories and anecdotes about that highly cultural, civilized region, inhabited since times immemorial. And all throughout the meetings he advised her, encouraged her, wrote and spoke for her, giving her all the best of his wisdom and experience.

One day she said to him:

"I have read your novel Sima, Mon Amour which unfolds in my country and in this region. I read about your love story for an old farmhouse near here which you restored and wrote about to Sima. I am dying to visit it. Why don't you invite me?"

He invited her there one evening to have a candle-light dinner. The house was located in an old celtic hamlet - St. Gix (the holy water) - near the spa of Divonne (the divine waters of the Romans), at the foot of the Jura mountains, only a quarter of an hour from the Palais des Nations. It was an unforgettable visit for her: an old farm restored by Parizot and his family to its medieval state and functioning. He told her the story of the farm and of the people who lived in it. He narrated many moving anecdotes. He showed her the stone from the Great Chinese Wall which he had brought from that country and incorporated into the entrance wall of the farm. She walked with delight through the old rooms with their wooden beams, their chimneys and other antiquities he had written about with such love in his book. She walked with him on the Roman road in front of the house, built by Julius Caesar when he invaded Helvetia. He told her about his dialogues with the ghost of Julius Caesar on that road, all recorded in his Journal.

She had this comment to him:

"You must be sad not to live here."

"Yes, we restored this home to be our place of retirement. But God wanted it differently. We are now on the other side of the planet, on my wife's continent. As an Alzheimer patient she is happy to be in her linguistic and cultural environment and in a beautiful climate. And instead of being "retired", I continue to be of service to one of the most promising new children of the UN: the University for Peace in Costa Rica. Contrary to the ending of my book Sima, Mon Amour, the readers of my works will not find my tomb in the cemetery of Divonne but in the cemetery of peacemakers in Costa Rica. As we say in French: L'homme propose, Dieu dispose. Man plans, God decides."

And among his many anecdotes he told her that one day, as they were vacationing in the farmhouse, a lady called him, all excited, saying: "Mr Parizot, I was looking for your tomb all over the cemetery of Divonne, after having read 'Sima, Mon Amour'. And then someone told me that you were still alive and they gave me your address. I am so happy that you are not dead and would love to meet you!"

Yes, it was a great, unforgettable month of learning, enlightenment and happiness for Lakshmi. She returned to New York, immensely enriched, loving this planet and humanity more than ever, ready to give her life for them, prepared to enter the scene of her first General Assembly in September. This magnificent planet and its noble human race merited a gallant battle against unnecessary world suffering, destruction, waste and injustice. She felt like an Amazon, like an Archangel or peace goddess determined to smother all evil on this planet. She was ready for her first General Assembly.

\* \* \*

# Chapter 11

Napoleon Ames had been hired by the UN Buildings and Management Service. Asked by the head of that Department if he had any wishes regarding his work he answered:

"Yes. I have read the Peace Plan 2010 of the Secretary-General and was struck by her brilliant and timely proposal for a World Peace Room at the UN. I would very much like to work on that."

"Excellent. I put you in charge of it. The Secretary-General will be happy to hear this good news."

"I have another wish: she apparently wants to have the Peace Room established on the thirty ninth floor of the UN which, for telecommunication purposes and security, would indeed be the best place. Could a room be foreseen for me on that floor, so that I can work right on the spot and draw my plans?"

"It will be done. You will be your own master-builder up there. I will give the necessary instructions."

Napoleon was overwhelmed. Within a few days he had a room on top of the UN, a floor higher than the Secretary-General, meaning to him symbolically that hatred ranked higher than decency and love.

He spent numerous delightful days on that floor, all alone, examining every corner of it, and scheming his resounding crime. He had reviewed many ways of committing it. To kill the Secretary-General was an easy affair. She was barely protected, just a personal guard accompanying her in her movements in the UN building and on her travels. It was close to nothing, compared with the protection any head of state, especially the President of the United States received. She could be killed at any time in a corridor, in a conference room, in the UN Restaurant, at a reception, taking or leaving her car. But it had to be better than that. There needed to be a special thrill and uniqueness which would arouse world attention, something for the media to feast on. And he knew how to do that:

He would commit his crime right in her office, face to face, dramatically, using the empty shaft meant many years ago for a personal elevator for the Secretary-General, now simply closed by a door in her office. That would be the thrilling, spectacular aspect which the media will love. He could already see the headlines: "Abandoned elevator shaft in the UN used to murder the Secretary-General." He would be interviewed by the press and TV. He could brag about it and describe every detail during his trial. The whole world would read about it and would be hungry for more details. Someone might even write a best-seller about him and sell hundreds of thousands of copies in several languages.

In order to live with intimacy and total dominion over his plan, he asked that his work-room on the thirty ninth floor be built right on top of the shaft, without anyone knowing it of course.

When that work-room was built, he had to do some serious planning: the shaft was covered with the concrete floor of the thirty ninth floor. He acquired special, silent equipment to break up and chip off the concrete. It took him several weeks, but it was a delightful occupation. No one cared about what he was doing on the thirty ninth floor. The question was: how to get rid of the concrete chips without being noticed? He concentrated first on boring a hole of a few square inches in the middle of the concrete. The chips from that operation he took out from the UN in his briefcase over a period of several days. When the hole was opened, he simply threw the rest of the chips into the shaft; there was no danger of any noise being made by the chips possibly scraping the walls as they fell into the cellar. There was no door down there, no one around. The shaft was behind a thick wall of concrete and everyone had long forgotten about it.

He completed the reopening of the elevator shaft at the end of August, covering each day the emplacement of the shaft with a thin but strong steel plate, itself hidden by a carpet. In order to remain undisturbed he had the thirty ninth floor declared off-limits and the yoga, gymnastics and art classes for the UN personnel moved elsewhere. In order to avoid having custodial personel clean his workshop, he decided to have his main office on the lower floor of the Building Management Service and to consider the room on the thirty ninth floor as being only his draftsman place.

The next question was how to get to the level of the Secretary-General's office through the shaft and, when the time came, to open the door of the closet into her office. He got himself appropriate climbing equipment to let him down the shaft, and during several nights when the Secretary-General's office was empty, he let himself down into the shaft and tried key after key until he found one that fitted. He could then relax and plan the exact timing of his act which had to attract world attention. In the meantime he was working with the UN Military Staff Committee and Buildings Services to lay out the plans for the famous World Peace Room. That kept him busy and amused until the return of the Secretary-General from Geneva and various state visits around Labor Day. He was called to a meeting in her office to report on his work. He acted in the most devoted, enthusiastic way to get the Secretary-General's friendship and interest. She was enthusiastic about the project and had many practical suggestions to offer. During that time he observed sharply every detail in the room in order to plan exactly how he would murder her. Her beauty and kindness left him unperturbed. His decision was irrevocable. The human being she was had nothing to do with it. Only her prominent position in the world did.

Andy Smith, the personal guard of Lakshmi, was present at this meeting and followed the discussion with interest, always drawn by the charm and the intelligence of the Secretary-General. He had checked out Napoleon Ames with US Security Services and had received full assurances about him. He also felt proud that a black man had been put in charge of one of the Secretary-General's dearest projects. Nevertheless, a little instinctive ping in his heart advised him to keep an eye on this fellow. There was something in his eyes he did not like. He promised himself to check him out again. As with the previous security check, he was assured that Mr. Ames was someone in whom the Secretary-General could place her entire trust.

\* \* \*

121

# Chapter 12

Tuesday 15, September 1992.  Opening of the forty seventh General Assembly with a minute of silence for prayer or meditation televised world-wide by CNN.  All the religions and more than a billion people joined in that moment of recollection with their delegates, praying God to bless their work for peace and for a better world.  Lakshmi was praying too with every cell of her heart, trying to bring the Gods down to Earth to perform many needed miracles.  To her this was a truly pentecostal meeting and in her mind she saw little tongues of fire, cosmic fire, flicker above the heads of the delegates.

The main items of the meeting were a speech by the outgoing President, the election of a new President,  a speech by the new President and his oath of office, and finally her own speech.  The meeting this year, due to the renewed cooperation of the big powers in the UN, was broadcast over most of the world.

A speech had been prepared for her by her staff.  She had worked on it intensively and was ready to deliver it with all her heart and soul.

Suddenly, a thought flashed through her mind: how will the peoples of the world react to a speech meant primarily for diplomats and governments?  They would not be moved.  They would turn off their television sets, tired by all these speeches not addressed to them. She intended to add a few emotional, personal feelings and appeals at the end of her speech. But would this be enough? The people would not wait for that end. Suddenly a new, bold idea arose in her mind, overthrowing all diplomacy and rationality: she would forget about her written speech which would be circulated anyway, and read instead to the delegates and to the peoples, her Peace Plan 2010. She always carried it in her purse. When the President gave her the floor, she simply said:

"Dear delegates, heads of states, and peoples of the world. As the first woman Secretary-General of the UN I feel it my duty to offer you a plan which would ensure that by the year 2010 no mother on Earth would any longer have to see her son in a uniform and be killed in a war."

And she read out slowly and distinctly with heart and vigor her entire plan, so that every sentence and idea would sink deeply into the minds of listeners and viewers. Delegates began to take notes, listening with fascination over their earphones. The media were jotting down notes frantically. At the end of her reading, she made this announcement:

"Under the rules of procedure of the General Assembly, I will submit today the request for the inscription of an additional item on the agenda of this Assembly entitled: 'Celebration of the Year 2000'. I invite the whole world to prepare that celebration which should usher us into a new millennium of peace, love and happiness on this beautiful planet in the universe."

When she finished, a profound, prolonged silence reigned in the vast Assembly Hall. Only the journalists were rushing out scrambling for telephones and teleprinters. Lakshmi thought that a bomb had fallen on the Assembly. But after a few minutes, blood begin to circulate again in the minds and hearts of the attendants. The whole body of delegates arose and broke out into a thunder of applause which lasted for several minutes, retransmitted all over the world. She simply stood there behind the green marble speaker's podium of the Assembly, facing the audience. Tears came down from her eyes. With folded hands she was saying, Om Shanti, Peace be with you, to the entire world. .....Only one individual in the room was outraged and fuming with rage: Napoleon Ames. He was standing in the back of the General Assembly to have a good overall view of her performance. She had won. The world's attention was focused on her. Through a simple act she had catapulted herself to the summit of fame. "The bitch is winning", he bitterly murmured to himself. But after a while he thought differently:

"This is all for the best. Now she is really famous and by killing her I will be equally famous, if not more. I must now select the ideal moment for her demise. And I think I know when it will be."

And he left the General Assembly Hall, exhilarated, grinning with satanic, satisfying delight.

\* \* \*

# Chapter 13

It was now middle of October, the time of the general debate in the Assembly, when heads of states and Ministers of Foreign Affairs gather at the UN to deliver their speeches and to transact a lot of business behind the scenes. As former Secretary of State Henry Kissinger once said: "During that period I settled at the UN more business in a week than in six months of travel in the world."

The President of the United States had decided to speak on 24 October, the UN anniversary day, to underline his esteem for an organization he knew first-hand from his time as a Permanent Representative of his country to it. He and his wife agreed to meet on that occasion with the young people who had won a world-wide essay contest on the subject: "What in your opinion is the most important problem facing the UN?"

The schedule for the President's visit was as follows: arrival at the UN at 11:00 am. He and his wife would be taken by the UN Chief of Protocol, accompanied by security, to the thirty eighth floor where the Secretary-General would welcome them at the elevator. Meeting in the Secretary-General's office, visit and refreshments in her little apartment; speech to the General Assembly at 11:30; announcement and presentation of the youths who had won the essay contest; luncheon offered by the Secretary-General for the President, his wife and the permanent members of the Security Council. Departure from the UN at 3:00 pm.

For Napoleon Ames that was the ideal day to commit his crime: he had first thought of acting just before the arrival of the President of the United States, in order to create an indescribable turmoil and confusion in world news. But after reflection, he thought that it would be even better afterwards: the world would have heard the proposals of the President of the United States; the UN officialdom would be happy and relaxed that all went well; US security would have gone with the President and UN security would be again at its minimum; nobody would ever think that anything could happen at that moment. He would be much more tranquil and the big news would break out in the world: Secretary-General of the UN murdered in her office just after visit of President of the United States.

Everything indeed went well with the visit of the President. He had a special birthday gift to the UN: he had ordered the destruction of 100 more nuclear missiles and the closing of an additional fifty US military bases. The savings from these measures would go to the UN Environment Program for oxygen-producing reforestation around the world. He suggested that henceforth every head of state in his yearly speech to the General Assembly, should announce some very specific actions taken by his country for peace and a better world, and never deliver anymore empty or philosophical speeches asking others to act. He supported a whole series of Lakshmi's proposals in her 2010 Peace Plan: for example the holding of two meetings of the Security Council each year at the head of state level; work to start immediately on high tech communications systems between heads of states, the US being ready to give several million dollars to that effect; the building of a World Peace Room at the UN; debt reduction and forgiveness to developing countries ready to reduce their armaments expenditures or to demilitarize; endorsement of the Secretary-General's suggestion to prepare and hold a world-wide celebration of the Year 2000. He also formally proposed the inclusion of a new item on the agenda of the next General Assembly: transformation of the UN into a true world community.

He also reported on his meetings with President Gorbachev and the determination of the two leaders to usher the world into a true Renaissance and an era of total peace.

It was a triumph. He and Gorbachev were really the new leaders of the world, expected for so long on the eve of the third millennium. For the media and the UN press corps it was a real heyday. They were running around like squirrels. The typewriter area provided by the UN for the journalists was filled with typists and the clicks of the machines. The whole UN building seemed to be emitting vibrations of good news, love and hope to the world.

The three speakers scheduled after the speech by the President of the United States went to see the President of the General Assembly and suggested that he suspend the afternoon meeting. They would be speaking to an empty room. Everyone had to take stock of the US speech. They wanted also to consult their capitals to introduce specific proposals in their speeches. They did not want to be the first to fall in the category of "empty speeches" or as the American Indians call them: "Much rain, little water." The President of the Assembly readily agreed and suspended the meeting for the rest of the day.

After kissing the US President and his wife goodbye at the UN's exit, Lakshmi Narayan went to the UN Meditation Room to thank God for this great day. She was overwhelmed with joy. Perhaps indeed the world was shedding its old skin and preparing itself for a new metamorphosis. Her life and proposals had perhaps not been in vain. She was remembering the words of Peter Marshall, the Chaplain of the US Senate: "It is better to fail in a cause that will ultimately succeed than to succeed in a cause that will ultimately fail." And she added in her mind: "And it is even better to succeed in a cause which will ultimately succeed." A new idea popped up in her mind: why don't we have a chaplain at the UN? I will arrange that every month a UN chaplain be designated by one of the religions and that all UN meetings will start with an invocation. I will designate Sri Chinmoy for the month of November."

She returned to her office, not very keen to work or to see visitors. She wanted to study the speech of the US President of which she had received a personally autographed and warmly inscribed copy. Andy accompanied her, enjoying her happiness and success, proud to be serving such a wonderful lady. She was a true miracle-maker, a blessed instrument of God, assisted and protected by all the saints in heaven. He was saying silently to himself: "I would like to serve her until my death."

During that time, Napoleon Ames, alone in his shack on the thirty ninth floor, was readying himself: he had decided to wear a tight, black leotard outfit, thinking of the pictures which will be taken of him by the world press after his arrest. He had also selected a black mask, the mask of Mozart's deceased father in the film Amadeus: she needed to see the features of hatred before dying. He would tear off the mask so that she could see that it was he, the man in charge of the World Peace Room, who was putting an end to her life.

He was hanging down in the shaft at the height of the closet door, listening and waiting for the right moment.

He heard the doors of her office open and an excited crowd coming in with her: the three secretaries, the chef de cabinet and several other officials. After a while, he heard her say: "I wish to be alone for at least a half-hour, undisturbed. I want to think and to read carefully the speech of the President of the United States."

The noises and the voices abated. Napoleon Ames's hour had struck. He had unlocked the cabinet door before her arrival and all he had to do was to open the latch, unhook himself from the straps and burst into the room.

That is exactly what he did. Unknown to him, Lakshmi had just pressed the button to ask Andy Smith to come in and take a message to the President of the General Assembly. As Andy opened the door of her office, his well-trained security eyes saw the latch of the closet door go down and he guessed in a flash that a pandemonium was about to break out. In an enormous jump, he fell over the desk of the Secretary-General, dragging her down on the floor and covering her with his body. Napoleon Ames, dumbstruck but determined, emptied his sub-machine gun into the pack of flesh, chair and papers behind the desk. The secretaries and security guards rushed in and saw with disbelief and horror the incredible carnage. Napoleon Ames was standing there, unperturbed, prepared to be handcuffed by UN guards. He had only one thought: "I hope that I got the bitch for good."

The UN Medical Service arrived within minutes with stretchers, and an ambulance rushed to the entrance of the UN building. The head of the Medical Service bent over the bodies covered with blood. Andy Smith was dead, but Lakshmi was still breathing, with awful gargles in her chest. She had to be rushed immediately to the nearest hospital for surgery.

\* \*

The whole world was dumfounded by the news. The old people were shaking their heads, saying: "It was too good to be true. Evil always prevails. The world will never change." The whole UN was in turmoil. Thousands of telegrams and telephone calls were flowing in and out. The media were going crazy. The hospital where Lakshmi had been taken was literally assailed by journalists, cameras and television crews. The Presidents of the US and the USSR appeared immediately on television, deploring the incredible act and praying for the recovery of the Secretary-General.

Thank God, after one and a half hours of surgery, the doctors made this announcement: "Secretary-General Lakshmi Narayan underwent surgery successfully. The bullets have been removed. She is in stable condition and is expected to recover slowly but surely. We thank God."

And in many villages and communities of the world, the priests and ministers ran to their churches and temples to ring the bells and gongs and announce the good news to the people and give thanks to God.

* * *

# Chapter 14

The President of the United States ordered immediately a special investigation of what had happened. Napoleon Ames, upon his arrest, in order to increase the attention to his case, declared that he had been hired by the Golden Age Foundation to commit the murder. This was a big blow to the extreme-right, isolationist elements in the United States. They would have an awful time to deny Ames' allegations, which sounded logical.

The man most deeply shocked by the drama was Alexander Rumacher. He asked John Fitzpatrick to fly in immediately from Washington to New York for explanations. After a long, stormy session, he was convinced that the Foundation had nothing to do with the crime and that Napoleon Ames had acted entirely on his own.

Nevertheless, Rumacher felt that his responsibility was involved: Ames had been nourished by the hatred of the Foundation for the UN, behind which stood his own animosity. This is where extremism and fundamentalism can lead to. He was shaken down to his innermost being. They had gone too far. He had followed the genuine efforts of Lakshmi Narayan, had read her World Peace Plan 2010, was shocked at first, but soon concluded that this candid, courageous, wonderful woman was basically right. His mother, not his father, would have approved of her one hundred percent. It would take him time to digest all that and to adjust, perhaps even change his beliefs and course of his life. Had his ideals been wrong? Was his father mistaken and part of a bygone world of values?

He called the hospital and talked to the surgeon who had operated on Lakshmi. The hospital had nothing to refuse him, because he was one of its main benefactors. He wanted to be sure that the very best was being done for her. He would make another substantial donation to the hospital, if all went well. He also insisted on being high up on her list of visitors, as soon as she would be allowed to receive visits.

That time came after a week. In the meantime he had visited the most prestigious antique shops in Manhattan to find an appropriate gift for her. The network of dealers got into action and they found for him an antique bronze of Goddess Lakshmi, smuggled out of India and worth a fortune.

Lakshmi had been told by the hospital about the man who was to visit her. She should be nice to him and express no bitterness. They made her beautiful to receive him. Alexander Rumacher entered the room, his heart wildly pounding. This woman could have been killed, partly through his fault. He introduced himself, greeted her, asked her how she felt and presented her with his beautifully wrapped gift surmounted by a bouquet of orchids.

She smiled at him, opened the gift and gasped in utmost wonder: "But this is impossible, a true miracle! It is the Lakshmi statue of the temple of Devanagar, a holy city near my village. I know it by heart. I have seen it, prayed it and admired it so many times during our pilgrimages to the temple. It was stolen a few years ago and no trace of it could be found, despite all the efforts of Interpol. How on Earth did you find it?"

He put a finger on his lips and said: "Shh. All that counts is that it has been found. It is all yours."

She made an effort to lift herself to thank him, but felt an acute pain in her chest and fell back on her cushions. He begged her to remain calm and still.

She held the statue lovingly in her arms and kissed her delicately with awe and respect. She asked him timidly:

"Would you allow me to return it to our temple?"

"Of course. It is all yours. You are its master."

"O thank you, thank you."

He then sat down next to her bed and told her about his life, his beliefs, his misgivings against all forms of government and especially against the UN, his sponsoring of anti-UN movements and the culpability he now felt. He could see how hatred could feed more hatred and lead to the most extreme and reprehensible acts. He looked sad, shaken, downcast and at one point he said: "Do you see that grey lock in my dark hair? It showed up overnight after I heard the horrible news of your attempted assassination. How will I ever be able to make it up to you? Will you ever be in a position to forgive me?"

"You are already forgiven. The last words of Gandhi were words of forgiveness, and I am not even dead!"

She reached for a card on her night-table and gave it to him:

"I have been reading this text time and again. It is an exhortation on forgiveness written by a dear UN colleague. Please read it aloud for you and for me, and keep it. I have more of them at the UN. I would like all people and nations to forgive each other."

And he read this text from a postcard showing an Indian war-hatchet to be buried and recommending that 24 October , UN Day, be observed as World Forgiveness Day:

Decide To Forgive
For resentment is negative
Resentment is poisonous
Resentment diminishes
    and devours the self.
Be the first to forgive
To smile and take the first step
And you will see happiness bloom
On the face of your human
    brother or sister.
Be always the first
Do not wait for others to forgive
For by forgiving
  You become the master of fate
  The fashioner of life
  A doer of miracles
To forgive is the highest
    most beautiful form of love.
In return you will receive
    untold peace and happiness.

After reading, he looked up at her. She was smiling and so beautiful. She simply said:

"You see, this is it. It is all so simple. You and all your colleagues, including Napoleon Ames, are all forgiven. I only hope that you will become our friends, our brothers, sisters and helpers on the difficult road to a peaceful and happy world. This is the best you could do for the memory of my poor colleague Andy Smith who gave his life for me."

He could barely take his eyes off her. But he had to leave and let her rest. He kissed her forehead and told her that he would come and see her soon again. He gave her his telephone number: "Anything you need, anything you wish, you just give me a ring."

She answered: "All I need is your love and concern for the world and humanity."

*　*

When he left the room he went to talk to the surgeon who had operated on her:

"What will be your next step? Will she fully recover? Will she be handicapped or diminished?"

"Not in the least. What she needs is to be spared the hardships of Manhattan and of her position. She must rest for several weeks in a peaceful place. She wants to go and convalesce at the Lake Mohonk Mountain House which will be indeed ideal for her. We will transport her there in about ten days, if there are no complications."

Alexander Rumacher left the hospital exclaiming: "Thank you, O God. What a sign You have given me! Thank You for not having made it worse. I promise You to draw the conclusions You expect from me. Thank You for Your kindness and love. I will become the servant of Your Peace and of Your beautiful planet."

*　*　*

# Chapter 15

Sometime later, Lakshmi was transferred to Lake Mohonk Mountain House where she was received by the Smileys and the whole staff with deep love and concern. She was feeling better every day and was convalescing well. The wonderful air, nature, peace and elevation of Mohonk Mountain were the perfect environment to foster the return of her health. She was thinking, meditating, reading and writing a lot. Telephone calls were prohibited. At the UN, the Director-General for International Economic Relations was acting in her place until the end of the General Assembly. In any case, she was there every day in mind, in heart and in spirit through her World Peace Plan 2010 which was actively discussed in the Assembly. She was allowed to receive only rare visitors, selected by her personally. Among those, she included Alexander Rumacher whom she wanted to win over to the causes of the UN and of the poor peoples of the world. He was so powerful and she had the womanly instinct that deep inside he was a good, kind, sentimental man. He had a role to play that could be very beneficial to the world.

Alexander Rumacher for his part loved to come and see her at Lake Mohonk. He had an immense property for the week-ends in Connecticut, but when he went there he had to oversee its management, build more and take care of many details. At Lake Mohonk, he had nothing to worry about. From the day of her transfer, he had rented a room at Mohonk for the rest of the year. He discovered what virtues and happiness can be in a simple room, comfortable but without any unnecessary encumbrances. Inside that room he found himself to be the main capital and value, and outside he found the immense riches and diversity of God's nature. He began to feel like a monk and understood why some of his harassed business friends chose to spend weekends in monastic retreats.

But Lakshmi was his main joy. He came to Mohonk every weekend and spent hours with her, talking, discussing, dreaming, trying to discover the ultimate mysteries and purposes of life, the meaning of this planet, of humanity and of our journey in the universe. He had never been a religious or spiritual person and as a youth he had listened to his religious instructors only with a distant, uninterested ear. But here was a person, deeply anchored in the most powerful cosmic philosophy ever devised on this planet by the sages of her country over thousands of years.

This was not life **and** spirituality but spirituality **as** life, matter and life being particular forms of the invisible cosmic energy that pervades the universe, of the immense body and constant new manifestations of the godhead.

What lessons he received from her! But he clung stubbornly to his belief in power, possession and wealth. To his surprise, she did not condemn that. She once explained to him the Hindu philosophy of happiness:

"One of our basic beliefs is that the self, the ego, the individual is much too small to be the object of perpetual enthusiasm. We believe that there are four stages of human happiness. The first stage is the pursuit of pleasure - you Westerners call it "hedonism". Our sages say to us, " do not hesitate, explore fully the pleasures of life." They even instruct us on the ways to increase pleasure, especially the sexual ones. The Kama Sutra, a religious book, is a treatise on how to achieve supreme sexual pleasure, as one of the ways to reach cosmic union. But with time, people get tired of the pursuit of pure pleasure. It might happen during the same life time, or it might happen in the next. Then they turn their attention to achieving wealth, fame and power. But with time, this again leads to dissatisfaction, because the self is too small for perpetual enthusiasm. Then they turn to selfless service, to philanthropy. But here again they make a difference between the self and the others, the giver and the receiver. As a result, it also leads to dissatisfaction. This is the moment Hindu philosophy has been waiting for. Then indeed comes the realization of the individual that he or she is one with God, one with the universe, one with the eternal stream of time. This releases the separateness of the self in favor of being a sentient, conscious, active part of the universe, of the total marvelous Creation which is never too small for perpetual  enthusiasm. This gives infinite bliss. Then you can enjoy your pleasures, your money and power fully because they are balanced by your awareness of the oneness with the whole. You find yourself to be a steward of everything you have on behalf of the whole. You enjoy constant peace, bliss and harmony, because you have found your right place and role in the universe. You act and live in righteousness, morality and justice because you have discovered the sense of your universal responsibility.  You are a properly functioning cell of the cosmos. This is the stage I would like to see you attain."

"Incidentally, we Hindus believe that mothers do not have to go through all these stages. They are right from the start in stage four through their love and care of the new cosmic units to whom they give birth. They incarnate the most perfect, advanced sense of cosmic, divine, universal responsibility."

He was astonished by her depth, yet so simple, genuine, etheric candor, almost that of a child. He began to wonder: could women and children be the real possessors of the truth, not men? Were men only on the first rung of the ladder of consciousness? But she reassured him that the other rungs would be climbed too and that after the material, intellectual successes of the human race, there would come a sentimental, moral and spiritual transcendence. "Our sages' theory of happiness applies not only to individuals but to the entire human family, you will see." And she explained to him how this evolution, this transcendence would take place primarily through the United Nations which was the ultimate, most universal place of convergence of humanity's search for fulfillment. Slowly but surely she was teaching him like a mother does her child in the ways of love and God.

He spent more and more time with her, leaving his business to his associates. In any event, the growth of his fortune was something automatic and did hardly ever stop. Every hour it grew by hundreds of thousands of dollars. He did not know what to do anymore with all that money and began to lose interest in keeping track of it.

But the talks with Lakshmi and the unique beauty of Lake Mohonk began to give him some ideas. One day, at luncheon with

Lakshmi and the Smileys he inquired about the many informal meetings between UN delegates which took place at Lake Mohonk, permitting them to consult each other, to exchange ideas, to get informal instructions from their capitals and to take decisions or come to agreements well in advance of the UN General Assembly. The history of Lake Mohonk Mountain House as a meeting ground for peace initiatives and arbitration favored this process. Delegates were at ease here, far from the Manhattan turmoil, they met as friends and human beings rather than as representatives of their governments. Here they felt the holiness of God's nature and of human efforts towards peace and harmony with all Creation.

He asked Keith and Lakshmi: "Would you like to see a permanent Center for UN consultations established here, as a well-financed going concern, rather than to depend on foundation grants for specific meetings? I would also like to bring together here the most prominent businessmen of the US and of multinational corporations to become better acquainted with the UN's work and efforts and to help build a peaceful and more satisfactory society. Peace is of most direct interest to the good functioning of world business."

The eyes of Keith Smiley and of Lakshmi were shining and they answered enthusiastically yes, because in their minds and hearts they had both been thinking of such a center. Keith had been dreaming for a long time of a better use of Lake Mohonk Mountain House for the advancement of peace, and Lakshmi had deplored the absence of even a Club in Manhattan where delegates could meet in privacy.

"O.K. said Alexander. It is done. I will ask my lawyers to get in touch with you and work out the details. We will create here the Lake Mohonk Peace Center, a permanent location to be used informally or formally by the United Nations with no constraints attached. I am ready to appropriate the necessary finances to it."

Lakshmi was looking at him with infinite delight, but had also a little feline smile lingering on her lips: She said to him: "Dear Alexander, could I add a little suggestion to your marvelous offer: the United Nations Archives are in jeopardy, spread over several warehouses in New York. We do not know where to go. They are the historical record of a new page of world history, but governments have little foresight and do not really care about it."

"We need proper UN Archives and a museum as was done for the League of Nations in Geneva thanks to a generous grant from the Rockefellers. Why don't you consider becoming the Rockefeller of the United Nations, helping to build the UN's Archives and peace museum in the Hudson Valley?"

"O.K. We will have this studied too and perhaps we can combine the two."

* *

In the evening, back in her room, Lakshmi was beaming with joy. God had wanted all this in His very mysterious ways. This decision alone of Alexander Rumacher made her Secretary-Generalship worthwhile. Her predecessors had tried in vain to obtain this result and here, right in the first year of her mandate it was becoming a reality. This could have incalculable benefits for the future of humanity, especially if the business world would be more understanding of the world's constraints and global needs. It was a dear, delightful dream, coming true.

She looked out of her window: the sky was pure and dark, offering a full display of stars and galaxies in its infinity. This was the realm of the Gods. Since it was an exceptionally warm Indian-summer night, Lakshmi could not resist the call of the heavens: she wrapped herself in a shawl, went outdoors and sat down in her preferred gazebo on top of a rock near the lake, in order to dream, meditate and give thanks to the Gods.

She was sitting there for a while, but then decided to lie flat on her back on a bench in order to have a full view of the starry heaven and start her incantations and prayers. As she was doing that, the whole universe penetrated her from head to feet. She felt one of those rare moments of yoga, of total union, of non-separateness with the universe.

When she arose from the bench she heard a little humming. She turned around and saw Alexander Rumacher standing there and observing her with most intensive, almost touchable emanations of love.

He came near her, took her resplendent face in his hands, did not say a word, kissed her and then pressed her warmly in his arms. The stars and Gods in heaven smiled and congratulated each other: the miracle of love had happened again on planet Earth and as a record a new star was born.

No human words are meaningful, feelingful and sweet enough to describe the mysterious phenomena and fluxes which went on between these two blessed beings during that divine hour. The

138

miraculous cosmic unity has fused them to each other, bound by the mysterious will of the Gods, eager to produce more life and pursue the incredible cosmic experiment and manifestations on planet Earth. Their union would in time produce new cosmic units through the miracle of love. The cosmos was continuing its growth and life. Many old cells were dying after having performed well or not their function, but new beautiful, better cells were endlessly produced by the miracle of love in the chains of ever more complex and diverse fabrics of life.

They walked and walked, they sat and sat, they kissed and kissed, they embraced and embraced throughout the flow of the fragrant night. When dawn arose, Lakshmi made Alexander participate in the Agni-Sutra welcoming rite for the resurrecting sun and day. He then took her back to her room and kissed her gently, knowing that their love had to culminate in the summit of marriage, pure and unspoiled by any previous, non-sacramented relations. And they slept in their separate rooms several heavenly hours.

* * *

# Chapter 16

The following morning they met for breakfast very late. The Smileys came by, wondering what had happened and they saw immediately what it was: the two were resplendent with joy, vibrating with love, radiating happiness. Both exclaimed at the same time:

"We have fallen in love!" And they looked at each other, delighted by this simultaneous outburst of their sentiments. The Smileys were enchanted: Lake Mohonk Mountain had once again produced a miracle and taken on more sacredness as a high-point of peace and love. The effects of this miracle could be far-reaching.

Alexander Rumacher rarely returned to Manhattan and to Connecticut. He practically lived in Mohonk, enjoying his bliss, his daily togetherness, talks and walks with his beloved new master in the art of living. They had their whole lives to tell each other, the entire world and humanity to assess, their entire future to plan.

They decided to get married shortly. The sooner the better. He was over forty and she was 35. There was no time to waste and they wanted to get wonderful children from their love, "new, divine, cosmic units", as Lakshmi called them.

She absolutely wanted to get married in India, in her village in Rhajastan, near Mt. Abu, the seat of the Brahma Kumari sisters, and not far from Lakshmi's temple to which they would bring back the precious stolen statue. She insisted on a full Hindu wedding with its colorful and meaningful pageantry. Marriage was the dominion of the bride, he thought. He had to be patient and he yielded to her wishes. The marriage would take place in January, one of the coolest months in Rhajastan. She would be quite well and ready for the voyage. Her convalescence was practically over. The doctors however recommended that she should not resume her duties at the UN until January or February and avoid being involved in the current General Assembly which would end just before Christmas.

With utmost delight they planned their honeymoon trip: there was no question anymore of following Alexander the Great's footsteps! She wanted him to see her world, her culture, her loves, her peoples' customs, her Gods. In India they planned to visit Agra, the city of love, Kajuraho, the city of temples and Benares, the city of the beyond.

She expressed one more wish:

"Alexander, there is one stopover, one pilgrimage on our way back I would like to make: a visit to Costa Rica, a demilitarized country, a heaven of peace where the UN has created the first supra-national University for Peace and where you will meet our western UN guru or sage who has inspired and helped me a lot in my Secretary-Generalship, a man whom you will fully appreciate and enjoy: his name is Louis Parizot, a Frenchman from Alsace-Lorraine. Years ago he stayed for several months in India for a world conference held by the UN in my country, fell in love with it and wrote a beautiful novel called 'Sima, Mon Amour' for which he received a major French literary award. We will take his book along as our love and travel guide. And I want you to meet him on our way back." Alexander agreed readily. He knew and loved Costa Rica for its democracy, sense of liberty, wonderful nature and deep attachment to human rights. He often thought that Costa Rica should be one of the first countries to join the United States of the World, of which he was sometimes dreaming.

Lakshmi got busy corresponding with her family in India and with the Brahma Kumaris to do all the necessary preparations for her wedding. Alexander, on his side, put his affairs in good order in Manhattan and in Connecticut to be free and worriless for several weeks. They decided to leave just after Christmas which they wanted to spend and enjoy in the snow-covered and warm fire-side atmosphere of Lake Mohonk.

Before leaving, there remained only one duty to perform: the President of the General Assembly invited Lakshmi to be present at the last, closing meeting of the Assembly, the day before Christmas. She could not refuse, quite the contrary. All delegates and UN staff members were anxious to see her and to express their loving wishes for her marriage.

When that day came, she and Alexander drove down to Manhattan. She was greeted at the entrance of the General Assembly Hall by the President of the Assembly who led her on the way usually reserved for heads of states. This lent her entrance the highest significance and majesty possible.

As she proceeded to the podium of the Assembly, the UN singers sang Jill Jackson Miller's famous song "Let There be Peace on Earth and Let it Begin with Me", joined by the entire attendance of the Assembly. Sri Chinmoy, the UN eastern guru, was standing on the podium, his hands folded in Namaster and his eyes turned to the heavens. When she sat down, he chanted a Hindu incantation which ended with the sacred cosmic word AUM, repeated by the attendance and vibrating from the immense gathering hall of nations into many homes of the planet through television, radio and the universe's ether.

The President of the General Assembly took the floor and said: "Beloved Sister Lakshmi, we are so happy to see you amongst us again, well and more radiant than ever. Every day we prayed for you and we worked for you. As our wedding gift, I have been entrusted with the delightful task, in the name of all delegates to this assembly of nations, to offer you this summary of the decisions taken by the Assembly on the basis of your courageous and inspiring World Peace Plan 2010."

And he read this text:

"1. The General Assembly has adopted a turning point declaration in which it asks the Secretary-General to prepare an eight-years plan for world peace by the year 2000 and total disarmament by the year 2010. All member states are to submit their proposals to the Secretary-General and all specialized agencies are to update their plans 2000 in order to be incorporated in the Secretary-General's year 2000 action plan;

2. The Trusteeship Council of the UN having successfully completed its work under the Charter, is replaced by a World

Environmental Security Council, to deal also with the prevention of world accidents;

3. A committee of the General Assembly has been established to prepare the celebration of the fiftieth anniversary of the UN in 1995, with the widest participation of the peoples of the world;

4. A committee of the General Assembly has been established to prepare a world-wide celebration of the year 2000 and our entry into a peaceful, better third millennium. All governments and peoples are invited to prepare and to participate in that celebration."

He added:

"As you have noticed, dear Sister Lakshmi, we have acted on all your four suggestions addressed to us. I pray that all other proposals in your Peace Plan 2010 will be similarly implemented and be blessed by God. We wish you peace and great happiness in your union."

He kissed her and handed her the parchment he had read. It was signed by the 166 chief delegates to the United Nations: He handed her also a big bouquet of blue carnations, the first UN flowers developed by horticulturists.

She thanked and kissed him and asked if she could say a few words.

He gave her the floor:

"Dear Mr. President, dear brothers and sisters, there are moments in life when words are insufficient to express our innermost feelings. Tears then come to our help as an expression of our joys and sorrows. I see you at this moment through such tears in my eyes. Tears of joy for being back in the world home and for seeing this magnificent manifestation of your love. Tears of sorrow for the loss of my first and dearest co-worker in the UN, Andy Smith who gave his precious life for mine. I have mourned a lot for him and yet the tears are still coming. He was so human, so loving, so helpful to me and to this organization which he loved so dearly. The decisions of the Assembly you just read are no less a tribute to him, a man who had constantly new ideas born from his heart. My promised husband and I have decided to establish an Andy Smith Memorial Foundation which will offer fellowships to young people who wish to learn about the UN security and peace-keeping services. I trust that this is what his heart would have wished.

I say goodbye to you for a little while. Since the UN has decided to hold in 1994 an International Year of the Family, I thought that I had better hurry and give the good example, as we should always do at the UN, and have a family at that time!"

Whereupon she sent a kiss and a resounding Om Shanti to all the Assembly and left the podium with her fiance, pressing lovingly her bouquet of UN carnations on her heart, while the UN singers and the attendance were singing Beethoven's Ode to Joy.

*  *  *

# Chapter 17

In India, Lakshmi and Alexander stayed at Mt. Abu as guests of the Brahma Kumaris, a congregation of Hindu sisters accredited to the UN as a non-governmental organization. While Lakshmi was busy in her village arranging for the marriage ceremony, the sisters took good care of Alexander in their fascinating mountain resort and World Spiritual University.

Mt. Abu is the equivalent, on a larger scale, of Lake Mohonk. Here the maharajahs and the wealthy built their summer houses and palaces to enjoy the cooler mountain air during the hot Indian summers, around lakes of volcanic origin like Lake Mohonk. The maharajahs are gone but their palaces remain, often transformed into hotels. Mt. Abu is now a mountain resort for the Indian middle class. It is also a chosen place for sages, gurus and hermits. There are numerous caves in which hermits live in solitude and silence, seeking and probably finding their union with God and the universe.

A rich jeweller, Prajapita Brahma from Bombay, lovingly called Baba by the sisters, decided a few years ago to buy property on Mt. Abu, to disinvest himself of his fortune and to start here his last period of life (Vanaprashta) as many Hindus do. He created a convent and monastic movement of Hindu sisters, many of whom are young, unmarried daughters of well-to-do families who want to devote their lives to service of God, to peace and to world cooperation. The main thrust of their philosophy is Jnana Yoga, the path to union with

God through intelligence or the transmutation of the intellect into the omniscient wisdom of the soul. He taught his world views, philosophy and spirituality to the sisters and since his death is worshipped as their Father in heaven who helps them establish peace on Earth. The Brahma Kumaris have followers in many countries and became in the 1970s one of the first oriental spiritual non-governmental organizations accredited to the UN. They have a World University on Mt. Abu where many UN officials and delegates have met, like at Lake Mohonk. They adopted a remarkable Charter of World Cooperation in the drafting of which UN officials participated. In 1985, year of the fortieth anniversary of the UN, they collected from people around the world pledges for 1 billion minutes of silence for prayer or meditation on the third Tuesday of September, day of the yearly opening of the General Assembly and International Day of Peace. Lakshmi told Alexander the story that on the day when Secretary General Javier Perez de Cuellar received a delegation from the Brahma Kumaris who reported to him this great result of their campaign, he met Louis Parizot in the UN corridors and told him the good news: "You will be very pleased to learn that 1 billion people have promised to observe a minute of silence for prayer or meditation at the same time as the delegates to the General Assembly." Parizot looked at him surprised and commented: "Only 1 billion? There are five billion people on this planet. That makes only one out of five. The day must come when **all** humanity will pray with their delegates." The Secretary-General smiled and said: "You will never change!" In 1989-90 the Brahma Kumaris were collecting visions and action proposals for peace and a better world to constitute a world data bank and to serve as a basis for a report on the peoples' visions for the year 2000 to the Secretary-General of the UN.

Lakshmi left Alexander in the good hands of the gentle, white-robed sisters and went to attend to the preparations of the wedding in her village down in the valley. She also had to perform the required prenuptial rites under the guidance of a Brahmine. In particular she had to undertake a trip to a sacred place on the Ganges to cleanse herself in the holy waters of the river said to descend from heaven. She chose to go to Hardiwar.

Alexander enjoyed profoundly these days of relaxation and spiritual inspiration on Mt. Abu. He woke up at dawn when the gongs called the sisters and people to early meditation. He visited he palaces and temples. He attended classes of the sisters and became acquainted with one of the world's most profound cosmic spiritualities. He was reminded of a remark by a young Hindu who had studied psychiatry in an ivy-league American University and who said to him: "I return to India with the conviction that western psychiatry finds itself only at the first basement of what any sage, guru, rishi, brahmine or holy man knows in India." Above all he was fascinated by the hermits. Most of them did not talk and the others did not know English. As a last resort, he selected a small cave near the Two Lovers' Rock to experience himself for a few hours what it meant to be a hermit. It was the beginning of quite a transformation. He began to doubt his father's philosophy and quest for wealth and power. These were Earthly ideals while his eyes, his mind and his soul were detached from Earth and merged with infinity and eternity when he was sitting in his cave. He began to see the remainder of his life differently: why not enter stage three of happiness and become one of the world's greatest philanthropists and gaiaphilists, to use a word loved by Lakshmi, thus helping his wonderful wife achieve her dreams of a peaceful and better world? And perhaps later try also stage 4, namely the selfless surrender to God. During his stay on Mr. Abu, he had a unique experience which confirmed him on this new path.

The Brahma Kumaris had amongst them a sister who was a medium. Usually in India, people are on the lookout for children who at an early age show the rare capacity of communicating with the heavens and God. Such children are trained by Brahmines and gurus to later become mediums in holy places and communities. During Alexander's stay, a medium session with Baba was arranged by the Brahma Kumaris. On an elevated podium, lit by floodlights, in their main conference room accommodating close to a thousand people, an immaculate white bed had been erected. On it rested the medium sister, all clad in white too. For more than an hour there were sacred chants and incantations and many Om Shantis, the cosmic mantra: peace be with you. At one point, when the medium was ready to enter into trance, a total silence fell upon the conference hall. The medium began to talk, transmitted over loudspeakers. She acquired the voice of a man, a strange deep voice: Baba was talking through her to the audience, giving his messages. Sisters were taking frantically notes. When the messages ended, a sister came and invited Alexander to accompany her to the podium to receive Baba's personal message to him. He thought that it was all utter nonsense but he wanted to be polite and he accompanied her. On the podium she asked him to kneel next to the medium and to listen to her. Without looking at him, her eyes closed, the medium transmitted Baba's message in Hindi while he was asking himself: "Why do I get involved in such nonsense? What would my business partners say if they saw me?" But someone tapped him on his shoulder: it was a Hindu gentleman, a former nuclear scientist who had abandoned his field and was now an adviser to the Brahma Kumaris. He said to Alexander: "Do not oppose, do not resist. Let go and ask a question."

Alexander did so and at that moment he felt an explosion in his chest, accompanied by a strong light, and he heard distinctly these words pounding heavily in his bosom: "work, work, work, give, give, give."

It was the answer to the question he had asked: how can I help Lakshmi achieve a better world?

He was quite shaken by the experience. When he returned to his seat, the Hindu scientist said to him: "I am glad that you did not oppose."

The following day, the Sisters gave him the transcript of Baba's message: it prophesied that he would see world peace reign on Earth during his life-time.

\* \*

The day and evening of the wedding finally came. Alexander had to dress up for the occasion in a sumptuous maharajah apparel. He had to walk through the village preceded by a group of musicians and a dozen of young boys carrying kerosene lamps on their shoulders. On his way he had to distribute to the villagers silken handkerchiefs on which the commemoration of the wedding was printed in Hindi. He arrived at the gardens where an open-air reception had brought together the relatives of Lakshmi and her friends, all clad in the most colorful garments. Lakshmi was led to him under an arch covered with flowers (Pandal). He looked at her: she was ravishingly dressed in the most sumptuous saree and covered with jewelry, as is the custom in India where brides even borrow jewelry from their friends for the occasion. He took lovingly her hand and they both walked under the Pandal arch. This preliminary rite accomplished, there followed a reception which lasted until close to midnight. The guests then left and only the relatives and a few friends remained to serve as witnesses of the betrothal. Lakshmi and Alexander were led to a gazebo covered with flowers in the middle of which a fire was burning in a metal bowl: it was Agni, the faithful resurrecting God of light, in the presence of which all Hindu marriages must be performed. A Brahmine dressed like Nehru was officiating. Lakshmi, Alexander and the Brahmine sat around the fire which they kept alive by adding melted butter and coconut once in awhile. Lakshmi first had to invoke God Ganesha's help to avoid any mistakes in the rites. The Brahmine then attached a piece of holy cloth between the two, as a sign of union. He then proceeded by reciting endless verses in Sanskrit which both had to repeat without understanding them. Once in a while he spread grains of rice, holy water and red powder over their heads or on their hands united under a holy strand of cloth. Friends and relatives were sitting around, witnessing the proceedings. Finally, the last ritual took place, the famous Saptapadi or "seven decisive steps": Alexander stood up, followed by Lakshmi still attached to him, and they took seven steps around the Agni fire, Alexander addressing these words to his beloved one:

"Take this first step to acquire strength; the second one to fortify your soul; the third to be blessed with prosperity; the fourth to enjoy good health; the fifth to ensure our descendance; the sixth for our old age; and the last one to be always my friend. Be faithful to me. May we have many children and reach an advanced age."

With this final rite, both were married under Hindu law. Alexander and Lakshmi were driven back to their hotel on Mt. Abu where they became united for life, blessed with heavenly joys. At dawn, when they rested in each other's arms, Lakshmi could not resist continuing his Hindu education. She murmured to his ear:

"You see, darling, love is the supreme union with the eternal, the most intensive, ecstatic consciousness of the universe. Nothing else on Earth can ever match the vital fluid (prana) and potential consciousness contained in love. The woman, the eternal feminine, is the divine place of encounter, the incarnation, the convergence of infinity and eternity. And why do you think we are given all this happiness and pleasure? God and the universe want us to produce new cosmic units, new children of God in order to pursue the eternal mysterious journey and constant Creation."

\* \*

Their honey-moon trip in India was a pure enchantment, a pilgrimage to human highpoints of love, beauty and spirituality, a trip they would remember with fondness all their life.

They both knew Agra and the Taj Mahal, but it was a different experience to visit it as a couple divinely in love. They first visited it under daylight in all its resplendent marble-cool whiteness under the bright Indian sun. As they walked towards the world's most beautiful monument, she read from Louis Parizot's book, translating passages from French to English:

"Towards the year 1200, Muslims came from Afghanistan and Persia, conquered the North of India and vanquished he Hindu kings. Only in the 16th century did they emerge from obscurity with Moghol emperors Babar, Humayun and Akbar the Great, one of the most-prestigious emperors the world has ever known. His grandson Shah Jahan whose name means Emperor of the World, surpassed him even in architectural genius and built numerous palaces in white marble adorned with precious jewels. Thus one of the biggest diamonds ever, the Koh-i-noor was embedded in the facade of his palace in New Delhi. He loved his wife Mumtaz Mahal (the Crown of the Palace) dearly, but she died very young and the Emperor built for her the most beautiful mausoleum on Earth. He had architects from all the Orient compete with their designs. The man who won was a blind Persian, named Ustad Isa, who brought the model of the Taj Mahal in white marble on a red velvet cushion. The Emperor intended to build also a replica of the Taj Mahal in black marble for himself, on the other side of the river Jamuna, which would have been linked by a bridge with his wife's mausoleum, as a sign of eternal love between the two."

When she finished reading, they were standing in front of the incredible monument, reflected in tranquil basins of water, Lakshmi said to Alexander:

"Perhaps such a masterpiece required indeed the internal, heavenly vision of a blind artist. Remember that some of the greatest poets, for example Homer and Milton were blind. Beethoven, when he became deaf, wrote in his famous testament that he would show the world what he had in himself, and it was then that he composed his immortal symphonies. There is a wonderful reactive power in some handicapped people. I am always thinking of my handicapped hero, Franklin Roosevelt who dared to dream of a United Nations. It gives me an idea: when I am back in New York, as part of the

United Nations International Decade for the Handicapped, I will ask governments to celebrate their great handicapped artists like Homer, Milton, Beethoven and others. They will serve as an inspiration to the 300 million handicapped we have on this planet and give them hope. Perhaps some of them will find deep in themselves the mysterious reactive power."

Alexander commented: "Is there ever a moment when you do not think about the United Nations and a better world?"

Lakshmi: "No, not even when I love you. Incidentally do you know that UNESCO has placed the Taj Mahal on its famous World Heritage Register? As a result it is to be protected as a common treasure of humanity and is out of bound of any conflicts or wars."

"No, I didn't have any idea. But I am sure that with UNESCO's prejudice against the United States there is nothing American on that register."

"Wrong you are. I know at least two of them: the Grand Canyon, a natural treasure, and the old historic center of Philadelphia with its Independence and Constitution Halls, a human treasure.

Perhaps if you pursue successfully your dream of a Constitution for a United States of the World, the building where it will be drafted and adopted will also become a world heritage and you will become the George Washington of our time, remembered with love and gratitude by all future generations."

"Well, I will have to revise my attitude towards UNESCO and learn more about their work."

"That is the first step to fairness."

They visited again the Taj Mahal during the night under a full moon, something to be wished to every human on this Earth. The incredible mausoleum was inundated in a dark blue silver atmosphere radiated by the moon. It was one of the greatest, most romantic sights on Earth. Alexander was sitting with Lakshmi on a cool marble bench, holding hands, totally muted by their inner emotions, each having his own thoughts. Lakshmi was thinking of the Hindu Gods in heaven and of this monument built to the belief in the immortality of the soul. She prayed fervently that Mumtaz Mahal be reincarnated in her and that Alexander would be the Shah Jahan of world philanthropy and peace. Alexander for his part was thinking that neither Alexander the Great nor Baron de Rothchild could measure up to the immortality of the artist and emperor who built this treasure.

Yes, the miracle of love embodied in the Taj would leave a definite mark on the course of their lives.

* *

When at Lake Mohonk they had planned their honey-moon trip in India, Lakshmi discovered that Alexander knew most of the cultural highpoints of her country. But as she reviewed with him her preferred places, she learned that he had never been in Kajuraho, an astonishing little village filled with temples, located in Madhya Pradesh (the land of the middle), 400 kilometers to the south-east of New Delhi. That tiny village of only 2000 people has probably the largest number of temples anywhere on Earth on such a small surface.

For no known reason, out of the blue, 85 temples were built there between the years 900 and 1000, by the most prodigious artists. Only twenty temples remain today but they give a good idea of what an extraordinary place this must have been. The culture, artists and rulers who prevailed there are gone, like those of Tikal and Baalbek, and for no known reason. The remaining temples were only found at the end of the nineteenth century in this remote, forgotten place. But since then they occupy the forefront of world sculpture. Alexander and Lakshmi visited every single temple. The imagination, audacity and sense of beauty of the artists was such that their work could inspire dozens of schools of sculpture. The temples are packed with statues and bas-reliefs, inside and outside. Every surface is a sculpture. Young maidens are represented in endless postures, some bending, others playing or dancing. One of the most famous statues is that of a maiden pulling a thorn from her foot, in the most delightful posture. The temples are devoted to several Gods: to Vichnou, Shiva and to the dark, fierce Goddess Kali. Around her temple there remain about thirty of the private rooms which belonged to her maiden servants (yoguinis). The dominant scenes of the sculptures are those of love making. Lakshmi told Alexander that there was no reason to be shocked. "Proper love making has never been reproved in my country. On the contrary, since life is insepara-ble from spirituality, and since love is inseparable from life, proper love making is inseparable from spirituality. This is the whole basis of the Kama Sutra, the Indian religious treatise of love making."

As they took a small plane back to New Delhi to continue their trip to Benares, Alexander commented to Lakshmi:

"Did you notice how the people in Mt. Abu were happy when you gave them back the ancient statue of Lakshmi? I am so glad that I thought of this gift for you. Regarding my wedding gift, I gave you the biggest diamond I could find in New York, but it is not yet my real gift. I do not know as yet what it will be. One of these days it will come to me. It will have to be something very special which you will like with all your soul."

Lakshmi: "You have been over-generous, and I was so happy to bring happiness to my people. It will be an unforgettable gesture for them and we will always remain in their prayers. I was thinking myself of the smuggling of stolen art treasures from the poor countries, hidden in the apartments of rich New Yorkers or Texans. More than that, look at the great museums of London, Paris, Berlin, Vienna, etc. They are filled with art treasures stolen by their conquerors, a Napoleon for example, or by their archaeologists. Look at the art treasures from Yucatan in the Peabody museum in Boston or at the Cypriot treasures in the Metropolitan Museum in New York. Many of these works of art should be returned to their place of origin. The bas-reliefs of the Parthenon should not be in the somber British Museum but on the sunny walls of Athena's glorious temple. I am so glad that the UN General Assembly adopted a few years ago a resolution asking for the return of art treasures, and each year a few returns are reported. Thus, the crown of St. Stephen was returned by the US to Hungary, and Moctezuma's coronation mantle of quetzal feathers was returned to Mexico by Austria. They are now displayed in the beautiful Parliament building in Budapest and in the splendid Art Museum of Mexico City, instead of Fort Knox and an obscure museum in Vienna. But there remains so much to be done. In some American and European museums there are more art treasures from Africa than in entire countries of that continent. Africa has been irremediably plundered, as it became independent so late. Take the case of the Ethiopian obelisk stolen by Mussolini in Addis Ababa. It stands on a corner in front of the building of the Food and Agriculture Organization in Rome, sorely missing as the third obelisk of the great central avenue of Addis Ababa. When the Ethiopian government wanted it back, Italy said: "Fine, come and get it". And since Ethiopia is too poor and not equipped to carry out such an operation, it still stands in Rome. When I am back in New

York, I will look into such situations and exhort governments to do something about them."

Alexander was thinking for his part: "Here is an excellent field for world philanthropy, and a good source of ideas for gifts to my beloved one. For her next birthday that obelisk in Rome will be back in Ethiopia."

* *

Their last visit in India was to Benares, the huge, astounding city of death and resurrection on the Ganges river. Alexander was not in favor of that visit, but she insisted. "It is important to be reminded of our temporary, passing incarnation on this Earth, the part of our soul in the universal soul, our return to it at the end of our lives and our reincarnation some day as avatars."

She was his cicerone and spiritual guide throughout the visit:

"Benares or Varanasi received its name from the two affluents of the Ganges, the Varuna and the Asi. For thousands of years it has been a famous place of pilgrimage. The water of the Ganges is said to be holy: it cleanses all sins and takes the dead straight to heaven. The legend says that a dog who fell in the Ganges went right to heaven. You will find here innumerable religious practices and adepts: Hindu brahmines, buddhist monks in yellow robes, fakirs covered with ashes, Muslims with turbans, Jains holding their robes in front of their mouths so that no insect can fly in and get killed, etc. Here you will find every possible means conceived by humans to reach out and achieve union with God: prayer, meditation, fasting, rituals, corporeal punishment, even sexual practices. Shiva, the dominant God of Benares, the Mahadeva or Great God, has more than 400 temples here. In Benares he possesses the three attributes of the trinity: creation, preservation and destruction. We Hindus have the right to revere in any of the three main Gods (Brahma, Vichnou and Shiva) the attributes of the two others. Shiva is also the Great White God of the Himalayas. Everywhere in Benares he is represented by the lingam or male sex organ."

And she took him to places which illustrated her explanations: the Wishwanath or Golden Temple of Shiva where from a copper vessel in the ceiling, water from the Ganges drops on a lingam of stone inserted in a yoni (female sex organ) and glides into a channel at the end of which women receive that water in the cup of their hands and drink it religiously, praying the God to grant them fertility;

the mosque of Aurangzeb on top of a hill where in ancient time a thirty meter high statue of the Mahadeva stood to inspire awe to the visitors. Alexander asked why the statue had disappeared and why there were not any real ancient temples in the city. She said that Benares had been erased by the Moghols when they conquered the North of India in the twelfth century and that it remained for quite a while a dead city.

He did not want to see the macabre sights of corpses wrapped in white cloth being burned along the river, and of human ashes being spread over the waters. This was one of the main occupations in the city. He could see pyres and columns of smoke all along the riverbanks. This was certainly not a honeymoon place! But Lakshmi continued to teach him Hindu philosophy and the customs of her country:

"We are not afraid of death. The rishis of ancient India explained death as the withdrawal of life energy from our material body, as electricity ceases to pass through a circuit and a light bulb. Our human flesh with its sensory and motor nerves causing outward expressions and actions no longer receives the universe's cosmic energy. Our material body returns to the Earth in the form of water, chemicals or smoke, depending on funeral practices. Our soul or life energy returns to its source and according to our behavior on Earth we are sooner or later reincarnated and given a new chance to progress towards immortality. Once we have found our total union with God, as many sages, rishis, gurus and hermits do, there is no further need for reincarnation. We remain in eternal bliss as parts of the permanent cosmic energy that pervades the whole universe. We become perfect cells in the universal body of God, of Brahma."

Alexander listened, flabbergasted, incredulous at these strange views. Nevertheless, he recognized that even the greatest minds had asked themselves such questions over the millennia.

He commented to Lakshmi: "Why don't you ask the second World Congress of Religions in Chicago in 1993 to come up with a common answer to the mystery of life and death? It would be interesting to see the results."

She answered: "That is an excellent idea. I intended already to ask them to draft the cosmic laws they have in common and which should rule humanity on this Earth. Can you imagine what it would mean if they adopted as the first cosmic commandment: 'Thou shall not kill, not even in the name of a nation or of a religion.' I also plan to ask the World Health Organization and UNESCO to organize the first world conference on death. There has never been one in the entire human history."

They had arrived In Benares in the morning and had toured the city all day. In the evening, after dinner at the hotel, Lakshmi invited Alexander for a stroll along the Ganges. She wanted him to see the extraordinary sight of crowds of pilgrims still bathing and launching on the river thousands of tiny boats made of leaves and carrying lighted candles. The whole river was sprinkling with these lights conveying the prayers of the pilgrims to the Mahadeva for their dead.

The following morning Lakshmi woke up Alexander before dawn. "Hurry, she said. We can have breakfast when we return. I want you to see the sunrise over the Ganges before we leave India."

This time, Alexander was really impressed and shaken to the core of his being: It was still dark when they arrived at the river. Thousands of people were gathering and moving about like ghosts. Numerous boats were waiting on the river, overloaded with people watching the horizon.

At the first flickers of the sun above the horizon, everyone became still and silent, attentive to something extraordinary about to happen. Yes it was the resurrection of Sun God Suryia, in a golden apotheosis. His appearance signalled prayers from thousands of worshippers. The gongs of all Benares temples resounded. Smoke mounted from the funeral pyres lit at this precise moment. And the sun contemplated once again one of the strangest human scenes on Earth.

Then the immense blanket of humans suddenly began to move. Battalions of men, women and children glided silently into the waters of the Ganges up to their breasts, and began their ablutions. They drank with ecstacy the sacred water from the cups of their hands, as if it were a heavenly nectar. Monks, hermits, fakirs were dipping themselves delightfully into the water. Each person was alone with his prayers, his God and his problems. Choirs of voices mounted to the heavens, sweet or guttural according to the worshippers. Men and women threw flower petals and garlands of marigolds onto the river. Children launched little boats made of leaves. Merchants began selling their religious goods, in particular little bronze statuettes of a kneeling God holding an offering in his right hand. Pilgrims threw them into the river to get their prayers conveyed to God. And the busy daily life on the banks of the river Ganges began. The sacredness of the morning hour abated and gave way once more to ordinary human bustling and agitation.

Alexander was glad after all that he had come to Benares. It was like living on another planet. Or were the skyscrapers of Manhattan on another planet? What would beings from outer-space say if they could compare a sunrise over New York City and one over Benares?

* * *

# Chapter 18

Louis Parizot was waiting at the San Jose airport in Costa Rica for the arrival of Lakshmi and Alexander who were flying in from India, halfway around the world. He was thinking about the significance of this first visit of a Secretary-General of the UN and of a powerful, wealthy businessman to his beloved, fledgling University for Peace, to which he had given so much care during the last years. Sometimes he felt discouraged when he saw the blindness of nations and their reluctance to give support and funding to this wonderful undertaking. But today he felt happy: a meeting of representatives of the Central American Republics was taking place at the University to launch a project proposed by the University, namely the transformation of Central America into a zone of peace, following the example of Costa Rica which had demilitarized itself by Constitution in 1949.

The proposal seemed unrealistic and dangerous to political observers. But that was the fate of any new political ideas. As Gandhi said: "When one tries to effect change, one has to go through five steps: first people will greet you with indifference; second they will ridicule you; third they will abuse you; next they may put you in jail or try to kill you; if you go through these four steps successfully, you get to the most dangerous phase: when people start respecting you. Then you can become your own enemy unless you are careful."

Parizot remembered on that day a young Mexican colleague at the UN many years ago who dreamt that the whole of Latin America should be declared an area free of nuclear weapons. Garcia Robles pressed relentlessly for his idea, got the Tlatelolco Treaty adopted and received the Nobel Prize for Peace.

The idea of the demilitarization of the planet was beginning to make progress. Since the western powers often complain that the poor countries are spending too much money on arms, the Minister of Foreign Affairs of Costa Rica proposed in the UN General Assembly that poor countries who would totally or partly disarm should get preferential aid or debt reduction. The European Community had informed the University that if some provinces in troubled Central America would declare themselves zones of peace, devoid of military and guerrillas, the Community would develop these provinces with massive aid. Something big had therefore been started by the University and he felt quite happy when Lakshmi and Alexander Rumacher landed in Costa Rica. He had insisted that the Costa Rican government should not send any protocol or high officials. It was primarily a private visit. They would of course meet President Calderon and former President Oscar Arias, the Nobel Prize winner, during their visit.

Lakshmi and Louis were very moved when they saw each other again. For him, she was the reincarnation of Sima, Mon Amour. For her, he was her beloved world teacher, guru and Babaji.

He drove them to the Chatelle resort where he had made reservations for them, and explained to them what it was:

"I wanted you to be away from the city and to enjoy your honeymoon in an ideal, inspiring place in the middle of Costa Rica's luxuriant nature. The resort was built by a remarkable Latin American businessman, a Bolivian, who lives there and whom you will like. He remembered that as a young boy in Bolivia he played with his little comrades in the ruins of the vanished Tihuanaco civilization. In his child's mind he tried to visualize the palace which had left these ruins behind. He later studied that civilization and learned interesting facts about their architecture. Their dwellings and temples were built in round shapes, like native American Indian tepees, because the horizon of the world is round, because the sun and the moon are round, because the whole universe is round. Human heads are also round to be in better communion with the Earth and the universe. They also believed that the heaven above us is infinite. Their round temples and dwellings ended therefore in pointed roofs, the lines of which could be drawn into the infinite. They believed in seven cardinal virtues and fourteen sub-virtues. The roofs therefore were made of seven converging beams, each of them strengthened by two abutting beams. The dwellers were thus reminded of the basic virtues of life in the universe. Arturo Otero built his own house and a number of cottages according to that cosmological architecture. They are built in wood and a minimum of bricks, and not with concrete which is a barrier to the telluric and cosmic energies which human beings need for their good health and equilibrium."

Louis Parizot had selected that resort hotel, somewhat remote from the city because his beloved wife was staying in a nearby nursing home. He told Lakshmi and Rumacher of his delight of having a circular view of nature and of the horizon from his cottage. He never felt so at ease, so in communion with the Earth, with nature and with the universe. He wondered sometimes why the western world had adopted rectangular and quadrangular rooms and shapes which cut straight across the natural forms of the universe. Moreover, the cottages were located in a paradise of nature, Arturo Otero having planted every tropical tree, flower and greenery he knew in Latin America. Parizot loved to walk in that beautiful nature, watching horses roam in freedom in wild meadows, listening to the morning songs of cocks, picking live, tropical fruits right from the trees, taking a swim in a pool heated naturally by the sun all year round, and enjoying a cosmic sunray-bath every morning. It was a true paradise for thinking, meditating and writing. He suggested to Arturo Otero to build several more chalets and to offer them to selected people in the world who held cosmological views, who would come and live here in a community, have meetings, know each other, exchange views and develop a new cosmology for the third millennium. Arturo Otero loved the idea and planned to devote his retirement to it.

"This is the place I wanted you to know and enjoy during your short stay in Costa Rica", Louis said to his two companions. And he added for Alexander Rumacher:

"And please do not follow the example of that American couple I saw one morning run around like squirrels, wanting to get a taxi and move to a hotel in the city because the cocks in the neighborhood woke them up and they could not sleep! The incident reminded me of my disappointment when we lived in the charming village of Dobbs Ferry in the Hudson Valley: as an Alsatian I was missing the crowing of the cocks at dawn and I asked why I could not hear any in the village. I was told that the businessmen from Manhattan who lived there could not sleep in the morning because of the cocks. The village boards of Dobbs Ferry and Hastings therefore adopted an ordinance prohibiting cocks in the two villages."

It was late when they arrived at the Chatelle cottages in La Garita on the former Camino Real of the Spaniards. Louis left the couple in their cosmic cottage wishing them a good rest and union with the universe.

* *

The following morning, he drove his two friends to the University for Peace, telling them about the University, its origin, its work and its difficulties. He gave them also information about Costa Rica, the world's first demilitarized country, and some of the special features of the nature which was unfolding along the way. On the highway from Santa Ana to Ciudad Colon, he asked them to observe two examples of Costa Rica's conservation efforts: a very ancient one and a recent one. The ancient one was performed by cows, horses and goats which were left by the peasants to graze along the highway. "You will never see here the enormous lawn-mowing tractors you have along the US highways. Animals take care of the vegetation. Along many roads the grasses are left growing during the entire rainy or winter season, and are then cut with machetes at the beginning of the summer. As a result these high grasses produce oxygen or feed animals, and are not cut or wasted unnecessarily. It saves the country also a lot of energy." He then pointed to a recent example: the strip of land separating the two ways of the highway had been planted with thousands of small shrubs by high-school students of the area. They are supposed to absorb much of the carbon dioxide emitted by cars on the highway.

When they arrived in Ciudad Colon and took the winding road up to the University for Peace, he had a lot more to tell:

"Here you have typical examples of the ecological wisdom of the peasants and of the ecological mistakes of western civilization. Observe for example how all these prosperous, healthy coffee plantations are interspersed with trees. Well, these trees whose characteristics are well known and tested by the peasants over centuries, have the properties of retaining the soil, of reducing with their foliage the impact of heavy tropical rains, of giving shadow to the coffee shrubs and of keeping moisture during the dry season. At the University for Peace we are offering courses on peace with nature, in particular agroforestry, i.e. the intelligent mixing of agriculture, pastures and forestry. Western man has separated the three: barely any trees are planted on agricultural land or on pastures, and no agriculture is attempted in forest areas. In the tropics this is a basic mistake, as every peasant will tell you. The first advice to our students is therefore: always listen first to the peasants. They are shown areas of Costa Rica where agroforestry has succeeded and others where disasters have been produced by wrong ideas. Observe also those fences: the old fences of the peasants are all made of nature itself: lines of trees or shrubs separate the properties or the fields. The poles of the fences are living stems. They are beautiful, cheap and produce oxygen. But look at the properties bought by city dwellers or foreigners: they are surrounded by concrete pillars, painted in ugly colors which are an insult to the greenery of nature. You could cry when you see such things. And yet these people think that they are smart with their concrete pillars, barbed wire and lawn-mowers. There exists in the US an association of fences producers who have adopted the motto: world-wide fencing. Indeed, this is what they are doing, at the precise time when the world wants to get rid of the fencing by nations! He turned to Alexander Rumacher and said: " I hope you are not investing in those fencing companies. Please don't. Let natural fences produce oxygen and absorb carbon dioxide. Hire an Iroquois to tell you about the effects of your investments on the seventh generation."

He drew their attention to several hills which were reddish-yellow, without trees or coffee bushes, covered only partly with pastures. On some of them, still a few rare cows were grazing on the sparse grass. "Here you have the typical case of the substantial deforestation which hit Costa Rica a few years ago: the huge demand for hamburger meat in the United States induced Costa Rican peasants to cut the trees on their hills to make pastures for cattle growing. The problem here in tropical areas, and he pointed at the soil structure which was beautifully visible on the high banks of the road-sides, is this: the topsoil here is only a few inches thick, but on it grow luxuriant quantities of vegetation under the protection of trees which retain that thin layer of top-soil. This enormous biomass renews itself endlessly without need for fertilizer. When you cut the trees and the shrubs, all this goes; grass is sown and the cows begin to walk on the slopes of the hills. They are very heavy. As a result, their hoofs leave triangular indents in the top-soil. When the strong tropical rains hit the unprotected soil and fill the cavities left by the cows, the top-soil is progressively washed down the hill, and after a few years, there are no trees, no shrubs, no vegetation, no grass, no cows. If early action is not taken, the top-soil is gone for ever and no reforestation is possible. He showed them two hills which a peasant had put up for sale near the University because his cows could no longer graze on them. He turned to Rumacher and said: "Of course this is the last thing to which Harvard economists and business school experts would pay any attention. And now the world cries that the tropical rain forests, our main source of oxygen are disappearing, after having deforested the northern hemisphere. A human being dies when he loses more than one third of his skin. Our living, breathing Earth might similarly die if she loses more than a third of her living skin. You will look very funny in your Manhattan skyscrapers trying to figure out what to do next." And in far away Costa Rica, amidst coffee plantations and tropical forests, the cartoon of a world of skyscrapers surrounded by deserts drawn by Felix White came back to Alexander Rumacher's mind!

* *

The sight of the University for Peace was a pure enchantment. On a vast hill it overlooks a magnificent scenery of mountains and valleys. Flags of a number of nations are flying at the entrance near a monument erected to Gandhi. Lakshmi and Alexander were looking forward to visiting the University and its grounds under the guidance of Parizot, but he said to them:

"I am sorry, a rather important meeting is opening this morning which I must attend. I invite you to come along. After a while we will be able to leave and I will show you the grounds."

He explained to them that it was a meeting of the Vice-Chancellors of the Central American Republics who had come to examine a plan for the transformation of Central America into a Zone of Peace.

After the formal opening of the meeting, the Professors of the University who had drawn up the plan, introduced their proposal and were followed by speeches and comments of the Vice-Chancellors. Lakshmi was fascinated. She was struck in particular by the statement of the Vice-Chancellor of Guatemala who said that this plan was a long-term utopia, but that it was the role of universities to dream far ahead and to produce utopias. "It is up to us politicians to agree with the principle and the dream, and to begin to work towards it in ways which might be different from those proposed by academia, with different stages and at a different pace, but never losing sight of the end objective. I am ready to propose that the Presidents of the Central American Republics should announce their decision to make our region a Zone of Peace, Democracy and Cooperation, and that a commission of experts be created by them to work on that project with the help of the University for Peace."

The intervention of the Vice-Chancellor of Nicaragua was no less interesting:

"Since the beginning of colonization, Central America has been known as an area of wards, revolutions, dictatorships, upheavals and guerrillas. But suddenly in the last few years a fundamental change has taken place: we have peace and democracy in Nicaragua where for the first time 19,000 men have been disarmed and their arms destroyed by the United Nations. Costa Rica has disarmed itself totally and has asked the United Nations to create this University for Peace. The Presidents of Central America are meeting every six months and take decisions in the common interest of the area. A Central American Parliament is being created. In a number of countries we will have common Embassies. In international fora we will have common positions as Central America and not as individual countries. Negotiations for internal peace have succeeded in El Salvador and continue in Guatemala under UN auspices. Free elections are being held in each Central American country. The thousands of Salvadorean refugees in Honduras have gone home. It was the Vice-Chancellor present here of that country who officially closed the camps. I wholeheartedly endorse the proposal of the University for Peace, because it inscribes itself well in this flowering of peace, democracy and cooperation which takes place at long last in our region."

After the Vice-Chancellors had spoken, Louis Parizot made some comments in his capacity as Chancellor of the University:

"I was struck by the remark of the Vice-Chancellor of Guatemala that in his country as in many others, universities are no longer partners with the political world, society and the business world. They have isolated themselves. This is a mistake which will not be made by the University for Peace. When former Secretary-General

U Thant proposed the creation of world universities, it was precisely in order to establish bridges between universities and the political world. The dreams of academia must enrich the political world and the needs of the political world must be heard by academia, so that everyone will cooperate on societal problems, including at the world level.

The remarks of the Vice-Chancellor of Nicaragua reminded me of a similar phenomenon that happened in Europe: our continent and region was probably the most war-torn area in the world and in all history. Until recently my family suffered from European divisions: my poor grandfather had five successive nationalities without leaving his village, and in my family half of my cousins wore German uniforms and the other half French ones. We could have killed each other. And yet it is that same Europe which now shows the world a new path, a new political model, a United Europe. My passport bears the title "European Community" and as a sub-title, France. History shows that it is often from utter chaos and strife that a new world is born. The miracle of Europe is now being repeated here in Central America, where a demilitarized Costa Rica and this University show a new way to the world. Another precedent comes to mind: that of America which as a Confederacy between 1777 and 1786 was a chaos. There were tariffs between most states. Each state had its militia or army. Seven states were printing their own money. The government in Washington was financed like the United Nations with contributions which were often withheld. New York state was massing its troops on the Vermont frontier and the army of Pennsylvania was committing atrocities against settlers from Connecticut. The situation led General George Washington to declare: "The primary cause of all disorders lies in the different state governments and in the tenacity of that power which pervades the whole of their system."

" Well, the same situation prevails today in the world, and perhaps out of this depth of chaos, a new human dream and Renaissance will flower, the same way as it happened in the US, in Europe and in Central America. The world is ready for major changes. I would dare to predict here today that before this century and millennium are over, we will see proposals and debates of a new political system for the planet, possibly the birth of a United States of the World."

Lakshmi was thinking for herself: "Is Parizot becoming unfaithful to the UN? Or is he thinking of a fundamental transformation of the UN?"

But Rumacher was all excited: "This man is entirely right. The world will never work under the system of the United Nations. We must extend the federal democratic system of balance of powers of the US to the entire world. I am going to commit myself to the creation of the United States of the World. It is up to the US to take the leadership. President Bush's proposal for an all-American common market and community is fine but not enough. It is a mere imitation of the Europeans. We need infinitely more. If not, the Russians who are now inside the system, will sooner or later come up with a bold proposal which will take us by surprise and put us on the defensive. We must lead, not follow. I am going to give up my admiration for Alexander the Great and take George Washington as my hero."

* *

They then left the meeting which established a drafting group to issue a declaration for adoption in the afternoon. The meeting lasted only one day instead of the three which had been scheduled.

Louis Parizot took his two friends on a tour of the University grounds, one of the most inspiring places on Earth: an immense area of more than 300 hectares of hills, covered with tropical forests, luxuriant vegetation, a few lakes, beautiful landscapes, places of retreat and isolation, children's playgrounds, picnic places, flowerbeds and open air greenhouses. He took them for a walk on his preferred nature-path in the nearby tropical forest, a real paradise of nature's sumptuous diversity of vegetation, birds and butterflies. He showed them, in a brook, big redstones carved out as reservoirs of water: "Our neighbors, the Indians who live on the other side of the hill carved out one hundred of these huge stones as reservoirs for the dry season. They come here to cut climbers out of which they make straw hats and baskets. We help them reforest their hills by planting trees which are grown on the University ground with help from the European community. A former Minister of Agriculture of Costa Rica is spending his retirement here, as I do, and is happy, as I am, to be still of service to humanity. He is the soul behind all this wonderful landscaping and projects of reforestation and water conservation."

On the way to the huge peace monument on a hill in the upper part of the University, they saw the grounds where each week Elderhostel people plant trees before hearing lectures at the University. There were many statues of great peacemakers: Gandhi, Tolstoy, Thomas Payne, Teilhard de Chardin, Andres Bello, Marti, etc. Parizot was explaining: "We want the students to walk and meditate in the midst of the world's greatest peacemakers. An Albert Schweitzer Chair has been announced recently at a symposium on great peacemakers held at the UN. We will have Chairs named after St. Francis, Eleanor Roosevelt, etc."

They arrived at the famous Peace Monument created by a Cuban woman artist who worked voluntarily at the University for a whole year sculpting it: in spiral form there are sculpted portraits of the Costa Rican Presidents who had contributed most to the peace of their country and area, the last one of Oscar Arias, the Nobel Prize winner. Visitors could read great thoughts on peace from these presidents and from people associated with the University. Lakshmi was struck by an inscription by a Japanese: "Happy the Costa Rican mother who, at giving birth, knows that her son will never be a soldier." She asked: "Who is this Sasakawa who had this beautiful thought?" "He is a Japanese who accused the wrong education by his government for having made him an airplane manufacturer and war criminal. He is now one of the United Nations greatest philanthropists. I obtained from him a million dollars for the University. He has his bust displayed on the campus, as has the landowner who gave this land for a peaceful purpose, on the condition that we would preserve for future generations the last primeval Pacific sierra rain forest at this altitude in the whole of Latin America. The government of Costa Rica now suggests to other governments concerned with the conservation of natural resources and the preservation of the planet's oxygen, to buy all the remaining forests up there, to donate them to the University and thus create the first supra-national world park or reserve. There are many intelligent ways to preserve nature and we have stimulated quite a few at the University. For example, there was a plan by the US Corps of Engineers to build strategic roads along the borders with Nicaragua and Panama for Costa Rica's protection. Instead, the University proposed and Costa Rica accepted to declare the natural area and forests along the borders to be Peace Parks.

167

Costa Rica will be defended by the sanctity of nature. Many peace parks and areas are being created around the world, including in cities. Thus, a lady who heard me speak on the subject started a campaign for the creation of a Peace Park in Washington D.C. which has many monuments to the glory of war and the military, but no monuments devoted to peace. The US Congress approved the project and Washington will thus have its peace park for citizens to enjoy along the Potomac River."

He became pensive and commented: "What one can do for peace is just endless. So far we see only the tip of the iceberg. Throughout human history war and the military were celebrated everywhere. Peace was the neglected orphan, but it is now becoming the main value and people begin to have lots of ideas. For example, many national hymns are being rewritten into peace hymns. I have a whole file of them. In France, a committee of citizens wants a new text of the Marseillaise, one of the bloodiest songs on Earth. Instead of starting with the words: 'Let us march, children of the fatherland...' it will start with 'Let us march, children of the planet'." He pointed at the highest sculpture of the Peace Monument, a dove ready to take its flight and dominating the other sculptures. He said:

"Here is another beautiful story. I once I heard former Secretary-General U Thant say after a trip to member countries: 'In every capital I visit they take me to a monument erected to the unknown soldier, but never to a monument to the unknown peacemaker'. This remark stuck in my mind. Well, our Peace Monument will also become the world's first monument to unknown peacemakers. Arrangements are being made so that the beak of the dove can be lit and when heads of states visit the University they will be asked to light this symbol to honor all the humble, unknown peacemakers of this planet. I am sure the soul of U Thant is pleased and will help this University succeed. It is he, indeed, the humble teacher from Burma, who proposed in 1970 for the first time the creation of a United Nations University."

He told them many more inspiring stories about the University. He took them to the bench where he loves to sit, to dream and to write as he did in Geneva on his bench near the "Dwarf with the Silver Hands". But Lakshmi and Alexander had one question on their mind: they were surprised to see only a small number of students and no dormitories on the grounds of the University. Parizot answered sadly:

"This is our main problem. We do not have the funds necessary to pay Professors and to build dormitories. After ten years, only thirty one governments out of 166 have ratified the basic instruments of the University and only a handful have given us any money. We have only about sixty students. It is the poorest University on Earth. I sometimes call it the Poverella, in rememberance of St. Francis, the Poverello who labored for peace and respect for God's Creation on the inspiring hills of Assisi. But it gives a great inspiration to existing Universities which are all creating peace chairs, peace studies and faculties or centers. Sooner or later it will succeed and will be the training ground for future heads of states, peacemakers, Ministers of External Affairs, diplomats and world servants. God's projects on this Earth have always a difficult start, but they all succeed and flourish with time. It will be the same with this University."

Alexander Rumacher asked him if the University had a tax-exempt Foundation to receive donations. He answered: "Yes, we have in the United States a foundation called Friends of the University for Peace which has tax-exemption."

After touring the buildings and conference halls of the University, the International Radio for Peace, the Gandhi Center for the production of peace videos, television programs and films, and the library, they were invited to luncheon with the Vice-Chancellors of the Central American Republics in the University's dining hall. The Vice-Rector of the University revealed to the guests that the Secretary-General of the United Nations was present, incognita on her honeymoon trip. She was greeted with much affection. At the end of the luncheon, Alexander Rumacher asked for the floor:

"Dear friends, you cannot imagine how impressed I am with this visit, with what I saw and heard. This is one of the greatest dreams I have ever come across in my life, a dream of a new world which will become a reality if we all work at it. I begin to believe that peace is really possible on this planet, that the military and armaments are obsolete and that we can afford a better world political system. I will do all I can, and as a first step, I want to announce here today the donation of one million dollars towards the creation of a Lakshmi Rumacher Foundation at the University for Peace. It is my wedding gift to the dear wife God has given me as my life companion."

And he turned to Lakshmi and handed her a check of one million dollars for the University for Peace. The whole attendance broke into applause, including the women working in the kitchen who had felt that something special was going on. And Louis Parizot was thinking for himself: "Thank you, dear God, once again You have done a miracle."

* *

During the rest of their short stay, Alexander Rumacher remained obsessed with the University and he bombarded Louis Parizot with questions:

"How come that only thirty one governments have ratified it and even fewer have given it any money?"

"It has to do with the built-in self-interest and self-promoting power of nations and of their agents, as George Washington pointed out for the states of his time. Money is given only for national projects, not for the world. Huge sums of money are spent by nations as subsidies to **their** Universities, to allow foreign students to come and study in **their** Universities in order to make friends with **their** young people, with **their** cultures, language, beliefs, systems, ways of life and ideologies. The aim is to gain friends for the nation, not for humanity and the world. There are only a very few first universities and colleges on this planet where students from all nations can come as equals and be trained in the needs and concerns of the planet and humanity, and not be programmed into any particular nation: there are the World Colleges created by the Quakers in a number of countries, there is a World University in Oregon which sponsors the International Radio for Peace here on the grounds of the University for Peace, there is the World Spiritual University of Mt. Abu, and there are the first world universities created by the United Nations: the United Nations University in Tokyo, the International Institute of Physics in Trieste, the World Maritime University in Sweden, and the University for Peace in Costa Rica. But many more are needed. From such truly global institutions of higher learning, graduates go home as friends of all nations and cultures, and as agents of the world and humanity. We plan to hold a conference of these first world universities in order to take stock of their experience and stimulate the creation of more of them to respond to the world's growing global needs. We must give the world back to the people, especially to youth. For example, there has been only once in the history of this planet a school for heads of states: Confucius established it in China which at that time was utterly divided as the world is today. We need

170

one desperately for the world of today and of tomorrow, if we want to avoid dictators and extremist leaders ready to go to war. Every head of state should know the world. If Hitler had been offered trips to Siberia and across the United States by train, he would have never dared to start a war. Show and teach leaders the world and they will see that they are only a small part of it, but a very responsible part. In 1990, the government of Costa Rica asked the UN General Assembly to celebrate the tenth anniversary of the University. A draft resolution endorsing the University was tabled by forty governments, but some of the largest and richest were notoriously absent from the list, most eminently the United States, a fact which would come as a shock to a Benjamin Franklin and George Washington if they were alive. The bigger the powers, the less they are interested in strengthening world instrumentalities, because they see themselves as the world's organizers and rulers, a notion that is dead for ever."

"And how about the support from Foundations? Have you tried that?"

"Of course. But unfortunately you find there the same disease. Most foundations are nation-oriented. They finance primarily projects which are in the interest or for the glory of **their** nation or of **their** universities, **their** alma maters. Their founders think that they owe their wealth to their nation or to the education they received in their university. So the gratitude and the money go to them. As a result, once again the world and humanity are orphans, and the gap between the rich and the poor increases, between nations as well as universities. Nobel, Andrew Carnegie and Sasakawa were rare and genial exceptions to that trend. On the occasion of John D. Rockefeller's 100th anniversary I was invited to a conference organized by the Rockefeller family on philanthropy in the 21st century. I spoke there in favor of world philanthropy and gaiaphily, above and beyond national philanthropy. The Earth and humanity were in my view the new priorities. Alas, I preached in a desert and had no results whatsoever, I had approached the Rockefellers with the plea to help the University, but their 'experts' advised them that the University was not yet a going concern and that consequently they should not help it. As if it was not precisely the very need of the University to be helped to become a going concern! My proposal to UNESCO to convene a world conference on philanthropy was not heard either. Believe me, sometimes I think that we should offer the campus of the University to the military who would get millions of dollars overnight,

171

or to Mac Donalds, Kentucky Fried Chicken, Hiltons or Ramada Inns. That is the world we live in."

"Have you tried to appeal directly to the people so as to get a large membership and number of small donations to the University?"

Parizot handed him a paper and said: "Every letter I send out has this appeal on the back side. It has helped a little, but they are only drops of water. The people pray for peace and pay for war."

And Alexander Rumacher read this text:

## AN APPEAL TO THE PEOPLE

The University for Peace is one of the most beautiful ideas born on the eve of the third Millennium, an idea whose time has come. It is not surprising that it came from Costa Rica, that paragon of peace, democracy, human rights, national parks, conceiver of the International Year and Day of Peace, 1987 winner of the Nobel Peace Prize (President Oscar Arias), the country that outlawed the military by Constitution in 1949, transformed its military buildings into schools and museums (former President Jose Figueres) and possesses the secret of peace and disarmament: no military budgets, i.e. no base to increase year after year with fears and menaces of conflicts. The General Assembly of the UN went along with the proposal of Costa Rica (former President Rodrigo Carazo). How could governments who are members of the UN not be in favor of a world peace University! But they gave the idea a kind of kiss of death, by saying: we will not finance it, go and seek your own financing. That is what has happened so far. The 166 sovereign nations of this Earth extract from their subjects a trillion dollars a year of taxes for the military but are unwilling to find 600,000 dollars (less than 3,800 per nation!!) to meet the operating expenses of the first and only peace university on this planet, compared with thousands of military academies! So, it is up to us the people to react, to take over and to break the national borders of financing and philanthropy. A small sum per well-do-do inhabitant of this planet will easily finance this magnificent instrument of peace which can change the course of the world by training young people to be the friendly and cooperating leaders of tomorrow. Peoples associations for the University for Peace have sprung up in several countries. Contribute what your heart tells you to, for the benefit of your children and grandchildren. Let us show governments what We The Peoples of this beautiful planet can do.

172

Probably they will even join us, for as the Chinese say: when the people lead, the leaders will follow. Do not miss this great opportunity for personal, grass-root world democracy. Let us make the University for Peace a resounding, historical success, a shining example of the will of the human family for peace and a better world. Contribute generously. And if you are very rich, this is your chance of obtaining world-wide visibility and recognition.

May peace begin with each of us."

Alexander commented:

"Isn't the peoples' reluctance due to the fact that you have only a few students to show?"

"Sure, that is one of the key problems: you cannot show students because you have no money to pay a faculty, and you get no money because you have few students! It is the classical vicious circle which has beset humanity since the beginnings of time".

"A last question: haven't you thought of creating an international city on the vast grounds you possess up here?"

"Yes, we have been approached by several investors, but so far nothing has happened."

Rumacher:

"Well, I think that I will buy the entire landholding around the University. It would be a pity to have this exploited for commercial purposes. This must remain something very pure and unique in the world, in full conformity and harmony with the noble purposes of the University. I am determined to buy it. I have the feeling that it will have a very special meaning to our lives, isn't it Lakshmi?"

Lakshmi was embarrassed and did not know what to say. She had listened with great care and was thinking what she could do as Secretary-General of the UN to help the University. She had a whole series of ideas, but not on the utilization of a piece of land. She simply said:

"In your plans, do not forget the spiritual side. God and the world's great spiritual traditions must have a place here. The third millennium must be a spiritual millennium."

And Louis Parizot was saying to himself: "Thank You again, O God. You are about to make another miracle, and a very big one."

He thanked Alexander for his thought and said:

"I cannot resist telling you a beautiful anecdote from French history of which your intention reminds me: we had in Paris in the 17th Century a priest who became a saint, St. Vincent de Paul. He created in Paris the hospital you see near the cathedral of Notre-Dame. He was the inventor of seminaries for priests, of hospitals and of missions abroad. He used the hospital in Paris to invite people to luncheon in the vast refectory and to hold discussions, especially on religion and God. One day, the manager of the hospital said to him: 'Monsieur Vincent, I do not know what to do anymore. You invite all Paris to luncheon, but we have run out of money. I do not know how to feed these people.' St. Vincent looked at his co-worker, a large happy smile appeared on his face and he exclaimed: 'How wonderful! This will give God an opportunity to do a miracle'."

Parizot added:

"This is exactly how I feel since you have come to Costa Rica, although I am not a saint."

* *

Lakshmi had remained silent during most of that exchange. But she had a question which was burning her lips. When they finished, she asked Parizot:

"I am dead curious: could you tell me by what miracle Costa Rica was able to demilitarize herself, a rare, almost Herculean achievement in our epoch?"

Parizot answered:

"It is a beautiful story which was told to us by the author of that extraordinary feat, Jose Figueres, the former President of Costa Rica. The story is this: Jose Figueres, like many Costa Ricans was studying law in Paris when he was young. He had a great liking for philosophy and had studied all the great philosophers of human history. One of his preferred modern authors was H.G. Wells of England, the advocate of world disarmament and world government, more known however for his *"War of Worlds"*, which was made into a famous film. Figueres was sad to learn that H.G. Wells had died disillusioned and bitter because none of his great ideas for a disarmed world had been accepted by governments. Figueres, after completing his studies, returned to Costa Rica where a dictator had seized power. Figueres was mad and left for the woods with friends to start an insurrectional army and oust the dictator. He became the general of that army. Their headquarters were located right here near the University. They defeated the troops of the dictator and Figueres found himself to be the new President of his country. One morning he woke up and remembered H.G. Wells's dream of a disarmed, demilitarized world. He said to himself: "Here I am, the President of a country and general of a victorious army. I can dismiss that army, because I am its commander in chief; and I can also dissolve the defeated army, they will be all too happy to go home. I am in a position to fulfill the dream of my preferred philosopher. He will be happy in heaven that at least one little country on Earth did what he had recommended all nations to do." He implemented his plan and obtained the ratification in 1949 of a new constitution which abolishes and prohibits permanently all armaments and military in the country. As a result, Costa Rica has enjoyed ever since peace and prosperity right in the middle of war-torn and dictator-ridden Central America. He had found the secret. You will now understand why Costa Rica proposed to the UN General Assembly to create on its soil the first supra-national peace University on Earth."

Parizot added these words for Lakshmi:

"It is up to you to expand the fulfillment of this dream to other countries. Many saints and philosophers in heaven are looking down to you as their main hope to be at long last heard and followed on this planet. I am sure that Pepe Figueres, as the Costa Ricans call him lovingly, who passed away, is part of the heavenly headquarters of peacemakers and that he will help you perform that miracle. It is written in the stars."

And since Parizot was an endless, impassioned world story-teller, he exclaimed:

"Oh, this reminds me of another beautiful story which I cannot resist telling you: Once when I talked to my compatriot Robert Schuman, the father of the European Community, I asked him how it came that he took up this marvelous idea. He told me the following story: 'When I became Minister of Foreign Affairs of France, I was approached by a very remarkable man, Jean Monnet, who said to me: "Mr. Schuman, as an Alsace-Lorrainer who was once a German and then a French soldier, you owe it to your region to reconcile France and Germany and build a new Europe. I have here a plan which I would like you to endorse. It should bear your name and be called The Schuman Plan. It is an idea for a European Coal and Steel Community in which France and Germany would cooperate because they have very concrete interests: France has the iron-ore of Lorraine and Germany has the excellent coking coal of the Ruhr.

175

Once they have learned to cooperate on that, we can extend the idea to a broader European community and then later to a united Europe, as a political entity. It is your duty to support that idea." Schuman did not really know what to do with the plan. It was very technical, and he was neither an economist nor a coal and steel expert. So he had it on his desk for several days, unable to make up his mind. Then one morning he woke up and remembered that when he was a little boy he lived in a part of Lorraine called Die Drei-Grenzen Ecke, the corner of three borders, where Germany, France and Luxembourg are bordering each other. And he was mad each time he rode his bicycle that he ran into border control. He swore to himself that if in his life he would ever be given a chance, he would suppress those damned borders. 'This was my occasion', he exclaimed, and he went to his office and signed the plan without finishing to read it."

"Schuman also said to me: 'Your thesis on the Saar Territory, of which you sent me a copy, has been my bedside reading on that issue. I swore to myself that once in power I would settle that problem right away with my friend Adenauer.' And he did. For my part I am glad today that I have been appointed member of a committee of Alsace-Lorrainers who have introduced with the Holy Father a petition to make Robert Schuman a saint. The petition is being processed, but we are being told that a number of individual miracles, such as healing at his tomb are needed. My answer is: What greater miracle do you need than the miracle of millions of humans being spared a new European or World War?"

Parizot became dreamy. He added:

"Why don't more people and heads of states understand that this is basically a Planet of Dreams, a Planet of the Spirit and of the Heart. Every mother dreams for her child. Our Mother Earth similarly dreams for us. We must fulfill the dreams of our mothers. If only Presidents Bush and Gorbachev and all leaders of this planet could dream for their children and grandchildren and discuss their dreams with their mothers and wives, with Mother Earth and with our Father in heaven Nothing would be more beneficial to this world."

* * *

176

# Chapter 19

After having visited San Jose and its museums, especially the fascinating jade and gold museums, and paid courtesy visits to the President of Costa Rica, Mr. Calderon Fournier, and to former President and Nobel Prize winner Oscar Arias, Lakshmi had one last wish before their departure for New York: to pay a visit to Mrs. Parizot who had done so much in the United Nations for the rights of women and who was now afflicted with Alzheimer's disease and staying in a Costa Rican nursing home.

As they drove to the Golden Valley geriatric home, Louis Parizot explained to his friends how he had come to select that particular place:

"My wife had a phenomenal memory when she was young. As a law student in Chile she was able to memorize entire chapters of the Chilean code. At her doctorate's exams she got the highest marks any student ever received and became one of Chile's first women diplomats. Her thesis on the rights of Chilean women is still a classic and thanks to her activism in the Chilean Christian Democratic Party, Chile soon became the country on Earth with the most advanced rights of women. Today they even have more rights than men! At the UN she worked on that subject with women like Eleanor Roosevelt and Gabriela Mistral, the Chilean Nobel Prize for Literature. She was, however, always concerned that with old age something adverse might happen to her, because her mother and her aunt had both developed arterio-sclerosis and died without recognizing the members of her family.

About six years ago it began to happen: we noticed that she was losing her glasses, her keys and her purse, sometimes not remembering where she was. She had difficulties to start the car, or forgot where she had left it. Thanks God this happened when I was able to take my retirement from the UN. She could not be left alone at any time, because she could get lost. We had nevertheless, some wonderful retirement years. Since I receive many requests for speeches, I accepted quite a few and we had beautiful trips to Africa, Latin America, Greece, Italy and many cities in the United States, as far as Alaska and Prudhoe Bay. I had to be with her day and night.

About a year ago it got worse: Airplane travel became more difficult; she would ask me in the middle of the night to stop the boat (!) and get a taxi to take her home. Incontinence was also a growing problem. We went to Chile to see her family before it was too late. When we returned to the United States, the problems compounded. Her walking became more difficult. I got the help of our children and of a maid. Finally she had to be hospitalized, and the doctors recommended that she should be placed in a nursing home. I could not get this over my heart. But with time I became myself a nervous wreck. Day and night I had to be on the look-out for possible mishaps. I could sleep only lightly because she woke up several times in the night and needed help.

It got constantly worse, without any hope for improvement. Every few months, her condition months back looked like paradise. I was seriously beginning to think of common suicide, remembering the case of a prominent writer who had done that with his wife afflicted with Alzheimer's disease. My children made me visit nursing homes in the Hudson Valley. While perfect from the scientific and technical points of view, I found them appalling, being overcrowded and insufficiently staffed. Furthermore, all the nursing homes I visited had long waiting lists.

I began to look abroad and called my friend Rodrigo Carazo, the former President of Costa Rica and founder of the University for Peace. I asked him: How do you take care of your elderly people in Costa Rica? He recommended that I call the head of the geriatric hospital in San Jose, Dr. Alpizar, who had started a new, special nursing home for Alzheimer patients.

I called Dr. Alpizar and in the light of what he told me, I decided to take a trip to Costa Rica and visit his nursing home. From the first moment, the conclusion jumped to my mind: this is the rare place where I could see Margarita being well taken care of, without me being miserable and sleepless about it. I brought her to Costa Rica and after a month of trial period, we decided that this was the solution for both of us. She would be taken care of in a most human, loving way and I would be able to continue to have a useful life as the Chancellor of the University for Peace."

In the meantime, Lakshmi, Alexander and Louis arrived at the nursing home and could see for themselves how the patients were taken care of. It was not a hospital, but a beautiful, substantial, spacious Spanish hacienda surrounded by a park, gardens, flowerbeds and even animal husbandry. The patients could sit outside or walk with the assistance of nurses or nursing helpers in a most beautiful surrounding, happy to see chickens whom they could feed and a horse which loved to be petted. The ratio of helpers to patients was almost one to one. Each of the twelve patients was constantly observed and assisted. Only one lady who had her leg amputated was in a wheelchair. Other patients who could hardly walk were, nevertheless, taken for walks, helped by two nursing aids. The whole group was sitting in a circle of armchairs and was listening to Chilean folk music. A couple of patients even got up to dance, remembering the good times of their youth. Margarita welcomed her husband with effusion. His daily visit was an event expected not only by her, but by other patients too. He had become a member of the family.

Dr. Alpizar happened to be present. It was one of his biweekly visits to check the condition of each patient on the basis of the daily reports and check-ups by the nurses. Parizot introduced him to Lakshmi and Alexander and he explained to them his approach:

"In my gerontological studies in several countries, especially Switzerland, I became primarily interested in Alzheimer's disease, for a simple reason: my father died of it, so did my mother and an uncle. We have it in the family and I know that I will get it too. One indication is that I have a remarkable memory, and it is known that most people with an exceptional memory are prone to Alzheimer's disease. It has to do with inter-cell brain connections which are the first to be affected. As a result, there is nothing in the world on Alzheimer's disease which I do not know, because it is in my own interest to know. On the basis of years of experience I have come to the conclusion that the sickness cannot be cured at this stage of our knowledge. Drugs and injections are of little help and must be used with extreme moderation. What helps is right nutrition, exercise, long rest and above all love. If we cannot heal the patients, we can at least give them happiness. This is why a natural surrounding and a non-hospital dwelling are so important. They want to be well-attended and constantly taken care of. Love is the most important assistance to them. All nurses and helpers are instructed and trained to smile, to be cheerful, encouraging, optimistic and loving towards each patient. A nurse who becomes bitter loses her job. I have made tests with nurses wearing masks showing bitterness and unhappiness. The effect is disastrous on the patients. It is also important to have only a small number of patients. Beyond twelve to fifteen it can no longer be the same care and atmosphere. In the United States the main problems are the large number of patients, the high costs of personnel and the incessant tests and precautions they have to take not to incur lawsuits from the families. Our costs and charges here are less than one-third of those in the United States."

He added that he had just been approached by the US informing him that several nursing homes were being closed in that country, and asking if Costa Rica could accommodate some of the 5000 Alzheimer patients who had to be placed in other nursing homes.

When he left, Parizot commented to Lakshmi and to Alexander Rumacher:

"There are 2 million people with Alzheimer's disease in the US and there will be 4 million by the year 2000. Longevity continuing to increase, this will become a very serious problem in a country like the US and in other rich countries too. Why not, therefore arrange that more Americans could be taken care of in poor countries where the labor and professional costs are much lower? This would be a source of income, of foreign exchange and of employment for these countries. Alexander should consider investing in such geriatric homes in large numbers in developing countries. The weather is nice here, it is not very different from living in Florida, and it is much cheaper. The US should consider this as a policy option. It is already being done for manufacturing. Why not consider it also in the field of services?" Turning to Lakshmi, he said: "You should raise this question in the World Health Organization, the same way as we favored manufacturing in poor countries in UN debates years ago."

Lakshmi talked to Margarita, holding her hand lovingly and thanking her for her work for women at the United Nations. But it is mostly her smile and affectionate face that Margarita could understand. They took her out for dinner in a nearby restaurant where Louis went with her several times a week. Her understanding and conversation were extremely limited, but she was happy to be surrounded by people and life.

When they drove back to the Chatelle cottages, Parizot said to them: "Life around them seems to be one of the most important elements of their happiness. They can no longer read, they can no longer follow a long television program. But to look around and see the movement of the other patients and of the nurses becomes the centerpiece of their life. I have spent countless hours with them and have come to love each of them and to know their individual limitations and likings. The same is happening to the nurses. They really love them. When their shift is over, they kiss each patient goodbye. Even the driver of the nursing home sits with the patients, talks to them and loves each of them."

He told them several stories which had moved him deeply:

"Last time, when I returned by plane from New York, I arrived late in the evening at the nursing home. They have no strict visiting hours. I can come there at any time. So I decided to drop by, just in case Margarita was still up. They asked me to wait. After a while she appeared all dressed up and made beautiful to receive me! The nurses had cared to do that, although they had just undressed her for the night! Where in the world can you find a nursing home like that!"

He continued:

"Since the Coue method of auto-suggestion has rendered me immense services and even saved my life during the war, I once asked the nurses if they could not consider using it with the patients. They answered: "But of course, we do. Every morning when the patients wake up, we open the windows and tell them: isn't it a beautiful day? Aren't you feeling happy and better than yesterday? It will be a great day. You will feel wonderful!"

Louis Parizot had fostered the use of spirituality in the home. Priests were coming to celebrate mass or the patients watched mass on television. Every day a rosary session was held at five o'clock in the afternoon. A small miracle even happened: a lady who never spoke anymore began to recite the rosary and even gave the lead!

181

This ability to pray unlocked something in her mind and since then, she is speaking again.

He said to his friends: "You cannot imagine how I have become attached to this home, to the patients, to the kindness of the personnel. Every day when I come there I am greeted with joy. I often think that if Thomas Mann were alive today he would write his Magic Mountain in an Alzheimer's home. And if God allows me to get very old and if I need help, I wish to end my life in this blessed home."

\* \* \*

# Chapter 20

When Lakshmi and Alexander returned to New York, they decided to live in the mansion of the two preceding Secretaries-General at Sutton Place. Alexander wanted to take full advantage of his wife's top world position and of this prestigious UN dwelling to give innumerable receptions and parties for prominent US business people, high US Administration officials and political personalities. His aim was to bring them closer to the UN, to better understand the ideals, world views and workings of the UN and to give their full support to that US-based world organization. Lakshmi kept her little Hindu apartment on the thirty eighth floor of the UN, but no longer stayed there in the evening after work. And they both agreed to keep a permanent secondary week-end residence at Lake Mohonk.

After a few months their first child was born. Lakshmi's wishes were fulfilled: it was a beautiful, healthy girl. Lakshmi had given extreme attention to the conception and development of that new cosmic unit born from her life: the astrologers had set the date of the union in order to benefit from the best lunar and astral influences and during her entire pregnancy she had led the most careful physical, mental, sentimental and spiritual lives to benefit the growth of her conceived child. She had programmed her nutritional and mental inputs, convinced that they permeated the common body of mother and child; she practiced love and spirituality to irrigate the being of the child with those qualities. She often talked to her, loudly or silently, telling her how beautiful, how intelligent, how loving and how deeply spiritual she would be, and what a wonderful world she was being born into to serve God and humanity. Throughout her pregnancy, UN diplomats and her colleagues were respectful of her needs for rest, peace, relaxation, avoidance of exertion, and moments of solitude.

Lakshmi was deeply convinced that children should be given meaningful names which would be guides for their entire life. In India, children are given names of Gods, Goddesses, heroes and heroines of the great Hindu epics, or of human virtues. The Catholics like to give their children names of saints. She decided, with Alexander's agreement, to select names close to the UN's noble ideals. So the baby girl was named Irene and Eleanor, Irene the Greek Goddess of peace, and Eleanor in honor of Lakshmi's heroin, Eleanor Roosevelt and her pathbreaking work for human rights. A few months later, during a visit to India, the Hindu astrologer performed the traditional name-giving ceremony (Namakarana) and on the basis of the horoscope, he came up with the name Indhira.

A year later, she gave birth to a second child, a boy this time, fulfilling her dream to give a boy and name-bearer to her beloved husband. He agreed that their son be named Alexander, although he had deviated a little from his admiration for the Greek hero. But Lakshmi convinced him that Alexander the Great would have unified the known world of his time and created the foundations of an everlasting peace if he had not lost his life so early. He was a true genius and she wished their son to be a reincarnation of the Greek hero. Perhaps he would fulfill Alexander the Great's dream of what life should be on Earth after peace has been established. Her beloved husband was overwhelmed: his son would be named Alexander Rumacher II, following American tradition. He agreed also that his second name would be Gandhi to guide his life along the path of non-violence, simple frugal living, and spirituality. The astrologer in India gave him the name of Purushottama (the seeker of the origin and cause of all things). Lakshmi was over-joyed that it happened to be Parizot's Hindu name! Her boy would thus have beautiful examples to follow.

Lakshmi and Alexander decided not to have any more children. Lakshmi felt that since the UN was recommending voluntary population restraint, she should give the good example, and Alexander agreed.

* *

Time passed quickly to the year 2000. In 1996, she was re-elected unanimously Secretary-General for another term including the extraordinarily important year 2000.

She accomplished great feats during her mandate, consolidating and expanding world cooperation to unprecedented degrees, building on the new era opened by the end of the cold war and the friendship between Presidents Gorbachev and Bush. Progress became easier and easier as is usually the case in human affairs once a take-off begins. Peace was no exception. For thousands of years, peace had been advocated only by a few solitary prophets: great religious leaders like the Buddha, Confucius and Jesus, philosophers like Socrates, Cicero, Virgil, Abbe de St. Pierre, Immanuel Kant, great writers like Tolstoy and H.G. Wells, and many others. Then in the 19th century the first people's movements appeared on the scene, culminating in the first International Peace Conference in the Hague in 1899. Then in this century, the first political peace institutions were born: the feeble and geographically very limited League of Nations, followed by the universal and stronger, but still largely impotent United Nations. Although a new world war was avoided for more than half a century, many limited conflicts occurred and new frightful weapons proliferated. It was during her mandate on the eve of the third millennium that things began to change radically: peace, demilitarization, disarmament, world cooperation, the birth of a new consciousness and philosophy and of new world institutions accelerated in every direction to an unbelievable degree. The miracle of the fall of the Berlin Wall and of US/USSR reconciliation repeated itself. Things had fallen so low in the world, depression, hopelessness and folly were so deep that a reaction occurred. The world shook itself and went into an upward self-feeding, accelerating healing process. It was one of the most extraordinary times in human history, an end-product and fulfillment of the dreams of the solitary ones who had seen right and prepared the ground over the millennia.

Practically all of Lakshmi's recommendations in her celebrated and widely diffused world plan 2010 were implemented in time and even sometimes sooner. This was particularly the case of disarmament, demilitarization and the dismantling of military bases around the world. The US also went much faster in the creation of an all-American community than anyone expected. By 1995 the Community was in effect. The European Community for its part included all Eastern-European countries and extended as far as the northern part of the Asian continent. There was a European currency and European Central Bank. Without being a federation, the joint collegium which manages Europe for the common good at the expense of national sovereignty, was a tremendous success and step in the right direction. It did not turn out to be a threat to world unity, because President Bush very early obtained the discussion and consideration by the UN of a true world community of all nations, above and beyond existing and planned regional or continental communities. The spirits of Jean Monnet and Robert Schuman exulted in heaven!

But this was not all. Perhaps Lakshmi's greatest contribution was to be the first person in this century who thought about life and the world **after** peace. Our century was deeply stifled in its thinking by the overwhelming realities and prejudices of power, national sovereignty, armaments and wars. At its best, thinking was concentrating on the new global challenges to our living on this planet: the population explosion, the energy crisis, the environment, the conservation of natural resources, impending climatic changes, etc. No one but Lakshmi dared to lift their eyes above and beyond these impediments and to ask this fundamental and timely question: how should we envisage human life on this planet **after** peace? What will be the Human Life Plan after the 2010 Peace Plan?

She thus opened the eyes and minds of innumerable people around the world. It gave rise to a renaissance of philosophy and spirituality, of the wisdom of ancient cultures. It carried the human story a gigantic step forward, relegating technology, economics and materialism to a merely supporting role and extending our journey and progress into higher moral, affective and spiritual spheres. She was the true prophet of the new cosmic age, of our first, universal, world-wide attempt to understand our meaning and purpose on this celestial body circling in the universe.

She brought East and West, North and south, everybody together; she put on the world agenda the four human virtues advocated by her oriental predecessor U Thant: physical, mental, moral and highest of all, spiritual. She wrote the story U Thant wanted to write, namely the synthesis of western science and technology with oriental philosophy and spirituality.

Lakshmi was all excited and deeply involved in this great, unprecedented visionary scheme. Louis Parizot continued to be her adviser and inspirer.

But she had her own ideas, big novel ones as well as small ones for the heart. She perfected and expanded her peace plan 2010 constantly. Just to give a few examples: sick and tired of all the delays or refusals by some nations to pay their dues to the UN, she took the bull by the horn, gave the example of the European Community which in 1990 had a budget of 74.4 billion dollars derived from an added tax on all imports into the community, and got the first UN taxes adopted: a 10% UN tax on all arms sales in the world and a 1% share in the sale for medical purposes of all seized drugs in the world; a 1% UN retail tax on all sales of alcohol and tobacco products; and a 1% surcharge on all stamps and postages in the world to go to a world fund for environmental conservation. This was an unheard triumph of hers, something which would have been unthinkable only a few years ago. She also got under way the study and consideration of a single world currency to be adopted at the entrance of the third millennium. World public opinion polls showed that 70% of the world's people favored this solution.

She had also her beloved little pet projects, such as the publication in a world paper-back of information on all existing peace prizes and awards for a better world. This alone prompted tens of thousands of people to work and to compete for such prizes, and it caused a mushrooming of new prizes in many countries and fields. Following Franklin Roosevelt's example, she got the whole world out of depression, lifting the minds and sights of the people to a peaceful and infinitely better world.

The spirits of St. Francis, Gandhi, Dag Hammarskjøld, U Thant and of all the unemployed saints and spirits floating around this planet rushed down to help the living who opened themselves and prayed to them. They had waited so long! The miraculous Earth was becoming at long last the Planet of God! Human life was acquiring a new sense. A harmonious world was in the making, now that peace was the normal, permanent state of the planet.

\* \*

Alexander Rumacher on his side was proceeding in his own way, working with what he knew best: the world of business, money and power. The people in those worlds wanted peace and happiness too. As a matter of fact they had hard, ungratifying lives securing the material base of human well-being. It was not always fun to spend one's life producing goods and bringing them to the people. Since God and the universe had not created humans to make money, in the end money-making was not a satisfying way of fulfilling life. Alexander complemented admirably the work of Lakshmi:

1. He bought a small building across from the United Nations on First Avenue, built it into a skyscraper and called it the UN Business Center, similar to the UN Church Center which houses many religious, peace and other non-governmental organizations. His building housed a number of business organizations following the work of the UN, such as the International Chamber of Commerce, the Business Council of the United Nations Association of America, US Business for the UN, etc. Several others were created in numerous specific fields of business. A host of multinational corporations established information offices in it, built a substantial conference center, library, information and a computer network permitting all business in the US and abroad to network with the UN and its agencies, to be properly informed, to get answers to their queries and establish contacts with diplomats and world officials. It became a real bridge with the UN. Postgraduate students in business administration could register for courses taught by the best UN experts and diplomats. A world core curriculum and course on planetary management, to serve as a model for all business administration schools in the world, was developed by Louis Parizot. The Center became the biggest, best organized network of organizations following the work of the UN system and cooperating with it. He thereafter created similar buildings next to the European Office of the United Nations in Geneva, to the Center of International Organizations in Vienna and at the seat of every specialized agency of the UN. At long last government, the people, religions and business were working together.

2. Having once heard Louis Parizot tell Lakshmi how Margaret Mead, the famous anthropologist had organized the first peoples' assembly parallel to the UN conference on population in Bucharest, a model followed subsequently for all UN world conferences, he decided to do the same for business: alongside with each conference, starting with the 1992 UN Conference on the Environment and Development in Brazil, business conferences

were organized by him to follow these conferences and submit to them the views, comments and proposals of business. At first, governments had been somewhat troubled by these parallel conferences, but they soon loved their input and welcomed their participation on issues of grave world concern requiring the perceptions and help of people and business.

3. He also took up one of Lakshmi's proposals in her Peace Plan 2010, namely the creation of a true World Foundation for philanthropy and gaiaphily. The Foundation was composed of the following: a President, namely Alexander Rumacher himself; an Executive Committee consisting of the most prestigious philanthropists and foundations in the world; an Advisory Board consisting of all the heads of the UN specialized agencies and world programs, headed by the Secretary General of the UN; world information services on philanthropy and gaiaphily; a public relations service.

Each year the Advisory Board met in session with the Executive Committee to outline the world's and humanity's greatest needs and priorities as seen from the global, universal vantage point of view of the UN and of its specialized agencies. The Committee then met in private session to decide the allocation of funds to the priority programs agreed upon.

The UN obtained from all member nations tax exemption of contributions to the World Foundation. As a result, the UN and its agencies were no longer one hundred percent under the severe constraints of exclusive governmental financing. Democratically, any person, group, business, institution in the world was enabled to help the UN achieve its objectives. Inheritances and estates were contributed in increasing numbers to the Foundation. A whole system of imaginative recognitions was instaured. Each year the Foundation awarded a prestigious World Philanthropy Prize to the most meritorious philanthropist or gaiaphilist in the world. It soon received the same world-wide publicity as the Nobel Prizes. Lakshmi was in heaven: she could now obtain money for some of her most cherished projects and organizations, many of which would otherwise be ignored by existing foundations for being too small and not glamorous enough.

4. But his biggest project of all, the one to which he gave his relentless, unreserved commitment was the creation of the United States of the World.

He had lengthy discussions with Lakshmi on that subject after studying her Peace Plan 2010. He said to her once:

"Your work at the UN, my darling, and the exertions of your colleagues - I am thinking in particular of Louis Parizot - will never be effective. You are hitting constantly a Berlin wall and ceiling which must ultimately fall. The UN is faced with the same faults as was the League of Nations, and before it the US Confederacy after the Declaration of Independence. And this time it is worse, because it is on a world-wide basis and at a time of maximum global threats. George Washington's worries in 1786 remain central and fundamental to our time, when he said:

'The primary cause of all disorders lies in the different state governments and in the tenacity of that power which pervades the whole of their systems.'

Every nation is sovereign, has an army (except Costa Rica), has its sovereign government, a supreme court, a central bank, its own currency, its ministers, including one of 'foreign affairs', its taxing and borrowing power. At the world level which is crying for help and concern, the UN has nothing of this sort: no territorial sovereignty, no legislative, no executive, no judicial, no taxing and no borrowing power! It barely can take any decisions, only recommendations! The International Court of Justice is a farce, since governments can refuse to appear before it, since no individual in the world can submit a case to it, and governments who condescend to appear can refuse to accept its judgments! It is the greatest joke on Earth, an insult to the planet and to human intelligence! I just cannot see how you have the patience to give your life to such institutions. And I admire the marvelous results you extract from them with your skills and devotion. You are like Iroquois on the peace path! But you will break your teeth on the two major issues before the UN: wars and armaments. Under the present nation-state system, armaments will never disappear from this planet. They cannot disappear, because they are the main instrument and guarantee of national sovereignty. Therefore, as long as there will be sovereign nations, there will be armaments. The contrary is wishful, useless, time-consuming thinking.

You have been at it since the League of Nations, and armaments are infinitely worse today than ever.

We must therefore do what George Washington did: accept the idea of a world sovereignty for the common good and create a world federation with large decentralized powers to the 166 states, except defense and the issue of currency. The federal system will provide largest freedom and protection of human rights and liberties to all citizens of the planet and to intermediary groups, but no armaments and currency power. We need no Ministry of Foreign Affairs at the top, because there will be no longer any foreign affairs. Nations can transform their Ministries of Foreign Affairs into Ministries of coordination and cooperation with other states, under a World Ministry of Coordination and Cooperation. Our wonderful US system of balance of power should be adopted for the whole world. It has worked wonders for the people of so many origins who make up the American society. May I read to you these words by Woodrow Wilson, the US President after World Ward I:

"We are the mediating nation of the world. We are compounded of the nations of the world; we mediate their blood, we mediate their traditions, we mediate their sentiments, their tastes, their passions, we are ourselves compounded of those things. We are, therefore, able to understand all nations. We are able to understand them in the compound, not separately, as partisans, but unitedly as knowing and comprehending and embodying them all."

Lakshmi interrupted his reading:

"Yes, but he was defeated and the US refused to become a member of the League of Nations, thus contributing to the rise of Hitler, Mussolini, the Japanese warlords, to the holocaust and World War II. And today, I feel that the American isolationists are as far away from that statement as they were at the end of World War I."

He responded:

"Yes, the American people rejected their prophet; but his soul and truth went marching on. There are few now who remember or who have read his words, but there was a depth in them which will prevail before this century is over. I will personally make sure of it. The creation of the United States of the World can give an enormous push to the much needed strengthening of the United Nations and to the creation of a true world community. Such a community will sooner or later have to convert itself into a world federal system. We have thus three ways before us which we must all try: the immediate

191

creation of the United States of the World; the birth of a world community; and the strengthening of the United Nations on the road to a world community and world federal system. This end result is inevitable. It is the only way to take the world out of the present chaos. To wait any longer would be criminal. It required the first world war to produce the League of Nations, and the second world war to bring about the United Nations. Is it really necessary to wait for a third world war to create a better world order and organization? And you will see the wonderful things which will become possible when national sovereignty has been reduced and when we can ensure the top productivity of the world economy and the preservation of the Earth for the benefit of all. Innumerable savings, not only from disarmament, will derive from this decisive quantum jump in human organization and government. You will see, it will be done, it will work and the whole world will have a sigh of relief and gratitude."

Lakshmi looked at him with astonishment. She had her doubts about such a course which she saw strewn with immense obstacles and opposition. She asked him for his views about such opposition. He answered:

"Of course, there will be opposition, as there was against the US Constitution. As a matter of fact, if you read the records of the debates which lasted ten years in Philadelphia, you would find that United Nations debates are benign and polite in comparison. But as with the US Constitution, the world constitutional debate will be marked by a host of imaginative thinking. It will be a tremendous, unprecedented exercise to which the greatest minds of this planet will contribute. We might get a constitution which is very different from what is envisaged at first. You will see how fantastic it will be. It will be in the news every day and the peoples of the world will follow it with excitement. Of course not everybody will be happy. As Vernon Nash wrote about the Philadelphia miracle:

"The intolerable anarchy which was swiftly created by the exercise of autonomous sovereignty by the thirteen states over matters of common concern drove our forefathers into union. Most of them took every step in that direction with misgivings, with reluctance, and often with repugnance."

He also told her the anecdote of Benjamin Franklin. When the US Constitution was adopted after ten years of debates he made a little speech in which he said that during the debates he had often contemplated the chair occupied by the President, which had on its back a half sun with golden rays. And he said: "I wondered if that sun was a rising sun or a setting one. I am glad, Mr. Chairman that it was a rising sun."

Lakshmi kissed him and said: "You are great. I love you. And as my next birthday gift you may wish to have that chair reproduced and to give it to me as my chair on the General Assembly podium. Perhaps it will bring luck to me and to the UN." And she added with a mischievous smile:

"You were dying to read the remainder of Woodrow Wilson's speech. Please read it. I would love to hear it."

Alexander read:

"See, my friends, what this means. It means that Americans have a consciousness different from the consciousness of every other nation in the world. I am not saying this with even the slightest thought of criticism of other nations. You know how it is with a family. A family gets centered on itself, it is not careful and is less interested in its neighbors than in its own members. So a nation that is not constantly renewed out of new sources is apt to have the narrowness and prejudice of a family; whereas America must have this consciousness, that on all sides it touches elbows and it touches hearts with all the nations of humankind. The example of America must be a special example. The example of America must be the example not merely of peace because it will not fight, but of peace because peace is the healing and elevating influence of the world and strife is not. There is such a thing as man being too proud to fight. There is such a thing as a nation being right that it does not need to convince others by force that it is right. I thank God that those who believe in America, who try to serve her people, are likely to be also what America herself from the first hoped and meant to be - the servant of humankind."

Alexander put down the text and said:

"Isn't that beautiful? That is the America we must restore to the leadership and enlightenment of the world."

Lakshmi was thinking inwardly:

"My God, how far this man has come from his days of the Potomac cruises and the Golden Age Foundation! I thank You, O Lord for this marvelous transformation."

And she heard God whispering sweetly to her: "I thank you, dear angel, for having been my instrument."

\* \*

193

Alexander's first step was to get all existing federalist, world government and world citizens movements together under the same roof in a building he bought in Philadelphia near Constitution Hall. He gave them a staff, huge revenues, a public relations agency, and as a first step he asked them to collect every proposal for a world government made since the beginning of human history. The more information they collected, the more he read, the more convinced he was that his objective was right and most timely. It would give the United States an admirable leadership in fashioning at long last a workable political system for the world; it would strengthen the hands of the US in its negotiations with the European Community for a world community; and last but not least it would check Japan from becoming the new Great Britain and from aggressively and deviously invading the world instead of becoming an honest partner in it.

He went to see his friend the President of the United States who saw immediately that there was no risk and commitment in trying and that on the contrary it gave the US a fabulous leadership and a host of bargaining possibilities. The President leaned back in his chair and smiled at the heavens: what a great page in human history it would be if the US were the founding country of the United States of the World, and to have this happen during his presidency!

The same way as he had announced the American Community from Alaska to the Tierra del Fuego, President Bush surprised humanity one morning when he announced his proposal for a United States of the World, citing George Washington and also Victor Hugo who was the first to advocate the US of the World.

People gasped in admiration. A World Constitutional Assembly was convened in Philadelphia and was given until 1999 to come up with a World constitution. They did the most involved, thorough, all-encompassing and imaginative work, trying to figure out how humans should govern themselves on this planet, achieve happiness in freedom, fulfill their miraculous lives in well-being and justice, respond to the will of God and take good care of their fabulous home in the universe. The Constitution had many fascinating novelties e.g.: to avoid autocracy it had no President but a Board of five rotating Presidents. It introduced world public opinion polls and referenda on major world issues. From the Greeks it took the idea of an Aeropage, a group of wise men and women to keep under review the toddling of this new child and to help it to adulthood.

In the year 2000, the World Constitution came into effect when more than thirty countries ratified it. The American countries were the first to do it, fulfilling Simon Bolivar's and George Washington's dreams. Now it was the turn of the European countries to integrate themselves into the USW. A chapter of the Constitution foresaw that the United Nations and its agencies would constitute the core of the new federal government. The tasks of Lakshmi and of Alexander were completed. They received jointly the Nobel Prize for Peace, the first ever given to a couple. And they donated it immediately to the World Foundation.

* * *

# Chapter 21

The year 2000 was an incredible event. Ever since the UN General Assembly recommended to hold this world-wide celebration, ideas, visions, programs, projects, movements, institutions, awards and publicity campaigns for the year 2000 and the advent of the third millennium sprang up all over the world. It was a universal outbidding of enthusiasm, inspiration, imagination, discussions, and conferences on the expected new age. The UN received news of dozens of conferences being held to contribute to the year. Every nation established a national committee for the preparation and celebration of the Bimillennium. Every TV network on Earth commissioned programs reviewing how the world had changed since the year 1000 or the beginning of the century and what humanity could dream for the next millennium. Books were published showing the state of the world and of humanity 3000, 2000, 1000 years before Christ, in the years 1, 1000 and 2000. Each Earth Day was bigger than the preceding. Ecologists and the youth of the sixties saw the triumph of many of their ideas. The Catholics started an Evangelic movement 2000. All religions cooperated in an ecumenic Council for the year 2000. The Pope presented his views on a third, spiritual millennium to the 1994 UN General Assembly, during the International Year of the Family. The whole UN and its agencies were busy updating and putting together their plans 2000 and beyond. School children had contests on their views of the year 2000 and the next millennium. Universities and research institutes were overflowing with theses and books on the third millennium in all realms of science, technology, social, political, ethical, moral, philosophical and spiritual concerns. It was simply unbelievable. The sports joined in and organized special events and competitions in 2000. The arts flourished with innumerable year 2000 productions, rediscovering the beauty and harmony all around us, repeating the miracle of the Italian Renaissance after the bewildered, chaotic, scared Middle Ages.

Every conceivable celebration took place in the world, in capitals, in cities, in villages, in churches, in hamlets, in families. The grand opening of the world celebration took place on New Year's eve, 31 December 1999. Festivities and world prayers were held all over the planet, retransmitted by all major television networks. Never had such a thing happened in the entire human history. It was really the birth of the human family. A second highpoint was on the 3rd Tuesday of September of 2000, International Day of Peace. The planet's entire 6 billion people joined in prayers at the exact time when their delegates stood up in the UN General Assembly to observe a minute of silence for prayer or meditation at the opening of their yearly debates. Thereafter, all the church bells, gongs, muezzins and chofars of the world rang their cosmic vibrations and took humanity's prayers to the heavens. The third highpoint was 24 October 2000, United Nations Day, proclaimed as the first World Holiday and Thanksgiving Day. And the climax of it all was New Year's eve, 31 December 2000, when the world's people were about to see the dawn of the year 2001.

Lakshmi and Alexander were the people's heroes throughout the year. Never had any couple reached such a height of fame. It was the time also when Lakshmi's second term as Secretary-General was nearing its end. All governments wanted to re-elect her for an unprecedented third term, but she and Alexander had discussed it thoroughly and had come to the conclusion that it was time to let in not only a new millennium but also new blood in the Secretary-Generalship. They were in full agreement. On 24 October, UN Day, in her speech to the General Assembly, Lakshmi had these words:

"Dear brothers and sisters of the human family. It is hard for me to express the joys and blessings I derived from serving you and the world during this last decade. You have been most kind and understanding to me. We have been united in work, in mind, in heart and in spirit for the achievement of a peaceful, more just and happier world. We have done a lot together: the world at long last has found its soul again; the people love and respect our warm and beautiful Mother Earth; we have become one human family in one planetary home; a new positive, hopeful philosophy was born; a new cosmology and vision of our future are at hand; the womanly qualities of human nature have been recognized and allowed to play their full part; our world after many millennia of strife is at long last beyond war; our planet is being preserved and increasingly cared for; the heart and the soul have been allowed to add their power to intelligence; we are no longer afraid to use the words love and God in this house; we recognize now that we are integral parts, miraculous living cells of the Earth; we know that we have been created for the Earth and not the Earth for us; Mammon is dethroned; we know now that the universe was not made for money; at the beginning was the word, not money; we are entering a new period of this celestial body's and of the noble human race's journey and evolution in the universe; the next age will be even greater, more transcendental and fulfilling; it will be the cosmic age, the age of total union with the universe and God in the eternal chain of time. Even more surprises and miracles expect us. The unique cosmic experiment of the universe on this blessed planet was not cut short by a nuclear holocaust or by an ecological disaster. We must praise God and the saints for having guided us and shown us the way. In a hundred years our age might look as retrograde and confused as does the year 1900 to us today, but we will have done our best.

As I have informed the members of the Security Council who offered me so warmly to consider a third term as Secretary-General, I cannot honestly accept such an unprecedented honor. At the onset of a new millenium, a new person, a younger person must enter this ominous function, educated and prepared as a member of the new generation whose millennium it will be. I and my beloved husband will never really leave you. We will think hard to see how best we can continue to serve you, humanity, this beautiful planet and the great United Nations. We love you all dearly, we love every person on this planet, especially the children who will replace us in the eternal chain of life as new cosmic instruments. Goodbye. I am sad to leave you. I will never forget you. May God bless you, your children and children's children on this most beautiful, heavenly body in the universe. I love you all. Om shanti. Peace be always with you."

And from the bright green elevated podium of the General Assembly, standing in front of her new chair with a golden rising sun, she sent kisses to the Assembly and broke into tears, while all delegates stood up in a minute of religious silence, followed by a thunderous applause.

* * *

# Chapter 22

Alexander and Lakshmi gave intensive thought during the following weeks to the planning of the remainder of their lives. Lakshmi was flooded with an avalanche of prestigious offers: University Presidencies, well paid senior fellowships in foundations, presidencies of world associations, etc. None of them satisfied her until she received a letter from Louis Parizot informing her that the Rectorship of the University for Peace in Costa Rica would become vacant on 1 January 2001. He suggested that she consider that position, even if it carried only a minimal pay. She discussed it with Alexander who loved the idea. They remembered with fondness their first and subsequent visits to that extraordinary, inspiring place. It was one of those sacred places on Earth where a cosmic column of energy links the Earth with heaven, a "vouivre", as the Celts called them as they searched for them all over Europe to build their menhirs and temples. Geomancists had measured and confirmed the powerful energies outflowing from the grounds of the University.

The couple got all excited about the project. Lakshmi called Parizot to ask if he had any suggestions for Alexander. He said: "Yes, the International Foundation for the University for Peace has been dormant for a number of years. We could never find a philanthropist of world stature to take its presidency. We would be delighted if Alexander could accept to be President."

Alexander agreed happily. He would divide his time between the World Federal Government, the World Foundation and the University for Peace Foundation. He had also some personal plans he would reveal to them once they were in Costa Rica.

Lakshmi made arrangements with UN Archives for the preservation of her official papers and obtained authorization to take to Costa Rica her personal papers and gifts received from governments and private persons. She wanted to create at the University a Center and museum at which students would receive fellowships to study her efforts and finish her unfinished business for a better world. She would hire a Secretary to put order in her papers, speeches, videotapes, correspondence, and begin publishing what was worthwhile and useful for the future.

The International Council of the University for Peace elected them both unanimously and enthusiastically to their respective positions. Louis Parizot was the first to be at the airport in San Jose to welcome them again and for good to Costa Rica. It was January, one of the most glorious, sunniest months in Costa Rica. Nature was exploding with flowers. They stayed for a short while at the Chatelle resort in La Garita, but soon moved to a rented house in Ciudad Colon, near the University for Peace. From there Alexander could direct the construction of a prestigious Rector's home for Lakshmi and himself, half blended with the tropical forest and overlooking the magnificent scenery of mountains and valleys.

While Lakshmi was getting familiar with her new job as Rector, Alexander went into action. He revealed his plans one evening to Lakshmi and to Louis as they were sitting on Parizot's beloved bench, admiring the sunset behind the hills:

"You remember that I bought all the land around the University during our first visit. It has remained in its pure natural state since that time. I will preserve most of it, but I have also three specific ideas to utilize part of it:

First, I want to build up here the first international city on this planet, following probably the plans of the French architect Le Corbusier who wanted to see the UN at the center of a world city or capital, with a world library, a world university and a cultural representation of all nations. When Rockefeller's little piece of land in Manhattan was accepted by the UN, Le Corbusier slammed the door and left the planning committee, because it was impossible to build a world capital on that restricted ground. He was right. Well, we have the possibility of fulfilling his dream here. We have already the University and we can build the rest. I will appoint a committee of the world's best architects and we will see what they have to propose. I envisage also the construction of several national villages, following in the footsteps of the Spanish Guadalupe village offered to the University by the government of Spain and inaugurated by the King of Spain. We will attract here the greatest artists and composers of the world.

Second, I want to fulfill Louis's dream of a school for heads of states, left in abeyance since the times of Confucius. As a matter of fact, the supra-national grounds of the University should become a preferred place of encounter for heads of states.

Third, I want to build a new Margarita and Louis Parizot Center on the campus. The present one is much too small and modest. You both deserve better, for you have done so much for the world. I also want to build Parizot schools in Costa Rica and in different countries of the world to teach your revolutionary and so timely world core curriculum."

Louis Parizot could not believe his ears. It was not possible that so many of his dreams would become true. Was the Earth perhaps an enchanted place on which humans so far have not yet discovered the mysterious power of dreams? After a silence, he said to Alexander and to Lakshmi:
"Can I ask you to do me a great favor? Could you accompany me to the cemetery down in the valley near Ciudad Colon where my poor Margarita rests since last year. I would like you, dear Alexander, to repeat for her at her tomb, the wonderful things you just said. I am sure her spirit will be so happy and that she will help us in our last earthly endeavors."
They drove down to Ciudad Colon and on the way Louis Parizot told them about the Cemetery of Peacemakers he got established near the little town. He said:
"The military have their great cemeteries in many countries of the world. I thought that there   should also be cemeteries of peacemakers, to start with in that first demilitarized country on Earth, Costa Rica. Here one can really rest in peace, for there has been total

peace in this country for the last 52 years. I wish to be buried here near my beloved Margarita and University for Peace, the same way as my compatriot Albert Schweitzer rests near his hospital in Lambarene, Africa. I stipulated that if Costa Rica should ever re-arm herself and reintroduce the military, our rests will be disinterred and strewn on the Pacific Ocean, the Ocean of Peace".

They visited Margarita's tomb. A beautiful bust of her by Mazzone was smiling with heavenly peace. Little patches of ground from various places of the Earth which she had loved during her life, were covering her tomb: from Santander, the place of her birth; from Iquique, the place of her youth; from Lake Success, the first seat of the United Nations where she began to work; from Geneva, from St-Gix-Divonne, from their beloved home in Dobbs Ferry, from the places where her children and grandchildren lived.

Louis, with tears in his eyes, asked Alexander to tell her his projects. When Alexander finished, Louis read aloud the inscription on her tomb:

"I will spend my heaven helping women on Earth."

The tomb was built in the form of a great white peace dove extending her wings. One wing was the tomb of Margarita. The other wing was meant for Louis. In the middle, in front of the heart of the dove there was a bust of the two lovers smiling at each other. Margarita had her bust in front of her wing and Louis would have his in front of the second wing, which had no inscription as yet.

Louis said to his friends: "I will rest here next to my love and my inscription will be:

"I will spend my heaven working for peace on Earth."

"As for you, dear Lakshmi and Alexander, think also of your last message to the living who will visit this cemetery. From my dear master U Thant, I learned this wise precept: 'Try to know how you want to be remembered after your death.' He wanted to be remembered as a man who always tried to be good and to understand others."

He shook off his tears and memories and said to his friends:

"Thank you for coming with me and paying your respect to my beloved Margarita. I hear her telling us: do not be sad, do not cry, you have a lot of work to do. Go forth and do it for the glory of God, for this beautiful planet and humanity, especially for our children and children's children. There is no real death. Life eternally renews itself.  Your soul will rejoin the universal soul and live eternally."

The three left silently the holy grounds of great peacemakers absorbed in their thoughts as to what they could still do during the remainder of their lives for the good of this beautiful planet circling in the unfathomable, mysterious universe.  They climbed the hill of the University for Peace, determined to make it the new Athens of the world, the pinnacle of civilization, the sacred place of peace, beauty and human fulfillment....

THE END

or

THE BEGINNING ?

*About the Author . . .*

ROBERT MULLER   "A Citizen of the World"

Wherever in the world there is a major peace initiative, a peace conference, a citizens movement or project for peace, or a new initiative for international cooperation, we encounter the name of Robert Muller. After 38 years of silent, behind the scenes work at the United Nations he has emerged as one of the foremost peacemakers of our time. He has inspired and given hope to innumerable people around the world through his action, idealism, and uplifting speaking and writings. He has been a model to his international colleagues, and he is the hero of innumerable young people because of his total devotion to the good of humankind.

Joining the UN in 1948, Robert Muller rose through the ranks to the position of Assistant-Secretary-General. He has been one of the main architects of the UN institutional system in the economic and social fields, the main idea person, and trusted collaborator of three Secretary-Generals. He has been called the philosopher and prophet of hope of the United Nations. Here is an outstanding international civil servant whose deep love of humanity and this planet merit being given recognition through every possible means.

Now Chancellor Emeritus of the University for Peace in Costa Rica, created by the United Nations in 1980, Robert Muller is concentrating his efforts to promote greater human understanding and global awareness. His world core curriculum for education is being adopted by schools around the globe, and earned him the 1989 UNESCO Education Peace Prize. Robert Muller is in great demand to make speeches to religious, educational, environmental, spiritual, and political symposiums and conferences around the world.

# WORKS BY ROBERT MULLER

## English

*Most of All, They Taught Me Happiness* (Doubleday and World Happiness and Cooperation, U.S.)

*New Genesis, Shaping a Global Spriituality* (Doubleday and World Happiness and Cooperation, U.S.)

*What War Taught Me About Peace, with a Peace Plan 2010* (Doubleday U.S.)

*Dialogues of Hope* (World Happiness and Cooperation, U.S.)

*Decide To* (World Happiness and Cooperation, U.S.)

*World Joke Book, Vol. 1* (Amity House, U.S.)

*The Birth of a Global Civilization* (World Happiness and Cooperation, U.S.)

*A Planet of Hope* (Amity House, U.S.)

*The Desire to Be Human, an international compendium on Teilhard de Chardin* (Mirananda, Wassenaar, Holland.)

*The World Core Curriculum in the Robert Muller School* (Arlington, Texas, U.S.)

*Essays on Education* (University for Peace, Costa Rica.)

*Margaret McGurn: Planetary Conciousness in the Thought of Teilhard de Chardin and Robert Muller, with a proposal for a Bimillenium celebration of life* (World Happiness and Cooperation, U.S.)

*(cont.)*

### German

*Ich Lernte zu Leben* (translation of *Most of All They Taught Me Happiness*) (Dianus- Trikont, Munchen, Germany)

*Die Neuerschaffung der Welt* (translation of *New Genesis*) (Goldman Verlag, Munchen, Germany)

*Planet der Hoffnung* (translation of *Planet of Hope*) (Goldman Verlag, Munchen, Germany)

### French

*Sima mon Amour*, an international novel in French, Erckman-Chartrian literary prize, 1983 (Editions Pierron, Sarreguemines, France)

*Au Bonheur, a l'Amour, a la Paix* (translation of *New Genesis*) (Pierron, France)

### Spanish

*Dialogos con Robert Muller*, by Hilda Berger (Lima, Peru)

### Polish

*New Genesis in Polish*, Instytut Wysawniczy, (Warsaw, Poland)

### Japanese

Japanese edition of *New Genesis*, University of the Sacred Heart (Catholic Press Center, Tokyo)

\*     \*
\*

### Soon to be Published by
### World Happiness and Cooperation

*My Testament to the UN*

*The Art of Living*

**United Nations**
United Nations, New York  10017
U.S.A


**United Nations** - (Geneva)
Palais des Nations
Geneva,  10  Switzerland


**University for Peace**
UNIPAZ
P.O.Box 138
Ciudad Colón, Costa Rica
C.A.

This book is available for $ 7.95 plus
$ 3.00 for shipping and handling in the U.S.A.
from:

WORLD HAPPINESS AND COOPERATION
P.O. Box 1153 Anacortes, WA. 98221
U.S.A.

Please write for our current catalog of the works by
Robert Muller

Many of Robert Muller's books are available
at the United Nations Bookshop
Room GA. 32 B
United Nations, New York 10017